Fred,
Enjoy every
moment!
Jill Starling

AT

THIS

MOMENT

A novel by Jill Starling

I dedicate this novel to my loving parents whose strength continues to amaze me.

ACKNOWLEDGMENTS

Many thanks to God for giving me the words to write, for bringing the right people into my life at the right time to make it all happen. To Him I give all the glory.

My wonderful husband, Jamie, I am truly blessed by your love, encouragement and support. Thank you for your perfection in creating a stellar website, and an entertaining video. You're the best husband and friend I could ever ask for!

My two sons, James and Matthew, You light up my life! I am so glad you're my sons!

My parents, Thank you for your continuous love, encouragement and support! It means the world to me!

Brenda Moeske and Karin Gardner, I couldn't think of two other women with whom I would want to share this journey with. Thank you for your encouragement and enthusiasm throughout each chapter. You ladies are the best!

Kristen Stroebel, My final eyes! You are Amazing! I can't thank you enough for your love, support, prayers, and encouragement! You're the best!

Kathryn Chiarelli, You never know who you are going to meet at the 59th St. Subway Station! You are truly a godsend! Thank you for being my editor! Your kindness went above and beyond, and I am truly grateful.

Miranda Nagell, Thank you so much for all your expertise you shared with me about horses. You are a beautiful person, and I am truly grateful for all the help you have given to me!

Gloria Herman of Tesoros Cafe in Schenectady, NY, Thank you so much for sharing your culture and loving kindness with me!

Corey John Snide, Words cannot express how grateful, honored and thankful I am for all the help you have given to me! You are a godsend and what it means to be a true, "Star!"

Wendy Blanchard, You hit another homerun! I knew you would! Thank you!

David Castle of Youthful Trends Photo in Clifton Park, NY, Thank you so much for your perfectionism, patience, and kindness! Awesome Job!

To my first readers: My aunt, Linda Landers, My aunt, Rita Prinzo, Ardyce Elmore, Christina Landers, and Leigh Lock, I thank you all from the bottom of my heart for your support and kind words!

Dr. Gerald W. Zaidman, Thank you so much for taking the time to answer all my medical questions. You taught me quite a bit! I am very grateful for your kindness.

Dr. Shahida Mirza, Thank you so much for your kindness and taking the time to answer all my medical questions.

To everyone who supports me and my writing, I thank you from the bottom of my heart!

At this Moment

First Edition

Copyright @ 2014 by Jill Starling

"At this Moment"

~ At this moment, you are enjoying the laughter of someone you love.

~ At this moment, they are no longer there.

~ At this moment, you may have lost faith, friends, and trust.

~ At this moment, you realize those who stand beside you in your darkest hours are the only people you truly need.

~ At this moment, you may never be the same person you once were.

This moment is all you have for now. Be present in it and enjoy!

This moment won't last forever.

Jill Starling

Readers,

Each of these chapters is told through the particular character's point of view.

One thing is certain—you never know what the moment may bring, which may change your life forever.

Enjoy!

Jill Starling

Flash Forward

"Sometimes the questions are complicated and the answers are simple." ~Dr. Seuss

Lauren

I trembled, praying for someone to pick up. Within a few rings, I heard my dad's familiar voice.

"Dad, listen to me. I'm going to die," I said as calmly as I could while steadily holding my cell phone.

"Lauren, what's going on?" my dad asked, confused with panic in his voice.

I could hear my mom in the background asking if everything was all right.

"Dad, my plane has been hijacked," I whispered as I sloped into the back of the seat in front of me.

"Oh my God, we need to do something!" he said in shock.

"Dad, it's too late. I love you, Dad."

"I love you, too," he responded tearfully.

"Please let me talk to Mom now." I heard my dad tell her that I was in trouble.

"Lauren, Lauren," my mom repeated in hysterics.

"Mom, I love you so much. I'm so sorry if I disappointed you!"

"Lauren, I love you, Oh Lauren, my baby girl," my mom said, barely audible.

My dad returned to the phone, "Lauren, I think we should pray."

My parents put the phone on speaker and we recited the Lord's Prayer together.

"I have to go now."

Suddenly my mom screamed, "Oh my God, Lauren! It's on the TV."

"Listen to me!" I interrupted. "I want to thank you both for giving me such a good life. I really have to go now," I said, my voice cracking as I hung up.

I knew I had to make this one last phone call. I punched the number in. I looked at the identifier on my cell phone, Steven Belezzi. The phone rang and then stopped. Suddenly the plane shook rapidly. I couldn't tell if we had lost connection. I felt nauseous knowing this would probably be the last time I would ever speak to him.

"Steven, I will probably never have the chance to see you again, but I love you."

There was silence. Then suddenly a voice came on, but it wasn't Steven's.

"Who is this?"

I quickly hung up.

Melanie

"Chill out! I'm just going to meet with him," I said.

"You can't leave Fillmore or me," Elnando said, with a look of pain in his eyes.

"Elnando, stop, you're being absurd! You know I will never leave you."

"Even so, every dancer's dream is to get into Fillmore. Out of the thousands who audition each year, only 7% are accepted. Do you realize how lucky we are to be here?"

Elnando's question seemed more like a statement.

"And why are we here, Elnando? We are here so that we can get our feet in the door of a great dance company," I answered for him.

"Why can't you be happy that a prestigious dance company has an interest in me? I hope you aren't jealous?"

"How can you even think that? You're my girl! You should know I want the best for you. I think it's wonderful that they took an interest in you."

"It certainly doesn't seem that way!" I said, walking toward the door.

"Mel, wait."

I turned around and looked at him.

"Can't you just enjoy your time here?" He solemnly asked.

I didn't answer him, and left.

I needed to be alone. I took a short walk over to the campus park. I sat under an oak tree and secretly prayed that no one I knew would come by. I noticed a couple of hippies strumming together with their guitars. Their harmonizing tones relaxed me and I became lost in it, forgetting about the time. I looked at my watch. I couldn't believe how long I had been sitting there. I knew I couldn't put this off another second, if I was ever going to make my appointment.

I put my headphones on and turned up my iPhone as I made my way through Lincoln Center toward Broadway. An obnoxious beep with a push notification interrupted Radiohead, just as I was starting to calm down to the music. The emergency broadcast news released a report of a possible hijacking that had just occurred on an American Airlines plane, Flight #214 from Los Angeles to New York.

Great! 9/11 all over again! I thought.

As I made my way across the busy intersection, my music stopped again.

I'm sure it's Elnando trying to mess with my head.

"We have some news for you," the text message read.

What is this all about? I thought as I looked down.

The last thing I remember was texting, "We?"

As I was trying to complete my message, I suddenly felt my body being pushed fifty feet across traffic and a careening yellow cab sliding into me.

Elnando

"Look who's here. It's Ballerina Boy," my best friend, Jewel, said. Jewel was like a brother to me. We both grew up together in the same project in Spanish Harlem and our mothers were the best of friends.

I laughed. "How *ya* doin', man?" I asked, leaning into him while we gave each other our signature handshake.

"Good. What's going down?" he asked, as we both took a seat at the bar.

"Oh man, it's rough. Where do I begin? Trouble with my girl, I'm in class from 9:00 in the morning until 9:00 at night, I'm broke, and I have no time for a job."

He smiled at me in a taunting manner and ordered us some beers, which I hoped would better my mood.

"Come on! I feel like kicking your ass tonight," he said, taking the pool sticks off the wall and handing one to me. "Go ahead, break."

"Man, I still have it," I said, proud of my perfect shot.

"Have you checked on Birdie lately?" he asked, moistening his stick.

"Jewel, I just told you I don't have time for nothing."

"She got you to where you are, and now she's barely making it, and you don't have the time," he said, taking his shot.

"Look, man, if you hadn't been half steppin', you would have had your chance, too! What's wrong with Birdie anyway? She sick or something?"

"Don't go there with me. You know I give you a hard time, but I'm proud of you. She ain't sick, but are you fucking blind? Man, look around you, they don't want our kind here no more! They're trying to get rid of us! They're trying to tear our crib down so they can put up some luxury condos. Our

5

people can barely pay their rent now as it is. They're driving all of us out of here."

"What do you want me to do?"

"What do you think I want you to do, go in the corner and do some pirouettes? I want you to get your ass over to her place and talk to her. Tell her that you care."

"All right, I'll go over as soon as I'm done kicking your ass."

The game continued and my mood lightened with the buzz from the beers that kept coming, courtesy of Jewel.

"Eight ball, side pocket, like I said, I kicked your ass and now I'm *outta* here."

"Listen, make sure you tell Birdie I love her," Jewel said.

I signaled him as I headed out the door.

As I made my way east of Fifth Avenue, on 116th Street the Spanish-flavored aromas beaming out of the store fronts and flashing lights captivated me.

I walked up the steps to the sixth floor of the run-down tenement that I grew up in. The loud banging noises and the sounds of couples at war made me sick to my stomach. Suddenly from behind, I heard a familiar voice of a gang member that goes by the street name, "Billion."

"Hey, look who's back."

"Hey, man, how you doin'?"

"Good! What brings you here?"

"I'm here to check on Birdie."

"Why don't you stop in my place for a second? I want to hear what's going on with you."

"Yeah, I can do that."

We made our way to his crib. I hadn't been there in a long time, and not a thing had changed. It was still the same pigsty I remembered.

"What's new with you?" he asked, lighting a cigarette and handing me one.

"A lot, my girl, school."

"Birdie gives me tidbits here and there on you...You interested in making some quick cash?"

"Man, I'm not into that shit anymore," I said.

"You think you're too good for us now?"

"No, that's not what I'm saying," I said, continuing to stand as he got comfortable on the couch.

"We need your help. There are some things that need to be taken care of."

"I can't. I just can't."

He slowly put out his cigarette and got up off the couch. He walked over to me and without any warning I was sucker-punched and knocked to the floor. Barely conscious, the last thing I remember was feeling my cell phone being yanked from my pocket and hearing the words, "Don't you ever forget you belong to us, forever!"

MaryAnn

I loved the intimacy Caleb and I shared as we molded the wet clay together.

He laughed. "This smells funny, Mommy!"

"You're right! It does smell funny, sweetie." I smiled as I cradled his hands.

"Let your hands become your eyes, Caleb. How does it feel?"

"It feels gooey. The wheel is going really fast!"

"It is," I said, kneading out the bumps.

"There's my buddy!" Steven said as he walked into the room.

"Daddy!" Caleb yelled, surprised.

"Keep on going, honey," I said.

"I'm coming right over to your other side," Steven said, putting his arms around him, and kissing the top of his head.

"What do you have going on here?" he asked.

"We're making a turtle," Caleb answered excitedly.

"I bet you it's going to turn out really neat," Steven said, messing his hair.

It was amazing how Caleb, with his small amount of sight, caressed and prodded the shapes as he saw them in his mind. I was so proud of his fine motor skills. I wanted him to be as independent as possible should he never regain his eyesight.

I readily agreed with his instructors in their recommendation to have Caleb put off using a cane for now and have him become fully proficient in focusing on sounds. He seemed to be fine in using his light perception to navigate through doorways and using his hands to feel the walls.

"You're home early," I said to Steven.

"They're still protesting. It will be nothing short of a miracle if this project gets off the ground."

"You have to understand it's their home. You're messing with their home. You and I wouldn't like it if anyone messed with our home, Steven."

"You're probably right."

"By the way, you look like hell."

"I feel like it," he answered, staring at the Caller ID on his vibrating phone.

"Great, it's Jack. He needs to start stepping up to the plate. I'm not answering it."

I looked at Steven as he put his cell phone on the table. He looked exhausted.

"We're almost done here. Why don't you go upstairs and lie down? Try to relax a bit. I'll make you something to eat."

"I'm not hungry and I can't relax."

"Why don't you at least try? Just lie back and close your eyes. Go, it will be good for you," I said, urging him on.

"I'll try. See you in a little bit, buddy," Steven said to Caleb.

"Are you going to take a nap, Daddy?"

"I'm going to try."

"I hate naps, Daddy."

"Trust me! When you're a grownup, you'll appreciate them," Steven said, walking sluggishly out the door.

Our hands moved together in perfect harmony, as we both seemed to get lost in the feel of the clay and the rhythm of the potter's wheel. Suddenly, our calm state was interrupted when Steven's cell phone vibrated.

Steven

I sat at the edge of the bed. I cradled my head in my arms and felt numb with despair. *How did I let everything get this far?* I asked myself. This wasn't the plan, but nothing in my life really felt planned. I got up and put ESPN on, anything to rest my mind as I lay back and started to drift off. I thought about my life so far play by play, much like the commentators who were discussing the major upsets in Sundays' games.

I loved MaryAnn ever since I met her in college. Her long golden blonde hair and deep brown eyes captivated me. She was as beautiful inside as she was out. At eighteen, I knew I had to have her for the rest of my life. We got married the summer after graduation, and she became pregnant with Melanie on our honeymoon. She supported me as I worked endless hours at my family's building company, in hopes of winning over my father's approval and taking it over someday. It worked, and even with the bad economy the company had never been more successful.

MaryAnn realized the gift our daughter Melanie had in dance. She traveled with her to all her competitions, which became a full-time job for her. I tried my best to make it to as many of her events as I could, but MaryAnn was always by her side.

Thirteen years later, Caleb was born six weeks premature with corneal blindness. We were distraught as any parents would be, but we were told that there was hope for him, that a corneal transplant might cure him. Two months later we were relieved to receive a donor. That relief turned to heartbreak when his body's immune system rejected it.

After the next two unsuccessful attempts to help Caleb, we tried our best to accept our son's deteriorating eye condition, putting on a brave front, especially for Melanie who adored her baby brother. The doctors informed MaryAnn and I that Caleb would probably see shades of gray and lightness, which might diminish over time.

His doctor, who was a world-renowned specialist in this type of surgery, would only perform this surgery four times on a patient. Caleb needed a miracle, and time was running out.

MaryAnn became a crusader for blind children. She organized a play group for blind children at the local community center. MaryAnn bought all the special toys needed. The kids especially loved the blocks with Braille lettering, which most of them were starting to learn. MaryAnn and Melanie encouraged Caleb. They told him about how exciting learning Braille would be and that he would be able to someday read all the stories they once enjoyed. Although our schedules were busy, MaryAnn made sure that both Melanie and I learned Braille as well.

Caleb lit up the room whenever he entered. He was incredibly lovable, and in spite of his struggles, he seemed to enjoy his life. Although I secretly longed for a son that I could throw a football with and watch sports with, Caleb was a beautiful soul, and I could only thank God for the beautiful gift He had given us.

Throughout the past few years, our marriage seemed to always focus on Melanie and Caleb. We waited with anticipation to see what schools Melanie would get into. When we learned of her acceptance to Fillmore we were overjoyed, yet we were both anxious about our little girl leaving home and living in the big city. Although my office is also in the city, not too far from Fillmore, the thought of her walking the streets of New York left me feeling unsettled.

MaryAnn devoted every ounce of her time to Caleb, and when night fell upon us she was left with little energy and no desire for sex. I still remember the first time I laid eyes on Lauren, my heart skipped a beat and I thought *what a nice rack.* The more time I spent with her, the more alive I felt.

Suddenly, I was startled out of my half-consciousness by the sound of our wooden bedroom door being shoved open. I opened my eyes to see MaryAnn standing before me with tears in her eyes and my cell phone in her hand.

Part 1

The Beginning

"A Dream is a Wish Your Heart Makes"
~Cinderella

Chapter 1

Melanie

I was shaking in my seat, unable to move.

How am I ever going to be able to dance for them?

The peach-colored room felt more like a torture chamber than a holding room for all of us who successfully made it to the final round. All of us dancers, Fillmore hopefuls, developed a solid camaraderie as we painfully made it to the final round. Now we were all silent as the intensity could be felt in the air. I looked around as dancers lay on the floor with their legs stretched apart, while others sat listening to their iPods. Each last name starting in the alphabet from A-G was being called randomly for a two-minute solo and a final interview. After that you were required to leave the school, and if you were one of the few lucky ones, you would receive a call by 10:00 the next morning.

"Calm down," said Elnando, a Fillmore hopeful who first introduced himself to me at the ballet barre within minutes of our arrival at Fillmore. "You gave it your all. You were great!"

I couldn't even answer. I was feeling incredibly nervous. The past few days I couldn't help noticing him in the lineup. Elnando was a beautiful dancer with dark brown eyes and short brown hair that he wore in cornrows. His body was muscular and strong, and his charisma shone through when he danced. He stood apart from all the other male dancers, many of whom were obviously gay, which showed through their effeminate moves.

"Belezzi," the woman announced as she entered the room.

"Show them what you got, Melanie!" Darnel, one of my dance partners, yelled out.

"Break a leg!" Elnando said with a mischievous smile.

"Thanks! That's what I needed to hear."

The woman led me to a small dressing room and told me to take my time. I knew this was it. Everything mattered from this point forward. I changed into a black leotard and white wrap. I knew everything I had worked for depended on this dance. I focused and became centered as I lay on the floor, stretched and adjusted my pointe shoes. I stood up, breathed in and gave myself a final glance in the mirror.

I walked out of the dressing room. I could feel the gaze of the panel of judges as they sat before me. A young woman, who I assumed was an upperclassman, asked for my CD. I handed it to her. She gave me a reassuring smile and said, "Whenever you're ready." I took first position and nodded. I felt almost out-of-body as I flew through the air, performing the allegro of quick moving steps and jumps to the heart-pounding beats of Tchaikovsky's *1812 Overture*. My lines were clean and my landings were perfect. As the music ended, I felt a sense of relief and a feeling of euphoria that I had nailed the very routine that I had poured my heart and soul into over the past few months.

The young woman brought over a bright red chair and placed it before the panel. I sat and caught my breath as one of the panel members asked, "What sets you apart from all the other dancers who are vying for a chance to dance at Fillmore?"

"Dance is who I am. I have to dance. It's my life."

~~~

I waved and smiled at my parents and Caleb, as they pulled up to the Trump Hotel. I agreed to call them as soon as it was over. Breathlessly, I told them they could come and get me and that "I nailed it!"

The hotel was within walking distance of Fillmore. I knew I could go there, catch my breath, and it would be an easy spot for them to pick me up.

I jumped into the car. "Hey, little man," I said, leaning over and giving Caleb, my baby brother, a big fat, wet kiss on his cheek.

Caleb rubbed his cheek, "Hi, Melanie!"

My mother peered at me in the backseat, "Congratulations, honey."

"Thank you, Mom, but we're not in the clear yet."

My dad smiled at me through the rear-view mirror and said, "You said you nailed it. You gave it your best. Your mom and I are very proud of you, no matter what. Melanie, you hear me back there?"

"Yeah, I hear you," I said barely audible as I became engulfed with the sites and sounds of the big city. I knew if my dream was to come true, I would be living in the city that never sleeps and going to a school that I had wanted to go to since attending Miss Elle's School of Dance.

"Remember, Melanie, there's a lot of other good colleges out there, if this doesn't work out," my mom said.

"I know, Mom, but it's Fillmore. It's every dancer's dream."

"I know, sweetheart, and it's the dream of all the others, too. And they only choose so many," my mother reminded me.

"I know," I said, staring out the window, amazed that Caleb could be falling asleep with everything illuminating outside our window.

Then I thought: *Reminder to self: Caleb is blind. And, Mom, the ultimate voice of reason, is always right; Fillmore is not only my dream, but the dream of every dancer who performed beside me today.*

~~~

I couldn't sleep that night. I mentally replayed the routine that I performed for the judges, confirming to myself that I didn't miss a beat. I got up at the crack of dawn and let Barkley, our precocious eight-year-old golden retriever, out. I lay on the couch, clicking the channels through the different morning shows as all of them repeated the same stories. I watched the clock minute by minute.

An hour later Caleb and my mom came down, as I lay paralyzed with fear.

My mom cheerfully asked, "Who wants Belgium waffles?"

"I do," Caleb yelled, cradled in her arms.

"Who wants to help me make them?"

"Mom, I can't even move."

"Oh, come on. Help me out. It will make the time go by."

I sluggishly rose from the couch and grabbed Caleb. We went to the kitchen and I put Caleb on the counter, as Mom retrieved the bowl, oil, eggs and mix. She preheated the iron, as I held my hand around Caleb's hand. We smashed the egg against the metal bowl. I purposely let part of the egg touch his finger, knowing how much he relied on touch.

"That's really gooey isn't it, Caleb?" I asked.

"It feels funny."

My mom brewed a pot of hazelnut coffee, and as the waffles began to heat up, a sweet aroma filtered the air.

Mom and Caleb retreated to the table. Caleb ate the waffles whole without syrup, as my mother slowly sipped her coffee. I continued making rounds of waffles to pass the time.

My dad appeared, still sleepy-eyed.

"Dad, it's almost 10 o'clock. I can't take this anymore."

With a wide-eyed grin, he said, "Today's your big day."

"Ugh," I said, rubbing my temples.

"Relax! Have a waffle with your brother," my mom said in a teasing manner.

"They're really good *waftills*, Melanie, and I'm still crossing my fingers."

Although I was nervous as hell, I couldn't help but laugh as Caleb pushed out his arms and crossed his fingers between bites.

After our trip home last night, Caleb had woken up again, so I offered to tuck him in and read him a story. I needed to get my mind on something else. I told him to keep his fingers crossed that I would hopefully receive a very important phone call the next day. He wanted me to show him how to do it. I positioned his fingers, and he drifted off to sleep. I was surprised this morning that he not only remembered our conversation but how to cross his fingers.

"I really can't eat anything now, Caleb."

My cell phone rang. I anxiously looked at the Caller ID. "Oh my God, oh my God, it's Fillmore!"

"It's Fillmore! It's Fillmore," Caleb repeated.

I answered, as my mom and dad huddled around me. "Hello. Yes, this is. Oh my gosh, thank you so much! Yes, I'm very excited! I will see you soon!"

"I'm in! I'm in!" I yelled. Both of my parents embraced me in a bear hug. Overwhelmed with excitement, I lifted Caleb out of his seat and twirled him around. "I did it, Caleb! I'm going to Fillmore! I'm going to Fillmore!"

"I crossed my fingers, Melanie, and now you're going to Fillmore."

"That's right, Caleb." I laughed.

Chapter 2

Elnando

Out of my blood-shot eyes, I saw the familiar faces, my brothers, gathering around trying their best to get as many punches and kicks in as they could physically muster. Out of sheer exhaustion, many of them stopped, only to be told that whoever stopped, without being told, would get hit too. The pain was excruciating. As I was about to take what I thought would be my last breath, at full throttle a final blow to my ribs left me seeing stars. As I lay dying, I could hear the start of the Yankees game and the same familiar voices cheering them on.

"Hey, wake up! Wake up! Your phone is going off."

I was glad to be awakened from my nightmare, not wanting to relive another moment of what I had once endured. I was surprised to see Shalonka still there. I was pissed, after I had told her several times not to smoke in my bed, there she was puffing away.

I looked at the Caller ID and took a deep breath.

"Hello. Great! I'll be ready to go by then. Thank you," I said, shocked.

"You get some good news?" Shalonka asked, as she continued taking drags off her cigarette.

"Yeah, now it's time for you to get your ass out of here."

"You got anything for me?" she asked, getting up and gathering her things.

I reached across the side table and grabbed a $20 bill out of my wallet.

"Here, go get yourself a cab."

"Geez thanks," she said, walking out the door.

I sat still for a moment, feeling paralyzed with fear.

I really made it in. I'm really that good. I can't believe this. I have to go tell Birdie.

~~~

Birdie opened the door. The once vibrant woman was starting to show her age. Since her husband Joe died, the years were starting to take their toll on her. Birdie was becoming more unrecognizable with each visit. Although her smile was broad, and I felt her love as I walked through the door, her movements were slow and her hands trembled.

"So, do you have some news for me?" she asked wide-eyed.

"Birdie, I made it. They want me. I really am that good."

Birdie placed her cold hands on my face. "Joe and I always told you that you're something special. I'm so happy for you, and he would be, too."

"What can I get you?" she asked sweetly.

"Nothing, I'm fine. Sit down and relax. I have some things I want to share with you. I received a partial scholarship, and I will be living on campus."

"That's wonderful! I can tell something's wrong. What is it?"

"I don't know, Birdie. It's going to be an awful lot of hard work."

"And you ain't used to hard work? All those days Joe and I dragged you to the studio and you danced, you danced your heart out. All that aggression you had built up inside, you let it out when you danced. Joe and I knew you had it in you. We knew you could make it. You walked away from all the nonsense that was going on around you. You worked hard in school and when others put you down, you just kept on dancing."

"I owe it all to you and Joe. You took a chance on me."

"I have to say, you sitting here today with this good news, it paid off. We all know the road was hard for you, with your papa being gone. But, your mama, Joe and I, we all believed in you. Now, you just keep doing what you're doing."

"I will," I said, smiling up at her.

"Did you call your mama with the good news?"

"I left a message on her phone, and I know she only checks it now and then when she's working on the cruise ship."

"She is going to be delighted to hear your good news. You have a whole new world that's going to open up to you. Don't be afraid of it."

"You're right," I said, getting up and hugging her tight.

If she only knew that what ate at me inside wasn't the new world, but the old life I was trying so desperately to leave behind, if they would actually let me.

Chapter 3

Lauren

I knew it was him before I even set eyes on him. His cologne lingered through the office. Knowing that I would see him made me look forward to getting ready for work at Belezzi Builders every morning.

"Hello, Lauren," he said with a big smile. "You think you can make some follow-up calls for me today? I need the run down on where we stand with everything in Spanish Harlem."

"I'll get right on it." I smiled back.

Since starting as an administrative assistant five months ago, I find myself falling more in love with him every day. Not only is he a super boss, but he is also absolutely gorgeous. I find myself feeling giddy just getting ready for work in the morning, carefully planning my outfits, hoping he will notice me. I know he's happily married to a beautiful woman, and his daughter is not much younger than me. He's a terrific dad to his son who is blind. He's perfect. Lately, it seems that my life has been made up of working, drinking and clubbing with my girlfriends. It seems like all the men I date are straight out of *Jersey Shore*, arrogant, with little motivation except in getting me in the sack, but, of course, this one has to be married. I'd played that game before; it never worked, but I was willing to take the risk.

"Who feels like going on a field trip?" Jack, the goofy construction coordinator, asked.

"What's going on?"

"Mr. Belezzi thinks it would be a good idea for all of us to go take a look at the area that hopefully we will get permission to build on. And I hear he's going to be buying rounds at Pugby's afterwards," Jack said, in his silly manner as Steven walked by.

"Free drinks? I'm in." Steven joked.

"Yeah, on your tab!" Jack said.

"Lauren, look at this guy! Do you think he needs any more drinks in him?" Steven asked, patting Jack's stomach.

I smiled and shook my head at the two of them. They made working in an office so much fun. It didn't hurt that Dolores, the office gossip, and I were the only two women in the office. Even though Dolores was a pain in the ass, she was the only woman I had to deal with. I believe that the more women, the more drama in an office. But, no matter how crazy things got around here, Steven was beautiful eye candy, with his olive skin, dark brown hair and eyes, and his physique—perfect.

"I'll drive and then we can head back here afterwards," Steven announced to the two architects who worked in the cubes next to mine, and to Dolores who happened to be wandering near my cube.

All of us walked together to the parking garage and got into his Escalade, our destination—Spanish Harlem.

The colorful graffiti on the old buildings and the sculptures on Museum Mile made Spanish Harlem feel cozy and inviting. Steven was lucky enough to find a parking spot on a side road. We walked a few blocks and saw a 21-story run-down housing project, with a plot of land overgrown with weeds and garbage next to it. It stood out like a sore thumb among the Latin-flavored storefronts and rehabbed buildings in the areas surrounding it.

We walked over to the area like uninvited guests, as everyone who passed us by looked us up and down. Steven, unfazed by the glares, announced, "If all goes right, my friends, this is where our beautiful condos and street-level stores will be built. And, in the weeded fields to your right, will be a park for the young ones to enjoy. If everything falls into place, we will be starting construction in the early spring. Does anyone have any questions?"

"What is going to happen to the folks living here?" Dolores asked.

Why on earth did Steven ask her to come?

"They can always opt to live in one of our condos, but I doubt any of them will be able to afford it, seeing that the government is paying most of their rent. The tenants should be aware that the area is changing. The bottom line is, if we don't build, someone else is going to. All of us, as a team, know we are the best. We missed out on the Barclay Center, and although this isn't nearly as big, we can't afford to miss this opportunity."

~~~

We all gathered at Pugby's Pub, as the day turned to dusk. Steven said the food and drinks were on him. All of us ordered light fare, and the only people who drank were Steven and Jack. It was a good time, as Jack did most of the talking. We headed back to the office just before 6 o'clock.

When we returned, Steven announced that it was time to close shop. Everyone grabbed their bags and cases, then hurried out.

I was the only one left. While checking my messages, Steven came over.

"Didn't you hear me? It's time to get the hell out of here."

"I know! I know! I just wanted to see if anyone got back to me."

"You can worry about that tomorrow."

"Okay! Okay! I'm leaving."

Steven turned off the lights and we walked out together.

"Why don't I give you a lift?"

"That's all right. I don't want to put you out."

"It's no bother. Plus, I can use some company, driving in this crazy city."

"I live in Williamsburg."

"Williamsburg, why not?"

I followed him to the parking garage, without a word being spoken between us.

"Hop in," he said.

"Thank you so much! I really appreciate this."

"No problem."

As we drove, we made small talk. Although it felt awkward, it also felt good at the same time.

"Very nice," he said, as he pulled up to my apartment. "Although we didn't build it," he said with a sly smile, "I know the builder who did this whole neighborhood. Large walk-in bedroom closets, right?"

"Very good, do you want to come in?" I was shocked that I just asked him that, and even more surprised when he said, "Yeah, I'd like to see the place."

I apologized for the mess and wished I had taken at least a few minutes this morning to clear off the kitchen counter and put the dishes in the dishwasher.

"Not too shabby! I must be paying you well."

I smiled at him and offered him a drink.

"What do you have?"

I opened the 'fridge. "I have beer, Diet Coke...."

"A glass of water will do."

"Sure! I can get that for you."

I brought him a glass of water, and we sat together on my loveseat and laughed while talking about the office. I could see that he was trying hard not to stare at my breasts.

"I should be going now. We both have to work tomorrow."

I grabbed his hand. "Wait! I thought you might want to check out the closets."

Chapter 4

Melanie

I was excited and not sure what to expect as I arrived at the campus center. I knew I would be meeting my roommate, Ming-Na. She stood out at the auditions as a classic contemporary artist with a style all her own. Although I didn't get a chance to actually talk with her, I had a feeling from watching her from afar at the auditions that we would hit it off. Everyone was told to wear comfortable shoes and have some spending money on hand. They said we were in for an adventure.

I gave my name at the check-in. I was told that we would be divided into groups, and on return we would get any additional housing information for when we officially moved in next weekend.

I was given an extra large red T-shirt to put on over my shirt and a canvas bag filled with who knows what. I was also the lucky one chosen to be in charge of a digital camera, provided by Fillmore, to use for our team's adventure. I was assigned to the red team, otherwise known as Team Orbit, which consisted of three other dance majors.

With a broad smile, the greeter said, "I see some red shirts lingering over there."

I turned and, to my surprise, it was Darnel, Elnando and Ming-Na.

I was extremely happy to see that Darnel made it into Fillmore, too! Darnel was tall, black and handsome. He was extremely funny, outspoken, and openly gay. I remembered how he had entertained all of us and lightened the mood at times during the audition process. As for Elnando, the beautiful man who had cheered me on, I was especially glad to see him.

"Hey girl, you made it," Darnel said, giving me a hug. "This here is Ming-Na and she's from San Fran."

"My new roommate!" I exclaimed.

"Congratulations!" she said, smiling at me.

I liked Ming-Na as soon as she smiled at me, and I knew immediately that my feelings were right-on. She seemed easy going and a lot of fun. I knew we were going to be fast friends.

"We made it!" I said cheerfully.

"And you remember Elnando? He's my roomie," Darnel said, with an emphasis on Elnando.

"I do."

"I knew you were going to make it!" he said.

We were interrupted by the enthusiastic shouts coming from a bull horn.

"Hello, everyone, I'm Rachael, and I am a senior in the dance department. I want to welcome all of you to Fillmore! Being here is a prestigious honor, and you should all be very proud of yourselves. Today we are going to have an ice-breaker, so you can get to know each other and become familiar with this fabulous city. Guess what all of you are going to do today?"

"What?" we all cheered.

"We are going on a New York City scavenger hunt. Yoo-hoo! In your packets are coupons to get in free to many of the city's biggest tourist spots, maps with the destinations, and what tasks must be done when you reach your destination. Any number of members from each team can be in the photo. Each of the places has assigned points, and whatever team has the most points at the end, wins! Only one member of your team was given a digital camera. We don't

29

want any pictures on your cell phones. We will keep these pictures as property of Fillmore. If you don't want to be in a pic, don't pose for it. It's as simple as that." She yelled enthusiastically, "Are you ready?"

I flashed the camera at all of them.

"The person with the camera is in charge of the camera and downloading the pictures. All of the information for this is in the travel bag. I want all of you to return back here by 8 pm. Any questions? We will post all of the 'pics and announce the winning team in the next few weeks. Are you ready?"

All of us shouted a great big "Yes!"

"I said! Are you ready?" she asked even louder into the bull horn.

We all cheered, "Yes!" even louder.

"Then go! The Big Apple is waiting for all of you!"

~ ~ ~

"Ming-Na, I think Elnando and Darnel should share a seat in that pink Barbie car. The picture is worth 20 points."

"Good idea!" Ming-Na said.

"Come on, big boy!" Darnel said to Elnando, as they made their way to the Ferris wheel inside Toys "R" Us.

Elnando yelled, "I'll get you back for this, Melanie!"

"Oh look! They're stopped at the top! It's time for a Kodak moment," I yelled up to them.

Darnel put his arm around Elnando and pretended to kiss him.

"Now, that's a perfect shot!" I said, laughing at them.

Elnando shook his head at me and Ming-Na.

Our next stop was Madame Tussauds. The wax figures were so similar to the actual stars, that it was creepy. I asked a nice young couple touring at the same time as us if they would take a picture of the four of us. They agreed. All of us bowed in front of Gandhi with serious expressions. We all burst out laughing as soon as the flash went off.

We agreed our last stop would be the lower east side to Russ and Daughters Specialty Store.

"I thought you two grew up in the city? I asked looking at Elnando and Darnel.

Darnel answered, "What's your point?"

"Then why are we having such a hard time finding this place?" I teased them.

"Listen, Jersey girl, you just worry about the camera!" Darnel kidded.

We arrived at Russ and Daughters. You could smell the smoked fish as soon as you entered the store. The glass cases were filled with caviar and a smorgasbord of Jewish delicacies that I would guess none of us had ever tried.

"It's your turn, Elnando," I said, handing him the unwrapped package of smoked fish. This is worth 30 points; this may win it for us."

"I don't do fish."

"You can do it. Think of your girlfriend," Darnel said, egging him on.

"I don't have a girlfriend."

I was extremely glad to hear that, as Darnel raised his eyebrows, smiling and asked animatedly, "Is that so?" Ming-Na and I started laughing.

"Come on, Ming-Na! You know you *wanna* try it!" Elnando pleaded.

Ming-Na just shook her head.

"Melanie, come on," he said, shoving the package toward me.

"No, it's your turn. You can do it!" I said.

We all cheered as he lifted a bite to his mouth. We agreed that Elnando's disgusted look was worth 1000 words and definitely the 30 points.

We all collapsed on the subway back to school. Although we were all dancers and used to being on our feet, exploring the big city was an exhausting workout.

When we arrived back at campus, Elnando and Darnel hung out at our dorm while Ming-Na helped me download the pictures. I was grateful that not only was she going to be my roommate, but she was incredibly patient, with great computer skills.

Ming-Na had moved into the dorm on Friday, along with all the people who came from other states and some from other countries. I was going to be moving in next week with all the other freshmen from the city and Jersey. All first-year students were required to live on campus. Ming-Na had her area neatly set up, with pictures of family and friends on her tiny desk. I couldn't wait to move in with her.

~ ~ ~

We returned to the campus center to receive any last minute housing information and instructions from Rachael, the bull-horn enthusiast. Elnando, Darnel and I walked Ming-Na back to our dorm.

Darnel announced, "I must be heading back to the hood. See you all next week."

Ming-Na and I gave him a hug goodbye.

"Where are you off to?" Elnando asked.

"I have a choice. Because it's early enough, I can make a call for my dad's company car and go home, or I can stay at the Trump Hotel."

They all looked at me like I had three heads. "My dad owns a building company. What can I say? He knows "*the Donald*."" I chuckled.

32

"You can stay here, if you like. I have extra blankets," Ming-Na said.

"No, that's all right. Thank you though. I'll let you get settled."

"Wow! The Trump Hotel or the company car back to Jersey! You must be some kind of rich girl," Elnando said teasingly.

"My family's a little comfortable, but the next four years I will be a struggling student dancer like the rest of you."

"I understand. I'll walk you out, while you make up your mind."

Elnando and I both said goodbye to Ming-Na. I told her how much fun I had with her today and that I look forward to us being roomies.

She said she absolutely loves New York, and she feels a lot more at ease knowing that I am her roommate.

Fillmore was beginning to be everything I dreamed it would be. The day was beautiful. The cool breeze coming off the campus fountains felt refreshing, and having Elnando by my side made me wish this night would never end. I felt an instant connection to Elnando and an attraction to him that was getting hard to hide.

"Did you decide what you wanted to do?" Elnando asked.

"I really don't feel like going home tonight. Would you mind walking me back to the hotel?"

Elnando looked at me with a sheepish grin.

Chapter 5

MaryAnn

What is taking him so long? I know he said he would be checking out the site today. I'm not going to text him again. Plus, it kind of feels good to sit here, relax and enjoy this glass of Chardonnay. I thought as I sat at the granite island going through the latest issue of *Ladies Home Journal.*

As I started to get into an article on "Can This Marriage Be Saved?" Barkley, our golden retriever, started barking.

"Barkley, calm down and get over here. You're going to wake Caleb."

Steven walked into the kitchen and greeted me as if he had just returned from war.

"I missed you so much tonight!" he said, putting his arms around me, kissing me up and down.

"What's with you?" I asked.

"Can't a man be happy to see his beautiful wife?" he asked, as he continued kissing me all over.

"Come on! Let's go upstairs," he said, grabbing my hand.

~~~

Steven was ferocious and animalistic as we made love. It had been a long time since we made love with such fervor that my orgasms were repetitious as he continued to devour me.

I was glad I had that glass of wine to relax my mood, and tonight without objection I offered myself up to Steven.

I looked at Steven as we lay naked between the sheets.

34

"You're so hot! I bet all the women in the office are crazy about you," I teased him, scratching my nails up and down his chest. I sat up. "I mean, I bet Dolores, the only woman in your office, is crazy about you."

"During the spring, I hired a new girl. I thought I told you."

Before I could even respond, Steven sat up and said, "Let's not talk now," as he playfully pushed me back down on the bed.

~ ~ ~

Like clockwork, Barkley was there to greet us at our bedside at 7 am, as the shrill sound of the alarm clock awakened us. I reached over and turned it off, as Barkley jumped up and started panting at the foot of our bed.

Steven was still in a deep sleep. I looked over at him.

How lucky I am to have such a gorgeous husband with such a lively personality. God truly has blessed me.

I got up and Barkley followed me as I checked on Caleb.

Caleb sat quietly playing with his Braille cubes.

"Good morning, Caleb," I said, as Barkley ran over to him.

Caleb rubbed his head, as Barkley nearly knocked him over with kisses.

"Would you like to come downstairs and have some breakfast?"

"I want to play," Caleb said, absorbed in his toys.

Suddenly Steven came to his door, "Hey, Caleb, why don't you come downstairs and have breakfast with me?"

"Daddy!" Caleb yelled as Steven walked over to him. He scooped him up in his arms and carried him down the stairs.

I let Barkley out the back door, started the coffee, and put the bread in the toaster.

I asked Steven, "Do you want some scrambled eggs?"

"No thanks. Toast and coffee will do. By the way, I'm not going to be home until late tonight. I have a lot of site visits to do, and a mountain of paperwork to go through back at the office. I figured I'd eat breakfast with my little man, seeing I'm not going to have dinner with him," Steven said, patting Caleb's back.

"Another late night? Melanie will be coming home tonight. I'm sure she'll want to tell you all about her student orientation. I hope she likes who she'll be rooming with, and I hope she made some nice friends."

"I'm sure Melanie did fine. She's just like her father," Steven answered.

Chapter 6

Elnando

I sat at the edge of my bed watching Jade and Piv play Grand Theft Auto. They put so much stamina into the game and pursued every turn with such mad skill that I could only imagine what could become of them if they applied themselves to something legit.

I wanted to share with them how I met the most incredible girl, how amazing the campus was at Fillmore and about my new roommate. I knew they couldn't relate to what I wanted to say, and I didn't feel like being mocked more than usual. But watching them play the game was starting to get boring, and at this point talking to a total stranger would have been better than no one.

Suddenly, there was a frantic knock on the front door. Jade and Piv stopped dead in their tracks.

"It's me open up!"

I unlocked the door and there stood Jewel and some kid that I didn't know, who appeared to be around fourteen-years-old. Jewel was out of breath, and the kid looked like he had just seen a ghost.

"Man, Tarvo—he was coming after us!"

"Slow down, man! What's going on?" I asked.

"I was just walking back from his turf. I didn't want no trouble. I just had to drop some stuff off for a girl I met. He saw us and started shooting. I didn't have no time to do nothing. I started running, and *Boy Blue* here started following me."

I asked, amazed by his stupidity, "What the hell were you thinking going there? What did you want, a piece of ass?

Shit, you have this kid following you like your some rock star! C'mon, Jewel! You're smarter than this."

"Yeah, I know," he said catching his breath. "I really have been trying to lay low lately. I guess I thought they might have forgotten about me."

I chuckled. "Jewel, you are unforgettable."

Jade and Piv put down their controllers, unnerved by Jewel's appearance. "Thanks for letting us use your game for the last time. You sure you need it at your new school?" Jade asked.

"Get the hell out of here, man," I said.

Jade put out his hand. "Seriously man, I wish you some good luck!" Piv did the same and said, "Don't forget us."

"Trust me! You two are unforgettable, too! I'll still be around. I have to keep my eye on my mama and Birdie, and keep this guy in check," I said, looking over at Jewel.

Jade said, "Take care." Both of them looked over at Jewel and signaled goodbye.

I went to the 'fridge and brought out a couple of Coronas for me and Jewel. The only time I had beer in the 'fridge, or friends or women over, was when my mama was away for work.

"I'd offer you one but I don't believe you're old enough to drink," I said, mocking the young kid. "Hell, we're not even old enough to be drink." I smirked and handed Jewel a beer and sat back on the couch, while Jewel and *Boy Blue* sat in the old worn-out chairs. I put my hands in back of my head, staring at Jewel, speechless.

Jewel returned the stare. "C'mon, man! Say whatever it is you got to say."

"Jewel, when are you *gonna* learn?"

"Learn what? How to do plies? Get a job in the major leagues? What?"

"Jewel, you're like a brother to me. I love you, man, but you're going to get yourself killed. You protected me for the longest time. Now, I feel like I should be protecting you, and I'm not going to be around to do it. You were street smart, while I was always naïve. I looked up to you, but now we *ain't* kids no more. You *gotta* get your shit together. You have mad skills! Use them!"

"What are you talking about?"

"You're a charmer; you have a way with people. Plus, you can fix just about anything. Look at all the things you fixed at Birdie's and the studio, and all the things you put together for her. You're a hard worker. When you work, you bust your ass. We're getting older. This gang-banging shit, you're getting too old for it. We're getting too old for it!"

"I told you I've been trying to lay low. You seem to forget, they are our family," Jewel said.

"No Jewel, Joe was family. Birdie, my mama, your mama and me, we are your family. We were lucky to have Joe around when we did. He was the papa you and I never had. He had high hopes for us. It's time you made him proud, and what are you doing bringing his punk ass around here? Don't bring him down. He deserves a chance," I said, looking over at the solemn kid, who looked at us starry-eyed.

"He's," Jewel started to say.

"I don't care," I interrupted him. "He needs to be in school, where your ass should be right now!"

"I agree with you, man. But, you know we can never leave," Jewel reminded me.

"I know that, but we can at least change the direction we are going."

Chapter 7

Lauren

If he had only wanted to see my closet, I would have attacked him like a cat in heat. I know he's my boss, and he's married, but I didn't care. I wanted him, and I know he wanted me just as much, but he just left me hanging with a wide-eyed grin and an 'I gotta go.'

Everyone started to arrive at the office in piecemeal. I couldn't wait for Steven to arrive, not only because he turned me on so much, but then I wouldn't have to listen to Dolores' mouth. This morning she came back to my cube to ask me a million questions about the proposals I was working on. Her mouth seemed to go a mile a minute. Not to mention, I am reminded every time we talk that she started with the company when Steven's dad was running it, and Steven was a baby still in diapers. Dolores was as old as the light fixtures, but they were actually better looking. Her out-of-style short, poufy hairdo, large glasses and grandma-looking white sweater that she draped around herself every day was as nauseating to look at as the smell of her old-lady tea rose perfume that fumigated the office. Thank God, she answered the phone up front.

Steven finally arrived and paraded through the office like a superstar greeting everyone. A lot was to take place today. We were expecting the final approval from the city to proceed with the company's mission to start tearing down the old housing project we visited in Spanish Harlem, so the company could start building luxury condominiums.

As I saw Steven enter my cube, I smiled softly.

"Hello, Miss Bennett. How are you doing this morning?"

"Good, and how are you doing, Mr. Belezzi?"

40

"I'm doing fabulous, thank you."

"I have a lot of projects for you to work on today." He looked at me with a smile and his head tilted. "I wouldn't want to see you get bored and get yourself into trouble."

"Trouble? But that's my middle name."

"For some reason, I believe you. I need you to follow up on some of these newer proposals, and I will check in with you later in the day to see how you're doing."

"I look forward to it," I said.

Steven looked at me with a sly grin.

~~~

As the day progressed, I missed Steven, as he was out and about meeting with clients and site managers. The other men in the office were boring compared to Steven, except for Jack, who was in his late fifties, funny and fat with a really bad comb-over.

It's Friday night and instead of venturing back to Brooklyn I might as well stay right here in the city and meet up with Tiffany and Katt at our favorite place, The Red Velvet Rope. I had a black sexy cami under my suit coat and tight black dress pants, and sexy stilettos in my bag. It was pay day, so I would have money in my account. I needed to burn off this sexual tension I was feeling.

I sent a text to Tiffany and Katt confirming our time for our Friday night *partay,* as we liked to call it.

A roar of laughter and chatter erupted in the office as Jack and Steven entered later in the afternoon with bottles of Champagne. Everyone stood up and looked over the cube to see what was going on. Steven and Jack announced, "Everyone in the conference room now!" Like dutiful soldiers, we entered the large conference room and filled the seats. Steven uncorked the bubbly Champagne, and as it let out a loud pop and poured to the floor, he exclaimed, "It looks like the walls may be coming down! We received our final approval! As long as everything goes smoothly, we are in business!" Jack passed out the plastic cups and everyone in the conference room raised their cups and cheered. Mike, the IT "go-to" guy, with the long blonde hair and an easy-going manner, announced, "And, we're all getting raises!"

"As soon as I put you in charge! And by the way, didn't I fire your ass yesterday?" Steven kidded along with him. The office laughed along as Steven said, "I'm going to be a nice boss for once. I want all of you to finish up what you're working on and get the hell out of here, because come Monday morning I'm going to be riding you hard!"

Everyone was pumped up as they returned to their cubes. As much as I was happy to be able to get out early, it meant I would no longer be in the same place as Steven. It also meant a change of plans, and I didn't feel like heading home to Brooklyn and then back to the city again.

Everyone had just about gone except for Steven, who was in his office with his door closed. Then I heard the beep of the microwave, and I knew Dolores was still there as well, making herself a cup of tea.

That lady really needs to get a life.

I texted Tiffany and Katt and told them to be on high alert, that there may be a change of plans.

I shuffled papers around, trying to look busy, even though no one could see me. About fifteen minutes later I heard the faint sound of a knock on Steven's door and the annoying sounds of Dolores wishing him a good weekend. It seemed like an eternity for her to shuffle her way out the door, and when I knew she was gone for sure, I breathed a sigh of relief.

It's officially the weekend and Steven and I are the only ones here.

Suddenly, I heard Steven's footsteps. I stood up and looked over my cube.

"Hey, what are you still doing here?" Steven asked. "I was just about to turn the lights off and lock up shop."

"I wanted to finish up some things I was working on."

"Didn't you hear me say that I wanted everyone *outta* here? I want you all to be good and rested this weekend, because next week I want everyone to be at their personal best."

"I understand," I said, looking up at him with a smile. "Oh, by the way, we never went over the proposals you wanted me to follow-up on."

"I say we talk about it on Monday, and both of us get the hell out of here," Steven insisted.

"That's fine with me," I said as I took out my Skechers and started putting them on.

"Are you going for a run?" Steven asked.

I laughed. "No, I have some time I have to kill before I meet up with my girlfriends."

"To be young and free," Steven said with a chuckle.

I smiled at him. "Seeing that I'm forced to leave early today, I will probably go shopping and spend most of my pay before I even order my first drink."

"Self control, that's what you need to have."

"Really, I'll remember that," I said as we left the office together.

As we entered the street I walked over to the motivated street vendor ringing a bell under his large tarp yelling, "Fresh fruit" in accented English. Steven followed me and said, "My little guy loves apples. I should pick him up some."

I looked over at the plump fruit and decided that I'd rather spend my money on alcohol.

Steven grabbed some apples and started juggling. The street vendor shook his head and probably would have protested if he only knew the words to say. Steven smiled, pulled the plastic bag down, filled it with shiny red apples, and paid him.

I giggled and said, "Now, that's some real talent."

"Oh, you haven't seen anything."

We walked several blocks together, peering over the counterfeit goods that filled the city streets. We each tried on a pair of knock-off Prada sunglasses. Steven bought a pair and said, "Seeing that they are 2 for $15, your pair is on me." We both put our new shades on and walked incognito down 5th Avenue. It seemed so natural the two of us walking side by side, that for a moment I forgot he was my boss and married. Then again, nothing had happened between us—yet.

We came upon a vendor with knock-off handbags, and I was in heaven. Although I'd walked past these vendors all week long, I never took the time to actually stop and look. I could have swooped up a dozen handbags in every shape and color. I decided not to buy any. The knock-offs were as gorgeous as the real things, but I preferred to be gifted with the real thing rather than a cheap version of the original.

A light mist started coming down.

"Great," I said, raising my hands up.

"Where are you headed anyway?" Steven asked.

"The Red Velvet Rope," I answered as the light mist started to turn into rain. "This is not what the weatherman predicted."

"That's about six blocks away. I'll hail you a cab," Steven said.

"You don't have to do that."

"It's no problem."

After several attempts, Steven was successful. The cab came to a screeching stop. Like a perfect gentleman, Steven opened the door for me. As I sat down, a loud thunderous boom shot through the air.

"Come in before you get struck by lightning." I inadvertently pulled on his tie.

I gave the address to the driver as Steven sat by my side.

We sat silently listening to the rip and roar of thunder, as the cab maneuvered through the rush-hour city traffic.

The Red Velvet Rope was Katt's, Tiffany's, and my favorite Friday night meeting place. It was well known and a replica of the famous Studio 54. Not too fancy for being in the city, although it did attract some of the city's wealthiest and hottest businessmen, who the three of us seduced with our charm in order to score free drinks.

"Why don't you join me? You are just going to get stuck in traffic, in the pouring rain."

"You're meeting your friends. I don't want to intrude."

"Come on! They have heard all about you!"

He laughed. "That's why I don't think I should join you."

Surprisingly, without further argument he paid the cab fare.

He followed me through the pristine red velvet rope. Seventies music blared, and the ambiance of glittered walls and mirrors made me want to hit the dance floor upon entering. Although it was still early and the real *partay* didn't start until after midnight, it wasn't unusual to find people cutting loose on the dance floor during Friday's happy hour.

45

After a few Rum and Cokes, Katt, Tiffany and I were usually the ones who owned the dance floor.

Steven took a seat at the bar. I excused myself to go use the ladies room. The ladies room was empty. I took off my jacket, put my stilettos on, put my shoulder-length light brown hair in a twist, and left a few highlighted strands out on the side. I put on a sparkly long chain that I had in my purse, quickly reapplied my makeup, and spritzed on some Tommy Hilfiger. I gathered everything in my bag and gave myself a final glance. I looked good and couldn't believe Steven, my hot boss, was waiting for me. Maybe tonight all my fantasies would come true.

I sent a text to Katt and Tiffany telling them what was going on. Katt texted back, "You are something else! Do you still want Tiffany and me to come?"

I texted back, "Yes," I had no idea how long Steven was going to stay. I knew that I could ditch the two of them at any moment, which wasn't uncommon if someone wanted to take one of us home.

I went back to the bar and took a seat next to Steven.

"I think it's time for me to go. I had planned on checking out some sites," he said.

"It's Friday night. How 'bout a few shots on me?"

"A few shots on you? You're barely legal."

"Please! I'm 25!" I signaled the bartender.

We chugged our shots in unison, and then as if we were playing a game, we took turns ordering more, on Steven's tab.

A few rounds later, Katt and Tiffany appeared by our side. They both had on stylish mini dresses, and Katt, with her short blonde hair, killer blue eyes, and athletic kick ass body, stood out from amongst the crowd, while Tiffany, with her girl-next-door look and long dark brown hair extensions, looked like a beauty queen. I thought I looked just as good, even with my attire spruced up from my day job.

After an awkward introduction, the shots continued. Finally as the bar filled up, the lights went down and the disco ball that centered the dance floor lit up.

We were hammered and feeling good, as Katt, Tiffany and I made our way to the dance floor as "Ladies' Night" by Kool and the Gang blared through the speakers. We danced as Steven watched us from afar.

The DJ played the next song, Donna Summer's "Love to Love You Baby." Steven walked over to the side of the dance floor with a bottle of beer in his hand and stood mesmerized as the three of us danced seductively.

Our eyes met. I smiled at him.

"I have to go," he mouthed, barely able to contain himself.

Chapter 8

Elnando

"Welcome home, homeboy! Now, bow to the Ga, bow to the Ga," Darnel said to me as I entered our dorm room. On the bare wall, was a stand alone, large, painted picture of Lady Gaga. "And, don't you be *puttin'* your crosses or Spanish flag anywhere near her."

I animatedly bowed and couldn't help but laugh. "How you doin', man?" I asked, shaking his hand.

"I'm doing fine. You need any help?" Darnel asked.

"No, I'm good. I don't have much." The past few weeks Darnel and I slowly moved our belongings in. I always returned home. My mama was still away for work, so I decided to enjoy the little bit of time alone while I could. Darnel mostly stayed, even though his family lived in the city, and he already seemed acclimated to the dorm room.

Darnel said, while admiring himself in the mirror, "If you don't need me, I'm going to lift some weights and see if there is any studio space free. I need to work on my moves. I'll be back in a few hours to get ready. I don't know if you remember, but there's a student get-together at the campus center tonight. I told Ming-Na we'd be there."

"I remember. I'm going to put away the rest of my things and chill out for a bit. It will be good to see Ming-Na and Melanie. I take it she'll be there?"

"Yeah, I'm sure. I'll see you later," he said, grinning at me as he walked through the door.

Great, I thought lying back on the bed.

I meet a beautiful dancer, who's down to earth and not nutty like most of the dancers I've encountered. We talk for hours, and I leave her with a kiss. A kiss like nothing I had ever experienced. As crazy as

48

it sounds, that alone was better than any sex I had ever had. And, what do I do? Nothing! I never even give her a call back or a simple text. Yep, she's probably thinking I'm some sort of player. Well, the truth is, I really am. Melanie is the type of girl I always dreamed of being with. I would always be faithful to a girl like her. I've never met a girl like her. She's wholesome, outgoing, and cute as hell. I can't stop thinking about her.

I had to endure a lot of shit in my life, and yet I made it into Fillmore. This is the time for me to stay focused on dance and getting into a premier dance company. Plus, this girl can do so much better than me. We aren't even in the same league, or the same universe for that matter. I do want to see her again. I would love to have a girl like that in my life, but then I would have to let her into my world.

I grabbed a pillow and put it over my face, and laid back.

Damn, why do I have to be falling in love with such a perfect girl?

Chapter 9

Melanie

Not a call, text or anything! Yep, he's a player! I should have known!

I looked through the 'pics on my laptop of our adventure in the city.

"Those 'pics are a riot! Ming-Na said looking over my shoulder. "Whenever you're ready, we can head over to the campus center."

I closed my laptop shut. "I think I'm going to attempt to put the rest of my stuff away. Do you mind if I meet up with all of you at the campus center when I'm done?"

"No, but I can help you with the rest of it."

"That's okay. I don't know where I'm going to put half the stuff anyway."

"Are you sure?"

"Positive."

Ming-Na was incredibly kind. She welcomed me as soon as I arrived with my belongings. She offered to rearrange any of her things to make more room for mine. I told her there was no need, but if she could help me arrange my work area I would appreciate it. She said she would be happy to help and, then without my asking, helped me fold my clothes and put them away.

I never told Ming-Na that Elnando spent almost the whole night with me the first day we all met. Elnando and I stayed up until the wee hours talking about everything from movies to dance. When it felt like something more was about to take place, he whispered in my ear that he had to go. We embraced in a kiss that left me weak in the knees. I felt like I had just been kissed by some sort of superhero, who had to leave suddenly to go save the world.

I thought we had such a connection with each other, but as much as we talked about everything that night, I now realize that I barely know anything about him.

As soon as Ming-Na left, I opened up my computer. I looked at all the 'pics, pausing at the ones Elnando was in. I was too drained to take on the task of putting away my last few boxes. I slowly put on a pair of jeans and a pink satin top I had just folded, and got myself ready. I flipped my head over and put gel through my long, wavy, sandy blonde hair to give it some extra shine. The humidity was making it look frizzy, so I decided to tie it up in a loose ponytail instead of fussing with my straightening iron. I reapplied some foundation over the tiny freckles that seemed to appear anytime I spent any amount of time outside in the sun. I looked at myself in the full-length mirror on the bathroom door.

I really am standing in a dorm room at Fillmore. I actually made it.

I decided it was now or never for me to make my way to the campus center. Elnando may not even be hanging with Darnel and Ming-Na. I would probably see him flirting with one of the dancers who barely spoke English. Either way, I was now in the mood for some fun, whoever I ended up hanging with.

I walked in. Elnando's eyes instantly met mine, as he was sitting with Darnel and Ming-Na on the arm of Ming-Na's chair.

"Hi, Melanie," Darnel yelled.

"Hey, Darnel."

"How ya doing, baby?"

"I'm doing good. How are you?"

"Did you get all your things put away?" Ming-Na asked.

"I didn't. Actually, I didn't even attempt it."

"Maybe I can help you later tonight."

"That might not be such a bad idea."

"I'm going to get something to drink. You want anything?" Ming-Na asked.

"Oh, no thank you."

Darnel followed her, swaggering his way to greet another male dancer.

Elnando and I just sat there in silence.

Finally he said, "Hi, Melanie."

"Hello, Elnando."

"I've been meaning to call you, but it's been crazy between moving in and..."

I interrupted him, "You don't have to explain to me."

The school's jazz band began to perform, as a perky couple who were clearly theatre majors began to sing, "I'll Take Manhattan."

"So, what do you think?" Elnando asked.

"What?" I asked, looking away from the dazzling duo who sang it like Broadway stars.

"I say we go take Manhattan," he said, grabbing my hand. "Again, I really am sorry I didn't..."

"Elnando, like I said, you don't have to explain," I said, interrupting him.

"If you don't let me explain to you, will you at least let me show you?"

"Show me what?"

Elnando put his arm around me and yelled over to Darnel, "We're *outta* here! Let Ming-Na know."

Darnel smiled and gave him two thumbs up.

I asked, "Where are you taking me?"

"I want to take you to my home, Spanish Harlem."

~~~

We got off the subway as the day turned to dusk. The sticky humidity died down, and the air felt cooler. Merengue music blared as children danced in the streets, and the stoops of the brownstones became rest stops for passersby.

I followed him up to a beautiful historic tall building with four long vertical narrow windows in front. The large horizontal sign which stood above the window read: New Visions Center for Dance and Moment.

"This is my home," Elnando explained.

"This is a dance studio?" I said, questioning him.

"But it is also my home," he said, unlocking the door.

Elnando turned on the lights as we walked in. The track lighting gave the studio a nice glow. The studio was beautiful with shiny, knotty pine wood floors. Through the tall, narrow windows the city street lamps shimmered against the coconut cream walls. The opposite side of the room was completely mirrored.

He turned on the speakers and the pulsating beat of Latin Salsa sounds filled the entire studio as Elnando proceeded to move about the dance floor. Suddenly, he pulled me in and twirled me around. He smiled as I shook my head back and started laughing. "I was never trained in this style of dance."

"Oh, you're a natural."

The music continued as I followed his lead. Elnando's hips moved sensually as he gyrated to the rhythm of the beat.

Once the music ended, Elnando grabbed my hand, and we both collapsed on the floor next to the mirror.

"You tired me out!" Elnando said.

"What? You tired me out!" I exclaimed. "This is where you call home?" I asked, turning and looking at him.

"I have to explain," Elnando said, catching his breath.

"Let me first get us some water," Elnando said, as he walked over to the water cooler that sat on the other side.

He returned to the floor. "Cheers," he said.

"Cheers!" I laughed as we hit our plastic cups together. "Now, what were you going to tell me?"

"This is much more than a dance studio. This place saved my life."

"You've got me confused, Elnando."

"Growing up in Spanish Harlem was not easy. I was always left alone, while my mama worked two jobs just to put food on the table. One day when I was around fourteen-years-old, me and my best friend, Jewel, who is like a brother to me, were causing trouble outside our home, which is in a housing project, and an older couple named Joe and Birdie saw what we were doing."

"What were you doing?" I asked.

"We were spraying graffiti on the side of the building. At that time, we were just doing it to pass the time, and also because at that time I was a punk. Anyway, they laid into us pretty bad. Looking back, I'm surprised they weren't afraid of us. But that night they introduced themselves to my mama and Jewel's mama, and they brought us food. From that point on, they became second parents to Jewel and me.

"They started this studio, and it's for the children of the community. The dance classes are free. It's so much more than a dance studio. It's a place for kids to hang out instead of the street. We also went on trips to places we would never have seen, if it wasn't for this place. Joe saw how athletic Jewel and I were. He even said I caught his eye once when I was bebopping on the street, and that was what really made him and Birdie stop and talk to us that summer day. At first, I thought dance was only for girls or sissy boys, but after being

54

convinced to try one class, I was hooked. Every waking minute I spent here. I didn't choose dance. Dance chose me and saved me. Now I try to give back any chance I can. Joe died a few years ago and Birdie is up in years, but they have a good team running it now, and I try to help them out any chance I can, mostly by teaching classes."

"I can't believe you started dance so late! You must be a natural."

"Thank you," he said, smiling softly at me. "We better head back. It's getting late."

As we were walking a few blocks past the studio, a large sign spray-painted with graffiti caught my eye in the weeded lot adjacent to a run-down housing project. It read: Future Home of Luxury Condos from Belezzi Builders.

Chapter 10

MaryAnn

I held on tight to Caleb's hand as we walked into the barn. The cool air mixed with the smell of hay and leather comforted me, as I looked over at the majestic horses trotting around the indoor ring. They looked so free in spirit and yet they carried themselves with such beauty and grace. I had never gotten really close to a horse before, except for the state fair that my family and I went to every year. My family and I would walk through the barns, looking for the prize-winning horse. I couldn't believe that I was actually here with my four-year-old son, who weighed 40 lbs. and was almost completely blind no less, so he could learn how to ride a horse, while I had never even sat on one. The owner of the barn seemed like such a sweetheart on the phone, normally they never allow a boy as young as Caleb to sit on a horse, but he said something in his heart told him Caleb must be an exception.

I would do anything to enhance Caleb's life, and this was one of those times. I knew we were blessed financially to be able to do it. I learned through my own research, and from speaking with several teachers at the center Caleb attended, that horses helped children with autism and with other disabilities such as blindness in many ways, both cognitively and socially.

"Mommy, it smells in here," Caleb said, trying to loosen my grip on his hand.

"You're right! It does smell in here. Caleb, you must hold my hand and stay close to me, because the horses are big animals and they might not be able to see you."

"Are they blind too, Mommy?"

"No, honey," I said with a chuckle.

A short, stout, country man with blue denim overalls and dirty brown muck boots limped toward us. He had a slight gray beard and balding hair, and he appeared to be in his late sixties.

In a cheerful voice he said, "You must be Caleb," as he patted his shoulder.

"That's me," Caleb said, wiggling my hand and trying his best to let go.

"I'm Hank," he said, extending his hand to mine.

"Hi, I'm MaryAnn, we spoke on the phone."

"Yes, and it's a pleasure to meet you! Caleb, I hear you want to ride a horse?"

"I want to ride a horse," Caleb said, jumping up and down, loosening my grip on his hand. "Can I ride one now?"

"Well, it's not that easy. First, you and the horse have to become acquainted. You and the horse have to build a trust with each other, and he needs to know you're not going to hurt him."

"I would never hurt a horse," Caleb assured him.

Hank looked over at me with a smile, "I know that, son."

"Let's walk over here and meet my princess."

I followed him to the grooming stall where she was cross-tied.

"You mind if I pick him up?" Hank asked me.

"Not at all," I answered.

"Caleb, Hank is going to pick you up," I said, letting go of Caleb.

Hank gently picked Caleb up. "This here is Misty Mae. She is a sweet soul. You want to always be real gentle with her," Hank said as he put his hand over Caleb's, and stroked the brown mare with big white splotches on her hind end.

"Misty Mae is a beauty, who happened to turn ten-years-old just a few days ago."

I smiled at Hank, enjoying his easy-going manner. Misty Mae did appear to be a gentle beauty, with kind, calm reassuring eyes.

"I can tell you and Misty Mae are going to be fast friends," Hank said.

"I like how she feels. She feels like Thumper!" Caleb exclaimed.

"Who's this Thumper, you speak of?" Hank asked.

"Thumper is my bunny!"

"Thumper is a stuffed animal," I said.

"Feel, Mommy! She feels just like Thumper."

"May I pet her, too?" I asked.

"Sure! This lucky lady is getting a lot of love today," Hank answered, while continuing to stroke her with Caleb's hand.

"You're right, Caleb! She feels just like Thumper."

Hank asked, "You know what, Caleb? I think Misty Mae is starting to get a little hungry. Did you hear her stomach growl?"

"I did hear her stomach growl! It went rumble, rumble!"

Hank laughed. "Misty Mae here has a big stomach," Hank said, patting her midsection. "And, she also has a big appetite. How 'bout we feed her some carrots, to tide her over until dinner time?"

"I want to feed her the carrots!" Caleb yelled.

"I happen to have some carrots right here in my pocket," Hank said, trying to balance Caleb in one arm, as he clumsily retrieved the carrots from his side pocket. "I say we feed them to her. Remember; always be gentle, because Misty Mae, like all animals are special gifts from God. Now I'm going to hold the carrots with you, and we're going to make Misty Mae real happy."

"Okay," Caleb said.

Together, Hank and Caleb fed Misty Mae the carrots, and for a moment I forgot Caleb was blind.

Hank opened up his palm full of carrots towards me. "Would you like to feed Misty Mae a carrot?"

"Sure," I said, taking a carrot from the palm of his hand.

"Here you go," I said, feeding her the carrot.

Hank asked Caleb, "Wow, wasn't I right? This pretty lady sure does have a big appetite!"

"She was hungry!" Caleb exclaimed.

"Now that she's had her snack, I bet she can use a nap," Hank said, putting Caleb down and holding his hand.

"I want to ride her now."

"I know you do, and before long you'll be sitting right up on her. It just takes some time. I promise next time I'll let you sit on top of her. Misty Mae rides English style, but you're going to ride her Western, like the cowboys."

"Can I do it now?"

"Not today! Misty Mae just met you and your mom, and a good relationship can't be rushed. But I'm a man of my word! Next time, I promise!"

"Thank you, Hank. It was great meeting you and Misty Mae," I said.

"It was my pleasure."

"Caleb, say thank you to Hank and goodbye to Misty Mae."

"Thank you, Hank! Bye, Misty Mae."

"You're welcome, and you both go walk ahead. Remember this always, because this is very important, you never get right behind a horse, the reason being, you never know when they are going to kick back. Always keep a comfortable distance."

"I understand," I said, holding on to Caleb's hand.

"After I put Misty Mae back in her stall for a nap, I'm going to watch my granddaughter, sweet Caroline, practice her jumps," Hank said, looking over at the indoor ring.

"I want to go, too!"

"If you like, you can sit over there on the bleachers and watch," Hank said, pointing to the bleachers.

"Sure," I said, wanting to remind Hank that Caleb is blind.

I walked Caleb over and we sat side by side on the cold bleachers. "Caleb honey, it's so cold," I said, lifting him up and putting him into my arms. "Why don't we go home now? You're going to get bored just sitting here."

"Mommy, I can smell the horses and feel everything around me. I like it here."

Just hearing those words, reminded me how Caleb sees things without the use of his eyes. I tightly wrapped my arms around him and held him close.

Chapter 11

Lauren

"Where did your friend go?" Katt asked.

"You mean my boss?"

"Your newest conquest, whatever you want to call him," she responded.

"I have no idea. He took off."

"The night is still young. Let's go enjoy ourselves," Katt said, grabbing my hand as Tiffany followed.

We walked back to the bar, as the group of young, hot executives sitting next to us ordered us a round of drinks. We gladly accepted, knowing it would be a nighttime of drinks, and we were already feeling pretty hammered.

I caught one of the guys checking me out. He was athletic looking, but with a pretty boy look. He was still sporting his day job attire, but I could see that he was an athlete with his broad chest and toned physique. He was clean-shaven with light brown hair, ocean blue eyes and a charming personality. He introduced himself as Matt and that he was the fastest-acting day trader on the floor of the New York Stock Exchange. By all accounts he was a dream, but when you crave something else, even if it's something you really shouldn't have, little else matters.

I introduced myself as Lauren, and "I do it all for a building company."

Matt smiled and raised his shot glass. "To Lauren, who does it all!"

I hit my glass against his. Matt and I flirted the whole night, as the two other men got to know Tiffany and Katt.

Eventually, Matt felt comfortable enough around me and followed me out to the dance floor. With a drink in his hand and the other around my hips, we swayed to the beat of the music.

I was wasted, as Tiffany and Katt still maintained some sense of clarity.

~~~

"You ready?" Tiffany asked, as I returned to the bar. "You can spend the night at my place."

"I can take her home," Matt said.

"How 'bout you take me to your place?" I asked, fully intoxicated at this point, standing up close to him and patting both hands on his chest.

"That sounds good to me!"

"Make sure you text me first thing in the morning," Katt said, as Tiffany came over and gave me a quick hug.

~~~

The next morning, I awoke as Matt lay sleepily by my side. I got up, feeling hung over, groggy, and barely remembering how I even got there. I looked over at him. He looked innocent and kind, although I knew the time we spent together hardly knowing one another wasn't. I picked up my clothes that were scattered about his cold, hardwood floor, and put everything back on. I walked over to the large bay window. I was somewhere in the upper east side of Manhattan, and it was a beautiful morning.

I grabbed my bag and purse off his kitchen counter. I quietly opened the door. Matt jostled in the bed and said, "Leaving already?"

I turned and mumbled, "I am. Goodbye, stranger. It was really nice."

Chapter 12

Steven

It was well past midnight as I walked through the red velvet ropes for the second time tonight.

What am I thinking, coming back here? What am I supposed to do, go up to her and ask her if I can take her home and have sex with her? I should be in my own bed now. Why can't I get this girl out of my mind?

I texted MaryAnn earlier, reminding her that I would be doing a bunch of site visits and then probably going back to the office to finish up some paperwork. I did partially honor what I said I would do. I did go back to the office to finish up some paperwork, but my motivation wasn't to leave the area for site visits. It was to go elsewhere, leaving behind the boundaries of my marriage.

I walked in. The club seemed darker, the music seemed louder and the crowd seemed more intoxicated than when I left hours ago. I desperately wanted to see Lauren, but I also felt a sense of relief that she was no longer there. I had never been unfaithful in my marriage. Looking around for Lauren and thinking of her made me feel excited, but at the same time guilty. I wondered how she got home, and if anyone other than her girlfriends were with her. I sat down and ordered a White Russian, and thought *nothing happened....Nothing happened...*

I slowly finished my drink and took one last look around the crowded bar. I wondered how many of these people would be hooking up tonight. For some of them it seemed like their night was just beginning, while mine was ending.

63

It's time now that I return home to my beautiful wife, MaryAnn.

Chapter 13

Melanie

"C'mon, Melanie, feel the movements, faster, faster!" Olivia yelled, while pounding her pole on the wood floor.

Olivia Phillips, the master dance teacher for all incoming freshmen, had a reputation for being no-holds-barred. Being students at Fillmore, we were expected to already be the best, and Olivia wanted that and more. At orientation she announced that being a student at Fillmore is a privilege like no other, and that we would have the chance to train with some of the best choreographers in the world, and to keep our heads on straight. She reminded all of us, "Dance is a short-lived career, so enjoy every moment of the sweat, tears, wear and tear. When the time comes and our bodies say it's over, and our minds fight it, we need every ounce of sanity we have left to be able to deal with it."

She knew best what we were going through. She was an alumna of Fillmore and went on to dance with several companies in Europe before having a long stay with the Alvin Ailey Dance Company, eventually becoming one of their main choreographers. She reminded me of a beautiful African queen, with her deep dark chocolate skin, piercing mocha eyes, and long jet black braided hair that she kept neatly twisted in a bun. The room fell silent whenever she entered. Her manner was intimidating, but her heart could be felt throughout the room. She was a veteran, and as if we were her prize-winning race horses, she wanted us to go the distance. I could tell everyone wanted to make her proud. When we mastered a short routine that we had learned in only a few short hours, if she was pleased, her smile lit up the room.

Olivia announced, "Wow, impressive! You all are looking good out there. Now we are going to have some fun! Freestyle!" Suddenly the song "Sexy Back" by Justin Timberlake blasted throughout the room.

We all twisted, turned and laughed, letting go of all our pent up tension. Ming-Na did some contemporary moves, while Elnando got low and shook his shoulders side to side, adding some innovative arm movements. Darnel busted a move, making his the most fun to watch because of his charisma and the way his body moved in space. When it was my turn, I had fun, and danced like I would be listening to it at a night club.

When the routine ended, Olivia clapped and said, "I believe you are ready for a live audience, and I am going to give you that opportunity as soon as you leave here."

We all started cheering and clapping along with her, as Darnel yelled, "Cally Auditorium, here we come!"

"Not so fast! I was thinking more like Union Square."

We all looked at her, puzzled and confused.

"Seeing this is your last class before the weekend begins, your assignment is to leave here and perform a flash mob dance in the open area of Union Square. This may be your toughest audience ever. You will perform the fun piece you learned at dance orientation to the song "Blurred Lines."

We all started laughing and cheering!

"Now, go get changed!" Olivia yelled.

As I was gathering my belongings, Olivia walked over to me, "Melanie, remember, don't use all your energy at the beginning."

I nodded, while toweling the sweat off my forehead.

"You looked good out there today."

"Thank you," I said, feeling a strong sense of relief.

~~~

We made our way to the open area of Union Square. We looked no different than any of the harried motley crew of people who drifted through. With Olivia's orchestration, the music began. Everyone around us stopped dead in their tracks.

We danced in perfect harmony and bounced up and down to the upbeat lyrics of the song. Each one of us was beaming with joy when it was our turn to shine with our minute solo.

I caught the eye of an old lady with a grocery cart, who looked like a deer in headlights. I gave her a huge reassuring smile, as many of the young people held up their phones to YouTube our performance. When we finished, an eruption of clapping, cheers and laughter filled the large open area. At that moment, I had never felt as proud or happy to be a dancer in all my life.

Chapter 14

Steven

"Mr. Belezzi, Lauren is on the line. She needs to speak to you," Dolores said, holding the phone out as I walked by her desk.

"I'm on my way back to my office. I'll take it in there," I said, knowing that Dolores would be listening to every word I said.

I quickly walked back to my office, anxious to hear Lauren's voice and why she hadn't arrived yet.

I put her on the line. "Hey Lauren, what's going on?"

"I'm sorry! I would have called earlier, but I wanted to speak to you directly and not have Dolores relay the message. I had some plumbing issues this morning, and I had to get the super, and you know how it goes. I was wondering if I can meet you at the site today instead of stopping in the office first?"

"I don't mind. Do you need anything here at the office?" I asked.

"No, I'm all set. Do you want to meet around 11:00? The city planner will be there around that time as well."

"That's good. Do you want me to pick you up? It would only make sense, seeing you're not coming to the office first."

"If you don't mind?"

"Not at all! I will pick you up in about an hour. We can go over some paperwork before we meet at the site, and that will give us plenty of time to make our way over there."

"That sounds good! I'll see you soon."

"Bye," I said hanging up the phone, noticing the smiling picture on my desk of MaryAnn with Caleb on her lap and Melanie in the back giving them bunny ears.

I really do have a beautiful family.

~~~

I took a deep breath as I walked up the steps to Lauren's apartment. Lauren met me at the doorway with a big smile on her face. "Come on in. I really appreciate you picking me up. You saved me a lot of time, not to mention the hassle."

She was wearing a short black skirt with a ruffled white, sleeveless see-through blouse. Her hair was pulled back and she smelled incredible.

"Are all your plumbing issues solved?"

"Sort of," she giggled, as she gathered up some papers off her coffee table.

"I just have to do some last minute touchups."

I wanted to tell her how beautiful she looked just the way she was, but I didn't want to sound inappropriate.

"Why don't you follow me," she said with a coy smile.

How ironic. I didn't think it was appropriate to tell her how beautiful she looked, but now I'm panting like a dog, following her to her bedroom.

She made herself comfortable at her huge armoire that looked like something out of the makeup department at Macy's.

"You can have a seat on my bed, if you like" she said, as I stood awkwardly in the middle of her bedroom.

"So, what do I need to know?" she turned around with a makeup brush in her hand and asked.

"Uh?"

She smiled. "Anything else I need to know before we meet with the planner?" she asked as she applied her makeup.

"Oh," I said, looking past her in disbelief that I was actually in her bedroom and sitting on her bed. "Just stress the fact that we are committed to this project and the time frame in which we will complete it. And, we honor what we say we are going to do, and that our track record speaks for itself."

Lauren gave herself a final look in the mirror, then got up and walked toward me.

"Sounds good, what about the paperwork? You said you wanted to go over it," she asked, taking down her ponytail and standing before me.

"I can't fight this feeling I am having for you," I said, looking passionately into her eyes.

"Then don't," she said, pushing me gently on to the bed.

We engaged in a kiss. I felt like I was going to explode. "I know I shouldn't be with you," I said.

She got off the bed and stood before me. As if dangling a carrot in front of my nose, she slowly removed each article of her clothing. Then she shook her head back and grinned.

I attacked her body from beginning to end.

In the middle of making love, I realized it was time to go. "We should be going."

"Whatever you say, boss."

Chapter 15

Elnando

"What are your dreams once you leave Fillmore?" Darnel asked, pointing the video camera straight at Ming-Na.

"My dream is to hopefully get a job with a prestigious dance company, preferably in Europe," she said.

"And what are your dreams, Melanie, once you leave the wonderful walls of Fillmore?" Darnel asked.

"My dream is probably the same as Ming-Na and every other dancer here at Fillmore. It's to gain employment as a dancer. I am willing to go anywhere that will hire me," she said with a chuckle.

Indian summer was beginning and the sun was hot. An orange ray filled the sky as we sat on the campus lawn drinking our protein shakes and eating our salads for lunch.

"Elnando, what are your dreams once you leave here?"

"To get as far away from this city as I possibly can," I said, stirring the remains of my shake.

"That's some New York City spirit," Melanie said, smacking my knee. I looked at her, smiled shyly and rolled my eyes.

"Sweet Ming-Na, what is the craziest thing you have ever done?" Darnel asked.

Ming-Na looked straight into the camera and bit down hard on her carrot. "Wouldn't you like to know?"

"Yeah girl, we want to know," Darnel egged her on.

"I actually went naked back home at Baker Beach."

We all laughed.

"Hey, why are all of you laughing at me? Is it the thought of me in the buff? Or the fact that I actually did it?" she asked in a teasing manner.

Darnel laughed and said, "We're laughing 'cuz that is the craziest thing you've ever done!"

"Hey, it leaves the door wide open for even wilder things to come!"

"That's right, girl," Darnel said, shaking his head.

"All right, Mel, it's your turn! What's the craziest thing you have ever done?"

"Well, there was this time at band camp," Melanie and the rest of us started laughing.

"It's actually back here," she said, slapping her backside.

"Oh you little tramp—stamp! Let's see it!" Darnel said, lying on the grass, angling the camera at her backside.

"Stop! You can't film this," she said laughing. "My parents still don't know about it."

I pushed my shoulders into her and we both looked at each other and smiled. I felt privileged to have been the only one who knew about her crazy little secret. On her lower back was a large star, colored in a hue of dark purples and pink, with three tiny aqua blue stars on each of the opposite sides.

"I had this done here in the city, not too long ago, right after graduation. My girlfriend's older sister knew the artist."

"And the meaning of it is?" Darnel asked.

"What do you think? Like everyone here at Fillmore, I want to be a star."

"What about you, Darnel? What's the craziest thing you have ever done?" Melanie asked while mixing up her salad.

"Do you really want to go there, Melanie?" I asked. We all laughed.

"Come on. Tell us," Melanie pleaded.

"Oh girl, you're opening up a big fat Pandora's box. Let me think about this, seeing I have to give you the clean version," he said laughing. "But on to Elnando. What's the craziest thing you have ever done?"

"You don't want to know."

"Oh come on, pretty boy. Open up and spill your guts," Darnel said, sticking the camera in my face.

"I don't want to talk about it."

"Oh, come on," Melanie said, urging me on.

"You don't want to hear it."

"Yes, we do! Don't we, Ming-Na?" Melanie asked her.

Ming-Na just shook her head and smiled as she packed up her lunch tote.

"I bet it's very interesting," Melanie said.

"It's nothing you want to hear and nothing I want to share. Now c'mon, man! Put that friggin' camera away," I said, putting my hand over the lens and pushing it down.

~~~

"What was that all about during lunch?" Melanie asked while sitting on the edge of her bed sifting through CDs.

"What?" I looked at her, lying back against the wall.

She stopped and gave me a hard stare.

"Oh, you want to know about my crazy adventures?"

"I believe the question was: What was the craziest thing you have ever done?"

I sat back without responding to her.

"Why were you acting so defensive?"

"I wasn't. I was just messing with him; he was starting to get annoying. It was the only time we had to chill out and he's sticking his damn camera in all our faces."

"You seemed awfully defensive to me."

"I didn't mean to be. Nothing is catching your eye?" I asked, trying to change the subject. "I have a ton of CDs and Darnel does too, if you can't find anything."

"Sometimes just picking out our practice music is a job in of itself," she said, gently throwing the CDs into the bin. "I suppose I could try going through Ming-Na's and if all else fails, yours and Darnel's."

"Come on now, my taste in music isn't that bad."

She smiled. "I know. Honestly, Elnando, when you do your solos, you stand out among the rest of us. Your choreography is amazing, with the perfect music that no one has ever used."

"Oh, your making me blush," I kidded. "You're pretty amazing yourself."

Melanie responded, "I am, but you baby, are a natural!"

I moved closer to her and pushed back her wavy curls. Looking into her eyes, I said, "Melanie, you're a beautiful dancer and a beautiful woman."

The look in her eyes told me I believed it much more than she did.

I grabbed her hand. "Listen, we don't have much time. If you want me to meet your parents tomorrow, I have to go work out the kinks in my routine. Do you want to come with me?"

"No, I think I'll make another attempt to go through these CDs."

"That's fine! I'll meet you back here in about an hour," I said, giving her a quick kiss on the forehead.

As I was getting up, she pulled my arm. "Wait! You never answered the question. What was the craziest thing you ever did?"

"I'm about to do it right now," I said, throwing her back on the bed.

She started to laugh. "You're STILL not answering the question."

I pretended to bite her neck.

"Hey, you know there are no marks allowed. It doesn't look good when I wear a bun," she said teasing. "Now, will you please answer my question?"

"What was that?" I kidded, pretending to be confused as I buttoned down her silky top.

"What was the craziest thing you ever did?"

"It was falling in love with a beautiful ballerina from Jersey."

"Good answer!" She laughed and pulled me closer into her.

~~~

We arrived in Jersey courtesy of Melanie's dad's company's car service. Melanie's home was like nothing I had ever seen before. I had never been to Franklin Lakes, and I would have never thought her home would be an enormous log cabin. I thought it would look like the outside of the homes in *The Real Housewives of New Jersey*, which I would never admit I watched now and them. In front of the cabin was a large circular driveway surrounded by a beautifully landscaped lawn. It sat nestled upon acres of land.

I was nervous about meeting her family. It was ironic how often I had been in difficult situations and had not even been aware of how I was feeling. Knowing I was about to meet her well-to-do Italian family made me uneasy, especially since I was a male dancer, not to mention from a different culture. I just prayed that they didn't have any preconceived stereotypes about either. In any case, I figured a bouquet of flowers would be a nice touch.

As we walked to the house, I grabbed Melanie's arm and said to her, "I really hope they like me, especially your dad."

"Oh, don't worry about my dad. He probably thinks you're gay."

"Uh," I said wide-eyed.

"I'm just kidding. Will you stop being so nervous? Come on! My family is really nice, and Caleb is very excited about meeting you."

Her father opened the front door as we were about to walk in. "Come on in. How you doing, sweetheart?" he said, giving Melanie a kiss on the cheek. "You must be Elnando. Are these for me?" He laughed, giving me a strong handshake.

"Nope, they're for the Mrs.," I said with a chuckle.

"Melanie has told us a lot about you and I hear you're a hell of a dancer."

"Thank you so much," I said, taken aback by the spacious open great room. It looked like it had been professionally decorated, with an indoor stone fire pit in the center with leather couches and hassocks around it and a huge sixty-inch wide-screen TV nestled on the wall. On the other side of the room was a huge Adirondack-style dining room table with matching wooden chairs, and against the wall stood a huge curio cabinet filled with nice china.

Although the room was furnished with nothing but the best, it had a homey feel about it.

"Your mom is in the kitchen with Caleb. She's waiting for you. I'll join you in a minute. I just have some things I need to take care of."

We walked what seemed like the length of a football field into a large kitchen with oakwood cabinets. In the center was an island with a sage-colored granite countertop with wooden stools around it. Shiny silver pots and pans hung from the ceiling.

"It must be Melanie!" her brother yelled, while sitting upon the countertop. He was a cute and skinny little guy with shoulder-length shaggy brown hair.

The kitchen was warm and inviting. Melanie's mother turned from the simmering pot, and put a sauce-covered wooden spoon on a small plate. She wiped her hands on her apron which read, "Skinny Cooks Are Boring." Like her daughter, she was beautiful with long wavy dirty blonde hair and brown eyes, and a petite figure. I was surprised to see how young she looked, although Melanie had told me how her parents married young and she was born not too long after they finished college.

I was anxious to meet her baby brother. I had only encountered blind adults usually around the subway, but I had never met a blind child.

Melanie grabbed her brother from the counter and held him to her hip.

"I'm so happy you're here," she said, as the young boy yelled, "Melanie."

Her brother was different than I had imagined. He was full of energy, and the only thing odd to me now was the huge age difference between Caleb and Melanie.

"Elnando, this is my mom."

"It's nice to meet you, Mrs. Belezzi. These are for you," I said, giving her the bouquet of colorful carnations.

Melanie looked over at me and grinned.

"These are beautiful. You didn't have to do this. I have heard so many nice things about you. Melanie says you are quite the dancer."

I smiled and looked over at Melanie. She smiled back. "Thank you so much. I work hard."

Melanie's mom looked down at the flowers and smiled. "I'm going to put these in some water. I'll be right back," she said, walking toward what I thought was a closet but was a huge old-fashioned pantry.

"Caleb, this is my friend, Elnando," Melanie said, grabbing Caleb's hand and rubbing it up and down on my face.

"Is he your boyfriend, Melanie?" he teased.

"Yes, Caleb, he is."

"It's nice to meet you," I said, admiring his Batman shirt. I wondered how he would even know about Batman or any other superheroes if he couldn't see them in action.

Melanie turned to me and said, "Lift up your sleeve."

"Why?" I asked, puzzled.

"Just do it!"

I lifted up my sleeve as ordered. Melanie took Caleb's hand and rubbed it up and down my forearm.

"Aren't these some big muscles, Caleb?" Melanie said.

"You got big *musculls*!" Caleb yelled, kicking his feet while Melanie held him close.

"Yeah, he does!" Melanie laughed.

"You must be strong, like Batman."

"I don't know if I'm as strong as Batman, but I guess I'm pretty strong."

"He wears a leotard like him sometimes, too," Melanie joked, pulling my sleeve down with her free hand.

"Oh, that was low," I said and we both laughed.

Caleb looked baffled by our banter as her mother returned with an antique vase.

"Would you two like some chili?" Melanie's mom asked.

"Sure," Melanie said, placing Caleb on the island and taking a seat on the stool.

I sat next to her.

"Caleb, do you want some chili?" Melanie asked.

"I already had some."

"Geez thanks! You couldn't wait for us?"

"He was my guinea pig," Melanie's mom said, placing bowls of hot chili in front of us. "What can I get you two to drink?"

"Do you have any lemonade made?" Melanie asked.

"I sure do."

"Do you like lemonade?" Melanie asked me.

"Who doesn't?"

Melanie's mom brought over the glass pitcher and poured our glasses, and then placed before us a small wicker basket with slices of Italian bread wrapped in a plaid red and white linen napkin. A butter dish had been preset and was already almost fully melted. Melanie raised her glass and said, "Let me explain. In the Belezzi home we drink lemonade every season of the year. It could be four below, and we will drink lemonade."

Suddenly, the door swung open and it was Melanie's dad. "Elnando, if you should experience any ill effects, she's to blame," he said, pointing to Melanie's mom.

Melanie's dad was incredibly self-confident and was in great shape. He had a good tan and his bronzed glow made him look even more Italian. Melanie's parents were hip, and what I liked the most about them, like Melanie, was that they lacked the tough New Jersey accent and attitude that I usually encountered.

"Oh, stop," her mom said, leaning on the counter.

"Dad, Mom makes a mean chili."

"Her chili is delicious. It's the after-effects you have to worry about," he said, rubbing his stomach.

"It's delicious, but thank you for the warning," I said, feeling comfortable and at home among her family.

"What do the two of you have planned for the day?" Melanie's mom asked while ladling out two more bowls of chili.

"I'm not sure. We might practice our routines," Melanie answered.

"Don't you two want a break? You work hard all week," she said, handing her dad a bowl.

"Mom, that's the life of a dancer."

"I bet your bodies are begging for a break," her dad said.

Melanie chuckled. "It is, and it reminds me every day with its aches and pains."

Her dad laughed. "Wait 'til you hit forty."

"Elnando, Melanie says you are from Spanish Harlem. My company recently received its final approval to tear down the Carver Housing Project and build modern condos in its place. If no more hurdles should spring up, we should be ready to go by spring. I must admit, I really like the culture there. I have been spending a lot of time in that area while trying to get things up and running."

I suddenly had a sick feeling in the pit of my stomach, and it wasn't the chili. Melanie's dad was the one who wanted to drive my family and the rest of the residents out of the only homes they had ever known and could afford. I didn't want to reveal to him that it was my home he planned on tearing down.

"Yeah," I stuttered. "There's a lot of history in Spanish Harlem. It was a tough place, but the older I get, the more I appreciate the culture that I was exposed to while growing up."

Melanie's dad leaned on the counter and said, "The place seems to be changing now. From the research, I found that crime has been down, a lot of young professionals are moving in because of the low rent, and I hope that will be a boost for the condos my company plans on building."

I wanted to ask him, "What about the low income people just trying to survive?" I didn't want to get on his bad side, and I believed he truly had no clue how the other side lived.

Melanie's mom brought over a plate of cookies and said, "We have some chocolate chip cookies. Caleb made them himself."

"I made them into balls and put them on the sheet."

Melanie smiled and rolled her eyes up at me as we both stared at the lopsided cookies. "They look good Caleb, but I have to pass. My tummy is way too full. How about you, Elnando? Would you like one of Caleb's delicious cookies?"

"Sure, why not," I said, taking one off the tray and taking a bite. "They are delicious. Thank you."

Melanie asked, "Caleb, do you want a cookie?"

"I already had one!" He giggled.

"You did!" Melanie said, tickling him at the counter. "You couldn't wait for me for the chili and for the cookies?"

He burst out in laughter, looking like he was going to fall off the counter, and said, "I couldn't wait. They smelled so good, Melanie."

Melanie picked him up. "What are we going to do with you?"

"Take me back to the zoo!"

"I think that's what we are going to do! In the meantime, let's go bounce on the trampoline and show Elnando what you got."

"Let's do it!" Caleb yelled.

Melanie's mom grabbed our dirty bowls and put them in the sink. "Melanie, be careful with him out there."

"Mom, I'm clumsier than he is, and there's a safety net surrounding it."

"Please, still be careful."

"Yes, Mom."

"Don't go teaching him how to do triple axels," her father quipped, coming over and giving Melanie a kiss on top of her head.

"I believe that's in ice skating, Dad."

Her dad smirked. "I have to be heading out. It was nice meeting you, Elnando."

"It was nice meeting you, too," I said.

"Be good, Melanie. Don't try to fly, Caleb."

Melanie's mom turned from the pan she was washing. "Where do you have to go now?"

"There are some places I have to see and people I have to meet."

"Don't be too late. You're going to work yourself to death."

"MaryAnn, I'll try to be back in a few hours. Are you staying here tonight, Melanie?"

"We're actually going to head back in a few hours."

"If I don't see you, be careful," Melanie's dad said, heading out the door.

Melanie sighed. "I really don't feel like hanging out in my dance studio today. Maybe we should take a little break."

I whispered, "You have a dance studio?"

Melanie answered nonchalantly, "It's a little studio my dad built in our basement."

"Melanie, you should give Elnando a tour of our home."

"Would you like to tour our casa?"

"Yes, I would love to."

"Caleb, come on! Let's give Elnando a tour of the house," Melanie said, grabbing him off the counter. I was amazed to see him trail behind us with his hands out in front of him.

As we strolled through each room, I turned to her and Caleb and said, "This isn't a home. It's a luxury hotel."

She laughed and said, "And I didn't even show you the pottery room or the dance studio yet."

"I make turtles," Caleb said.

"Wow! That's pretty neat," I said.

We walked down the long stairway to the basement, which was completely made into a dance studio. It had shimmery hardwood floors, a long horizontal mirror on one side, and was complete with a full length ballet barre.

"This is something else," I said.

"Thank you," Melanie said modestly. "Most teenage girls spend their time holed up in their bedrooms. All of my time was spent in here."

"This is incredible. So where's the bowling alley?" I kidded.

"Don't have that, but I bet if you mention it to my dad, and you promise to come over and play with him, I'm sure he would put one in."

I smiled. "I'll remember that."

We walked out of the house to a large backyard, which was complete with a fenced-in pool with large cascading rocks and a waterfall. A concrete patio surrounded it with top-of-the-line wicker outdoor furniture. In the distance were acres upon acres of land. To the side of the house was an oversized trampoline.

Melanie picked Caleb up, put him in, and joined him. They bounced up and down giggling with every fall they took.

"Come on, Elnando! Join us."

"No, thank you! I'm having way too much fun watching the two of you."

"Come on," she said, opening the net and putting her hand out to me.

I took it and bounced up and down, being very careful of where Caleb was, but he seemed to consume his own space, enjoying every moment.

I was having the time of my life!

These people have perfect lives!

Chapter 16

Lauren

I watched him grab his cell phone off my side table and read it.

Yep, it must be his wife, and away he goes.

"I have to leave now."

"Is it because of your wife?"

"Does it matter?"

I shook my head, as he grabbed his clothes off the floor and put them next to him on my bed.

"Why can't you just stay here with me?"

"I'm married, Lauren. What part of that don't you understand?"

"Why are you here, if you're married?" I asked, exaggerating the word married.

"Please, Lauren! What do you want from me?"

I want you to tell me how much more beautiful I am than her, how you love me so much more and are planning on leaving her, I thought.

"Steven, leave. You have to eventually."

Steven turned toward me and gave me a goofy smile and said, "Can we hug it out?"

I sadly rolled my eyes as he hugged me and pushed me back down. He tickled my side and I started laughing, getting lost in the moment, forgetting how disappointed I was that he was taking off.

"Do you really have to leave?"

"Yes, I really must go," he said, kissing my forehead.

"You just pick yourself up and leave. It isn't fair," I said, sitting up and draping the sheets around me.

"I'm sorry, Lauren."

"What exactly are you sorry about?"

"That it has to be this way," he said, putting on his jeans.

"It doesn't. Please stay," I said, leaning over and pulling him back down to my bed.

He resisted and pulled back. "I can't, because you, my pretty lady, have work tomorrow morning and you need your rest."

"I think I deserve a day off."

"No way, we have deadlines to meet," he said, as he buttoned his shirt.

"Great," I said reaching over and grabbing my cigarettes and lighter off the side table. "You are one wrinkly mess. Good luck explaining that one."

Steven didn't answer and grabbed my hand. "No smoking. It's not good for you."

I took out a cigarette and lit it. "Neither is sleeping with a married man."

Steven smiled gently at me and caressed the side of my face.

I stared back at him and looked intently into his beautiful dark brown eyes and seductively blew out the smoke. Then he slowly turned and walked away.

Chapter 17

MaryAnn

"MaryAnn, I am going to be leaving now," Steven yelled, opening the sliding glass door. It was a sunny fall morning with a crisp coolness in the air. I lay back on my lounge chair, taking sips of my hot pumpkin flavored coffee, watching Caleb in the distance. Caleb could keep himself occupied for hours playing in the small dirt pile I put out for him. It was a joy to see him get filthy dirty while he pushed cups, cars, and action figures through the dirt. I often thought of how much fun he was having using just his sense of touch and his imagination, and how much greater the experience would be for him if he could actually see.

"Steven, I didn't even realize you made it home last night," I yelled up to him.

Steven walked down the stairs and stood by my side as I slowly sipped my coffee.

"What's that supposed to mean?"

"It means you're working way too hard. I'm sorry I didn't wait up for you yesterday, but I was beat," I said, getting up and giving him a hug.

"I have a lot on my plate, MaryAnn."

I rubbed his shoulder. "I understand."

"Daddy is leaving, Caleb. I love you," Steven yelled over to him.

"Bye, I love you, too!" Caleb yelled back, as he was now on all fours and covered in dirt.

"I'm not going to walk over to you because I have a meeting and I don't want to get myself dirty."

Caleb laughed. "But it's so much fun!"

"I bet it is! You enjoy yourself!"

"Look at him, MaryAnn. It's a shame he can't even see a thing."

"At least he's keeping himself occupied and having fun," MaryAnn responded.

"It sucks. He can't see this house, my buildings, or his own sister dance."

I put my coffee down and got up. I whispered, "Remember, Steven, he's blind, not deaf! I thought we were long past this. What's going on with you?"

Steven stared straight ahead at Caleb as he continued to be absorbed in the dirt. "It took so long for us to have a baby after Melanie. At least God could have thrown us a bone and not given us damaged goods."

Without thinking and with full force, I struck Steven across the face. "How dare you say that!" Steven's face became bright red, as my emotions boiled. "Caleb is nothing but a blessing."

For what seemed like eternity Steven and I stared at each other, as tears began to well up in his eyes.

Softly and barely able to get the words out, he said, "I know he's a blessing, MaryAnn, but it all still hurts."

"Get out of here, Steven. Go to work!"

Chapter 18

Melanie

The wind was whipping through our hair as we jumped aboard just in time.

"I feel like we're skipping class," Elnando said.

"We're not skipping—we're just not practicing."

"You're a crazy girl, Melanie. You're going to get us in trouble," Elnando said, grabbing my hand.

The overpowering honk of the horn blew, as the huge charter tour boat departed on its journey through the Hudson River. The boat was bustling with foreigners and school groups, who gathered next to the railings with their cameras in hand.

We found two corner seats on the lower deck. We put our feet against the railings and stared at the city views surrounding us.

"Maybe we should have planned ahead. It's chilly out here," I said, wrapping my arms around my body.

"You saw the boat, and you said, 'Let's go.' Come on, you can sit on me. I'll keep you warm," Elnando said, patting his lap.

As I got up he started taking off his royal blue fleece. "Are you crazy? All you have is a T-shirt under that. You'll freeze to death!"

"I'm warm-blooded. Here, take it."

Elnando handed me the cozy fleece.

"Are you sure?"

"Yes, plus you're going to keep me warm," he said, lifting me upon his lap. I cradled on him in a fetal position. He pushed my hair to one side and rested his head on my shoulder.

"New York is so beautiful. I bet there is no other place like this," I said.

Elnando squeezed me tight. "You're probably right. Are you warming up?"

"I am. Thank you."

"Elnando, we need a picture, and my phone is dead."

An older couple walked by. Elnando wiggled and grabbed his cell phone out of his side pocket.

"Would you folks be so kind as to take our picture?" he asked.

"You're so polite." I whispered in his ear.

"I would love to," the old man answered.

The man looked at the phone with a puzzled stare. "What do I do?"

Elnando smiled, took back his phone and adjusted it.

"You're going to aim it at us. You'll be able to see us through here, and press this little button," Elnando said, handing him back the phone.

"I'll give it a try. Okay now, say "Cheese.""

"Cheese," we both laughed.

The old man handed Elnando back his phone. Elnando looked at it and showed it to me and said, "Nice job. You like it, Melanie?"

"It's perfect!"

"Where are you two from?" I asked.

"Birmingham, Alabama," the old man answered in a southern drawl.

"We always wanted to visit the big city," the old lady answered sweetly.

"I'm sure you won't be disappointed. Thank you again for taking our picture," Elnando said, extending his hand to the old man.

"Thank you," I said.

"You two enjoy your day," the woman said as they walked by us.

"You, too," Elnando and I said in unison.

Over the muffled loud speaker the announcer announced, "If you look to your right you would see what once stood as the skyline of the majestic towers of the World Trade Center."

As everyone stared off in that direction, for just a few seconds it seemed like the boat was suddenly quiet. You could hear a pin drop, as everyone stared in disbelief at what once was.

I sat up and turned to Elnando, "Where were you at that moment?"

"What moment?" he asked.

"The moment the towers went down. Everyone remembers that moment. I remember that day like it was yesterday. I was around six-years-old and my dad used to drive me to school, but he was running late. That meant we were both late. Just as he was about to drop me off the announcement came on the radio about the first plane. I remember how puzzled I was as he blared the radio and said, 'We have to go back home.' When we arrived home my mother ran toward my father and me. I remember her saying, 'Steven that could have been you.' The next few days my parents refused to have the TV on when I was around. I'm not sure if I told you, but my dad's office is not too far from Fillmore. It was a big scare for both of them, and I think they wanted to shield me from everything. Where were you when the towers came down?"

"Melanie, I'll never forget that day. It changed my life forever. My mama returned home from her time spent away working on the cruise line. I was so happy to see her and I begged to stay home with her. I still remember my papa saying, 'No, Elnando, you must go to school. That's what you need to do today.'

"I was so mad at my papa. I pouted and didn't even say goodbye to him as he walked out the door early that morning. My mama said, 'You can stay home with me, if you promise to keep our little secret.'

"I remember swearing to my mama that my papa will never know. I remember watching her bending her head and putting her index finger to her mouth. She smiled and I giggled at what I thought was an enormous secret we both now shared.

"My mama cleaned around the house, as I played with second-hand toys that gathered in a cracked bin on the floor in our living room.

"Some celebrity caught my mama's eye on the *Today Show*, and she sat on the couch. I remember jumping up on the couch and joining her with one of my toys.

"Suddenly, the show was interrupted as news of the first plane hit.

"My mama fell to the floor, screaming, 'Javier, Javier.'

"I was so young I couldn't comprehend what was going on and why my mama was screaming my papa's name. Our neighbors took turns keeping their eye on me over the next few days, as my mama knelt with her rosary before a small statue of the Virgin Mary we had on a hutch, praying for my papa's safe return. My papa worked as a waiter since coming to this country at Windows of the World on the 106th floor of the North Tower, and I never saw him again."

"Oh my God, Elnando! I am so sorry. I didn't know," I said, putting my arms around him.

"That is one of the many reasons why I want to get the hell out of New York once we graduate."

"Elnando, what is going to happen to us when we graduate? We might get offers to join dance companies on opposite sides of the world."

Elnando grabbed my hand. "Mel, let's worry about it when the time comes."

I hugged Elnando tight. "I don't want to lose you, Elnando."

"Who says you're going to lose me? Mel, let's just enjoy this moment. Okay?"

I nodded.

How unscathed my life has been growing up in affluent Franklin Lakes. My family's greatest struggle was Caleb's blindness and the many surgeries he had to endure thus far. But he seemed to handle everything better than any of us. Elnando had to endure so much just to get where he is today. Something inside me told me there was more, and he was the type of person you couldn't push, but would have to wait for it to come out bit by bit. I couldn't imagine anything worse than losing my dad. Elnando came from such a different world than me and his experiences have far outweighed mine. Maybe he feared losing me if he exposed his heartaches. I was so in love with him that there wasn't a thing I believed could tear us apart.

~~~

A few days later, it was the dreadful day of September 11. I wanted to see Elnando first thing that morning so he would know that I was here for him and truly understood his pain.

I walked into his dorm room. Darnel was lying on the floor stretching. "Mel, Elnando is off practicing."

"I should have known. Even before class, he practices," I said as Darnel ignored me, absorbed in his stretches.

There was an awkward silence as I walked through the campus. Most of the dancers were either still sleeping or sitting half-awake as flashbacks of 9/11 permeated the screens of the morning shows that played on the televisions hung throughout the campus center.

I walked to the rehearsal hall. Ella Fitzgerald's rendition of "My Funny Valentine" could be heard. I slowly pushed on the door and watched Elnando gracefully move across the floor.

"I believe this is a dance for two." He smiled, seeing my entrance. As we twirled together in perfect harmony, it seemed as if we were dancing in slow motion as the innocent romantic lyrics of the song played on.

When the song ended, Elnando jostled my body on top of the ballet barre. The sweat continued to pour down his smooth skin. He lifted up my cotton skirt and lowered his shorts. As his body penetrated mine, I was left breathless as Elnando came. He held my body in place as it shook uncontrollably.

When my body finally calmed, Elnando gently lifted me down and we both collapsed in each other's arms.

As I caught my breath, I said, "I came here to make sure you were okay."

Elnando rubbed my leg. "I'm feeling a lot better now."

We both let out a slight chuckle.

Elnando said, "How 'bout you treat me to one of those weird drinks that you drink?" Catching his breath, he turned and looked at me. "You wore me out. I need something that's going to zap some energy into me if I'm going to make it through class."

"You mean a latte?"

"Yeah, let's go have a latte."

"Well come on," I jumped up and lifted Elnando's hand. "We don't have much time."

We quickly walked to the campus' Starbucks. I ordered us two double shot mocha lattes. As the café started to fill, we decided to grab our drinks and go for a quick walk outside around the campus. We found a bench near the annex; the one my father's company built and donated a few years back. I gazed in disbelief that it was my very own father who was responsible for the exquisite architecture and building of the huge annex that stood out among all the other buildings on the campus.

I took the lid off of my drink and, as the steam rose in the air, Elnando followed and took a sip.

"This is what you pay five dollars for?"

I smiled at his sour expression. "When it cools, you'll like it. I promise. It's delicious," I said, taking a slow sip.

"I think I need to go to the campus store and get me a Red Bull."

Blowing into my cup to cool it down, I said, "I know this is a hard day for you."

"It's a hard day for a lot of people, Melanie."

"I know it's an especially hard day for you, and I'm here for you."

"I know you are. In more ways than one! Thank you, Melanie."

My latte was finally cooling down, and I took bigger gulps, knowing that it was almost time for class, and I would need all the artificial pick-me-up just to get through my first class of Contemporary Dance with Miss "no mercy" Olivia.

I looked over again at the annex and felt a feeling of surreal joy come over me. It was hard to believe I was sitting here as a student at the world-renowned Fillmore School, staring at a building that my father was responsible for, with a wonderful guy that I was in love with.

"You know my dad's company built the annex. He even designed it himself."

"Wow," Elnando said, looking straight ahead. "That's pretty impressive. No wonder your family's rich."

"His company actually donated it. I guess my dad knew some people on the board here, and they had brought a lot of business his way in the past."

Elnando didn't respond and sat slowly sipping his latte.

"We should start heading to class," I said, getting up and walking over to the trash can to discard my completely empty cup.

"I think they put the wrong stuff in my drink. I'm ready for a nap."

"Come on! The day just started."

"Melanie, there's something I have to tell you."

I sat, hoping that he would make it quick, knowing that the last thing I needed was to be late for Miss Olivia's class.

"Thank you. I mean it. Today is a very hard day for me for more reasons than one."

"What do you mean? Elnando, what is it?"

"Melanie, I was involved in some horrible things."

I looked into Elnando's eyes, as a feeling of dread came over me.

"After my papa died, my mama was a wreck, and I was one really messed-up kid. And although I lived in a housing project filled with people, I felt very lonely. When I was only twelve-years-old, I got involved with a gang. They were like a family to me when I needed one most. I was very angry and vulnerable at the time. I did a lot of things I am ashamed of."

Elnando paused. I saw fear in his eyes as he continued to explain, "During that time I was involved in a lot of robberies."

Although I was shocked, I felt that I needed to comfort him. "You were a kid."

"I know, Melanie. Let me go on. On one of the days, a year after I joined, something went terribly wrong. We were apparently on another gang's turf, and they started shooting at us. We started shooting back. Yes, I had a gun."

I sat paralyzed, as Elnando continued, "You have to understand we had no choice but to shoot back. Melanie, one of them fell to the ground and..."

"What are you saying, Elnando?"

"Melanie, he died. I don't know if I was the one who killed him. We were all ducking behind the cars and shooting wildly."

"Oh, Elnando!"

"I'm sorry, Melanie. You're a good girl. You don't need this."

In disbelief I asked, "What changed?"

"About two years later, Birdie and Joe, the couple I told you about before, who own the dance studio, came into my life. They never knew anything about me being in a gang, although they may have suspected. They just saw me as a troubled kid with some promise."

"You're past all that, right, Elnando? It's all behind you, right?"

"Melanie, when you're in a gang, it's forever. There's no way out. It will never be behind me."

I was numb as the words flowed from Elnando's lips to the core of my soul. One thing I knew for sure was the thought of being late to Miss Olivia's class was the very least of my troubles.

Chapter 19

Elnando

I had finally confessed what had been burdening my heart all these years. I felt like a parakeet in a cage with the door slightly ajar, not fully able to fly free. I loved Melanie and, most of all, I trusted her. I didn't give her all the intimate details, nor did she ask, being too shocked by the confession of what I participated in and the life I may or may not have ended. Throughout the years, I tried to rationalize what I did; I was young and I was protecting myself. But then my conscience would remind me, the real threat was those standing around me who would ultimately do me the most harm.

The shame of the small robberies never weighed heavily on me, probably because the bigger event ripped away my soul. As the years went by, my time, and who I was with, was strictly guarded by Birdie and Joe. It was very hard for anyone to even get close to me. They shielded me and my best friend, Jewel, as we were both fatherless, and our mamas worked day and night just to make ends meet. As the neighborhood grew and became more impoverished, the greater the young prospects to invite in, and the fact that I was incredibly timid made me easily forgotten among the gun-happy strewn young men and women vying for a place to belong.

I danced and danced until the only thoughts that would permeate my mind were the aches and pains of my body being overused. Dance became my drug of choice to erase the pain of my past. As my heart grew more in love with Melanie, it also ached with guilt. I knew I needed to be free, and the drug of dance would no longer be a panacea for it. I would tell Melanie, my mama, Birdie, Jewel, and Anita that I would be going to the authorities. I still had my gun hidden behind a wall tile in Birdie's bathroom. Soon the walls of Birdie's home and mine will be coming down, so the gun needed to be removed. It was time for me to tear down my inner walls, as well and set myself free.

My main concern was Jewel. He was still active in the Latin Knights and was there that day as well. Like myself, Birdie and Joe gave Jewel every opportunity in the world, but he could never resist the allure of gang life. I needed to tell him what I planned to do and offer him the opportunity to come with me.

I knew from this moment on, things would never be the same, but not knowing if they would turn out better or worse, felt excruciating.

Chapter 20

Steven

Lauren and I arrived at Spanish Harlem. The surveyor met us at the site to go over a few technical things, and within a half hour our meeting was done. The overgrown weeded lot was over strewn with beer bottles, and in the center of it, lying on its side was an old commercial refrigerator. The old, run-down tenement and uncared-for lot played with my imagination. There was so much my company could do. Visions of swing sets, a community garden, and street-level stores raced through my mind. Reality quickly broke through as I turned and saw Lauren.

Lauren was incredibly irresistible and left me powerless, but lately the very thought of her made me feel guilty. I escaped to another place when thoughts of how I was destroying my wife and family overcame me. The crime had been committed several times. The temporary thrill with Lauren was starting to wane, as guilt waged war on me. I felt the urge to relieve my conscience, but the very thought of hurting MaryAnn, let alone her leaving me, was overwhelming.

"What are we doing?" I asked.

"What do you mean?"

"I mean, we can't keep doing what we're doing."

"You've never cheated on your wife before?" Lauren asked nonchalantly, as she reached into her purse and pulled out a small mirror and lipstick. She reapplied her lipstick and took a quick look into the mirror, reassuring herself of her beauty before clicking it shut.

"No, I haven't, Lauren."

With a chuckle, she responded, "How cute. I'm your first."

"You've done this before?"

Lauren smirked, "Don't look so surprised."

"I don't understand. You can get any guy you want."

Lauren put her arms around me, "And I did. I got you."

"But, I'm married."

"It doesn't seem to bother you when we're in the sack together."

I abruptly pushed her away from me. "I love my wife very much, Lauren."

"I'm sure you do. That's why you keep running off to me."

"I don't know what I'm doing, Lauren."

"Oh, Mr. Belezzi, I think you do!" she said mockingly.

"We've got to end all this."

"Why, when we've already started?"

"Like I said, 'I love my wife.'"

"Yeah, yeah, yeah, you love your wife!"

"I do!"

"What about me? Am I some casual lay to you? Do you think you can use me, and then run back to your wife with your tail between your legs? I don't think so!"

"What are you saying, Lauren?"

"I'm telling you, Steven, I care a lot about you. I can give you everything you need."

I didn't answer. I suddenly felt a feeling of fear towards Lauren. We stood together in awkward silence. Only the sounds of Latin music from the passing cars could be heard. A couple of old women coming out of the tenement, pulling on wobbly carts, gave us curious looks. I stared at the

101

vandalized Belezzi building sign, as Lauren angrily dug her heels into the dirt.

Out of the side of the lot, I noticed a tall, well-built Hispanic young man walking toward us.

"Hello, Mr. Belezzi."

I was surprised to see the man my daughter was involved with. I never expected her to be involved with someone from Spanish Harlem, and I secretly prayed that this was just a short-lived romance, like all of Melanie's high school flings.

"Elnando, how are you? I didn't recognize you at first."

"I'm good. I'm on my way to visit my mama and a very dear lady who helped raise me."

"They live here?"

"Yes, they do...for now. Mr. Belezzi it's your company that plans on tearing down our home."

"Yes. It's my company. I believe I mentioned that to you when we first met. I didn't know this was your home."

"I hate to say this to you, but it's your company that plans on driving my mama and so many people that I love away."

I looked at the run-down tenement.

They should be happy to be leaving here; any place has to be better than this shithole.

"I'm very sorry, Elnando. Our intention is not to drive anyone away, and everyone is welcome to stay. The condominiums will be beautiful, and this lot is going to be a great place for children to play. Elnando, really, if you or your people want to be angry with anyone, be angry with the investors who are going to benefit the most in the end, when all is said and done, and the government leaders who gave this their blessing. I attended a lot of the rallies and meetings.

102

I saw everyone give it a good fight. But the cold hard truth is the government always wins. They contend it's too run-down and basically unsafe to live in. Twenty percent of the condos are going to be made available for public housing."

Elnando looked at me with disgust. "Twenty percent! What about the rest of them?"

"Like they said at the meetings, 'Vouchers will be given to fund other suitable housing, and agencies have been set up to help anyone find suitable housing.' Elnando, I'm only the builder. Other builders have started building around here. If my company doesn't build here, trust me, another one will."

Elnando grinned. "You're just a regular "Bob the Builder!" I care a lot about your daughter, Mr. Belezzi, and being that you are Melanie's father, I mean no disrespect, but you are playing with these people's lives. Spanish Harlem is home to them. They're not going to be able to afford to live here or anywhere else in Spanish Harlem."

"I'm sorry, Elnando. Your home is going to be torn down one way or another."

"I understand that, but I'm afraid you may regret this Mr. Belezzi," he said with a glare.

"I don't think so, Elnando," I said in a stern tone, standing my ground.

Walking past Lauren and I, he said, "Mr. Belezzi, I wonder how Melanie would feel about what you're up to?"

"What's that supposed to mean?"

"Think about what I said Mr. Belezzi."

Chapter 21

Elnando

As I walked into the building, I felt angry, scared and a little guilty knowing how I had spoken to Mr. Belezzi, the father of the girl I love more than anything in the world. I already gave Melanie enough reasons to leave me. Now my confrontation with her dad was icing on the cake. Maybe I should put off going to the authorities until my mama, Anita and Birdie are settled into a new place. Jewel and I would have to be the ones to help them move. They would need my help, and I would have to be there for them. I lived with my dirty little secret this long. What were a few more months in the grand scheme of things? I just wanted to confess my sin and clear my conscience once and for all. The consequences of my confession would lead to serious implications on not only my life, but my mama's, Birdie's, Anita's, Jewel's and ultimately Melanie's, if she decides to hang in there with me for the long run. I was a minor when I took part in the shooting. I hoped that would be taken into consideration. I didn't even fear prison if I confessed. I was more afraid of being killed by the members of my gang.

I decided to put off my confession and just pay them a friendly visit. I felt shaky and I knew they would soon realize that there was something wrong with me. I decided that the best thing to do was turn around and go see Melanie. I would discuss my plan with her. Maybe she would try to talk me out of it.

~~~

I sat on the subway, closing my eyes with my earphones on and without the music, blocking out everyone around me. No music played, but I wanted to be alone in my thoughts of how I was going to tell Melanie my plan. I texted her and told her that I would be arriving back on campus soon and that I would meet her at her dorm as soon as I arrive. We hadn't been together long, but the love we had for each other and the passion we felt together was something that couldn't be denied.

~~~

A slow rain drizzled down as I made my way to Melanie's dorm. The dark, gloomy sky matched my dreary mood. I gently knocked on the door. Melanie answered, wearing a pair of LOVE PINK sweatpants and an off-the-shoulder gray sweatshirt, with her long wavy hair pinned at the top and flowing in the back. She looked like a natural beauty.

"Hey," she said, greeting me and giving me a kiss. Noticing my sad expression she asked, "Is everything all right?"

"I need to talk to you about a few things."

"Oh no," she said, walking over and taking a seat on her bed. "Have a seat. Ming-Na's not going to be back for a while."

I took a seat next to her. "Remember what I confessed to you the other day?"

Melanie nodded, with a scared look on her face.

"I decided I want to go to the authorities and tell them what happened. I want to know if I killed that boy. I need to free my conscience, Melanie."

Melanie sat for a few seconds at a loss for words. "What? What are you going to say to them? I was a thirteen-year-old gang banger and I may have shot someone to death!"

"Yes, Mel! I want to come clean."

"Why? Why now? You're at Fillmore. You are probably one of the greatest dancers this school has ever seen. In four years, you can move to another country. We can move to another country together and be dancers. We can live out our dream, together!"

"I don't want to be haunted by this anymore."

"Do you understand by doing this that you might as well forget any dreams you may have for your future? You may have to do some jail time, whether your bullet killed him or not. Are you going to tell them about the robberies as well?"

"I will probably mention it to them, but stealing hubcaps and bags of chips from the corner bodega will probably not be high on their list of priorities. I was just a minor when everything went down. Hopefully, they will take that into consideration. Mel, I don't really know what's going to happen to me." I bent over and hugged her tight, as tears filled her eyes.

"What about the other gang members? What if they find out you went to the police? What will they do?" she asked in barely a whisper, as I continued to hold her in my arms.

"They will probably try to kill me."

She abruptly pushed me out of her arms. "No, Elnando! No! You can't do this. I won't let you."

"Mel, I'm going to come clean, one way or another. I understand if you decide you don't want to be with me anymore. I understand, really I do! You don't need this shit in your life."

"I'm not leaving you, Elnando," she said, rubbing her mascara-smeared eyes. "Maybe my family can help you out. We can get you a lawyer or something..."

I grabbed her hand. "I actually ran into your dad today."

"What?"

"I went home this morning. I was planning on telling my mama and Birdie about what I did and my decision to go to the police, but at the last minute I changed my mind. I decided it was only right to discuss things with you first. I was there, but I couldn't even bring myself to go up to their place and pay them a visit."

"And you saw my dad?"

"He was outside my home. He must have been there to check things out."

"What are you talking about?"

"Your dad's company is the one that is going to tear down the housing project I grew up in to build some fancy condominiums. I spoke with your dad, not about my situation, but about his plans for his company to tear down my home."

"I feel terrible about this. We passed your home on the way back from the dance studio, didn't we? I do remember seeing my dad's company's sign. I'm so sorry."

"It's not your fault. Like he told me, Melanie, if he doesn't tear it down, someone else will."

"Elnando, can't you just enjoy where you are now? You have me. You're at a great school. You worked so hard to get here."

"Melanie, I can't. I need to come clean, in order to enjoy the rest of my life. I need to do this."

"Fine, I'm with you, but we need a plan!"

Chapter 22

Lauren

I decided to pay a surprise visit to my parents. I arrived at my parents' simple ranch style home in northeast Yonkers.

"Look who's here! My beautiful baby girl," my father said to me, as I walked through the door. It was nice to be home. Although I loved being on my own, I sometimes missed being around my parents. They were what I considered to be the best parents a girl could ever ask for. Growing up I was constantly reminded, as long as I could remember, that I was born in my mother's heart and I was daddy's little girl. My parents adopted both me and my older sister, Stefani, when they were in their late thirties. My parents were both old souls, and I tried my best to conceal my wild club-hopping way of living from them, along with my laundry list of intermittent romances with both single and married men. When I picked up the phone, hung over on most Saturday mornings, they quickly learned that I wasn't knitting afghans on Friday nights.

I wanted to tell them about Steven. I felt differently about him than all the rest of the men I had been with. I could see myself settling down with him and being by his side as his company continued to grow. I would be the cool stepmom to his daughter, and I would spoil his blind son. I could continue to meet Steven's needs, both inside the bedroom and out. I would be his young trophy wife and love Steven as much as I would love the affluent lifestyle that he could afford to give me. If he was in my bed as much as he was, why didn't he just stay?

"Lauren, when are you going to settle down and give me some grandbabies?" my father kidded, as I took off my coat, threw it on the couch and joined him in a seat next to him at the head of the kitchen table.

"Why would I want to do that when I am having so much fun?" I chuckled. "And, if you think I'm having a good time, think of how much fun Stefani's having in L.A."

My mom reminded me, "I talked to your sister briefly today. She seems to be settling down; unfortunately it's with her job. From the way she talks, she's working 24/7."

Stefani was two years older than me and had been living in L.A. for a couple of years now. She loved living there, and is going to be making it her permanent home. She's a production assistant, and from what she had told me, she's the low man on the totem pole that was mostly controlled by men with big egos. She was adopted as well; we share the same biological parents, whom we know nothing about.

"Who says I'm not seeing anyone?"

My father rose from the table. "Lauren, I would love to hear all about it. Please make sure I'm the first to know when it gets closer to me writing the big check! Weddings are ridiculously expensive, and thankfully you and your sister have kept me from filing for bankruptcy thus far."

"I'll remember that Daddy! Where are you headed?" I asked, rising to give him a kiss goodbye.

"I am going to the library to play some chess. You keep in touch, sweetheart!"

"I will! Have fun! Don't keep Mom waiting up for you!"

"I'll try not to!"

When he left, my mom offered me a drink. As we shared our glasses of ginger ale, she leaned closer into me and whispered, as if there was someone else present, "Lauren, tell me what's new with you? Are you really seeing someone?"

I leaned forward and animatedly whispered, "Yes, he's my boss!"

My mom sat back as if at a loss for words and stuttered, "Lauren, I...I thought the man you work for was married."

"He is!" My mom sat speechless at a loss for words, shaking her head disapprovingly.

"Stop looking at me like that, Mom!"

"Lauren, we taught you better!"

"It sounds worse than it is. He loves me. He spends more time with me than he does with his own wife."

"But, you're not his wife!"

"I know that, but I hope to be someday!"

"Lauren, this isn't right! You have to end it!"

"Why?"

"What do you mean by 'Why,' Lauren? You're going to get hurt. One way or another, you're going to get hurt, not to mention what you are doing to his family."

"What I'm doing, Mom, he's doing, too!"

"It's wrong, Lauren, and he's not going to leave his wife for you. Trust me!"

"How do you know?"

"Lauren, that's not the way it works."

"Well, Mom, in that case, at least I'm having fun!"

Chapter 23

MaryAnn

I was very relieved to finally have at least part of the day with Steven by my side, even if it meant Caleb was around, and part of the day would be spent taking him to his horseback riding lesson. I missed Steven so much, and I knew Caleb did as well by his continual asking lately of "When's Daddy coming home?" There had been an uncomfortable distance between Steven and me. His mind seemed somewhere else. I understood that this was an important and crazy time for him and he was fully responsible for his company. His dad no longer had his foot in the door to help him out, since last year he and Steven's mom started living part of the year in Florida. All the responsibility now fell on Steven, as well as the pressure, and to add to it, competition was fierce.

Something inside of me made me feel that there was something else going on with Steven. He always took care of himself, but lately I noticed him taking more of an interest in his appearance. The few times he did make it home for dinner, he immediately left afterwards to go workout at the gym. He seemed to be checking his phone more often, and when he did, he was always very secretive about it.

Steven never gave me reason to question him. I was truly proud of all he had accomplished throughout the years as a provider, father and husband. If something was bothering him, I would hope that he would share it with me. I was his wife and best friend. From our early unexpected pregnancy with Melanie, to our years of infertility, which no doctor could explain, to finally having Caleb, a child with a disability, we had been through a lot. I believed that there was nothing we couldn't get through and conquer.

We arrived at the cold, damp barn. Hank waved us over; to the same spot we met him at the last time we were there. He had Misty Mae cross tied, but this time she was wearing a saddle with a horn on the front. The musky hay smell filled the air, plugging my sinuses, and Caleb was bouncing with delight, knowing that today would be his big day; he would be able to get on top of Misty Mae and ride her, while Hank led them around the ring.

"Hey, big guy," Hank said.

"Hi, Hank! Hi, Misty Mae! I get to ride you today!"

"She's been talking about it all day!" Hank said.

"Misty Mae talks?"

"Sure she does. Didn't you ever hear of Mr. Ed, the talking horse? That's her father." Hank chuckled.

Caleb laughed. "You're funny!"

"Hey," Steven said, approaching us moments later, barely looking in my direction.

"Daddy," Caleb yelled, jumping up and down.

"Hay is for horses, and my name is Hank," Hank said, extending his hand to Steven. "Good to meet *ya*. Today is your son's big day. He gets to ride my beauty, Misty Mae."

Steven responded, "I know," and patted Caleb's head, while admiring the large mare. "You're going to get on top of her. You're brave. She's really big."

"I know! Can I ride her now?"

Hank chuckled and limped his way over to a large, black plastic pail and pulled out a stiff-bristled brush with a handle.

Hank started brushing Misty Mae's middle and said, "Before we go for our ride, Misty Mae likes to look good. I'm going to have your daddy pick you up."

Steven picked up Caleb.

Hank put Caleb's tiny right hand over the big, bulky brush. Then he guided Steven's hand over Caleb's.

"Now, Caleb, you and your daddy are going to give Misty Mae a good brushing," Hank said, putting his hand over both of theirs, showing them the proper way of brushing Misty Mae.

Hank stepped back and said, "The two of you are doing a great job! Misty Mae is looking prettier already! Now it's important to be relaxed when dealing with a horse. 'Cause they can tell if you're nervous, happy or excited, or if you're hiding something. Just like a woman!"

I gave Hank a soft smile.

Hank continued, "You have to be true to your horse. Trust is important; you want to give the horse a feeling of security. They need to know you won't hurt them. So always be gentle. Or else, they will go galloping off out of control, and you don't want that."

"Can I ride him now?" Caleb asked.

"Caleb, I think she's ready. But, guess what we have to do first?"

"What?" Caleb said responding anxiously to the question.

"You must always wear a protective helmet before getting on any horse," he said reaching down and grabbing a small helmet that was sitting close by on a tackle box. "I'm going to put this helmet on you, and make sure it's nice and secure. I need you to stay nice and still."

Caleb stood still at his demand.

"Now, I'm going to have your daddy put you on top of Misty Mae, and both your mom and dad are going to hold on to you while I untie her."

Steven very carefully lifted Caleb onto the mare, while I spotted him on the other side.

Hank said, "I am going to guide your hands. This here is the saddle horn, you are going to keep this hand firmly on it and the other hand is going to hold on tight to these rubber reins, while your parents and I guide you and Misty Mae out to the ring.

Caleb's body bounced back and forth as Steven tried to balance him. I stood, as directed, on the other side, ready to catch Caleb if he should fall.

Hank pulled the bridle as Misty Mae moved at a snail's pace.

"How's it feel, Caleb?" Hank asked.

"Good," Caleb answered. It was evident he was nervous and struggled to keep his balance.

Awed by what I was seeing, I said, "You're riding a horse, Caleb! Mommy's very proud of you!"

Caleb didn't answer, while he continued to keep his focus.

As we made our way halfway around the ring, Hank guided the horse to an opening in the gate.

Hank said, "Caleb, I think you wore Misty Mae out. She said she's ready for her nap."

"No, she didn't," Caleb said.

"She did. You just didn't hear her." Hank smiled, as he led the horse toward the stall. He effortlessly tied her in place and helped Steven grab Caleb off the horse.

The horse let out a whinny, and Caleb laughed.

"Caleb, you did great today!" Hank said.

Steven echoed his words, rubbing Caleb's shoulder.

I turned toward Hank and said, "Thank you, Hank. This meant a lot to Caleb, and I think he is going to really benefit by coming here."

"It was my and Misty Mae's pleasure."

I bent down and whispered in Caleb's ear, "What do we say, Caleb?"

"Thank you, Hank. Thank you, Misty Mae!"

"You're welcome, Caleb."

Steven extended his hand to Hank. "This is wonderful. I would have never thought…"

Hank firmly shook Steven's hand, smiled and said, "A person doesn't look at a horse with their eyes. They see them with their heart."

Chapter 24

Melanie

"Elnando, we need this! A day out of the city would be good for the both of us while we try to figure things out," I said as I stretched on the cold hardwood floor.

"I have to admit I am a little nervous about seeing your dad after our last meeting," Elnando said, as he settled into first position at the barre.

I got up, feeling achy in every part of my body, and positioned myself in back of Elnando as we both continued with our ballet warm-up. "I promise you it will be fun!"

Olivia abruptly walked over to us, "Do I need to separate the two of you? Focus. Focus. Do you hear me, everyone? Focus!"

Olivia took front center stage as we continued to our places. We danced to a medley of Beethoven. I pushed myself harder than I ever have. I felt like a race horse trying to take the lead, as sweat perspired from every pore in my body.

As the music came to an end, we all stood frozen in position. Within a few awkward seconds, Olivia clapped as if in slow motion. "Looking good out there, ladies and gents', but I must say some of you are looking a lot better than others. It's time to step up your game. As you train your bodies and minds in the next few weeks, keep in mind that I will be casting the roles for the holiday dance showcase. This year we will be performing the Russian Ballet, *The Firebird*, with choreography from some of our senior dancers. This is your time to shine. Continue working hard. This is your weekend to rest. If you think its hard now, you have no idea what's in store for you."

She pounded her pole on the floor and slowly glanced down the line across the room. "You're dismissed! See you all on Monday."

~~~

Elnando looked at me with a sly grin on his face, as he sat on the end of his bed.

"What is it, Elnando?" I asked as I did some ballet moves in place.

He chuckled.

"What?" I asked. "What is so funny?"

"No disrespect and I don't mean to be wise, but you bought your five-year-old brother a sweatshirt that says, "Fillmore.""

"So?"

"He's five years old. What five-year-old wants a sweatshirt for his birthday? Why couldn't we go to Toys "R" Us or FAO Schwartz and buy him a toy?"

"Because he's blind, Elnando, and my mom said she would pick up a toy he could use from the both of us. She knows best."

"That's very nice of your mother. My point is, he can't see, let alone read. Why did you get him a sweatshirt from our school?"

"It's the thought that counts, and I always talk to him about how proud I am to be going to Fillmore. And trust me; Caleb sees more than any of us can see."

"I *gotcha*. I am going to feel extremely out of place there."

"Don't! My grandparents will be there and you will love them, and all the people from my dad's company will be there, too."

"And, that's why I will feel out of place."

117

"They are all really nice, Elnando. We have been doing this every year for Caleb's birthday. We have a party with family and my dad's employees, and then Caleb has a party at his preschool."

I bent over and put both of my hands on the back of Elnando's hair and held it in a pony tail. "Just play nice, Elnando. Let's have a good weekend and forget everything else that is going on in our lives."

Elnando pulled me on to the bed and kissed my neck. "I'm always good, Melanie."

~~~

Batman balloons blowing in the wind greeted us at the large brick mailbox, as the car service my dad ordered for us swerved into the front of my house.

The hickory barbecue smell of my mom's famous baked beans whiffed through the air, as my mom greeted us at the front door with Caleb in her arms.

She gently put him down and said, "Melanie and Elnando are here."

Caleb yelled, "It's my birthday."

"It is, Caleb!" I said, bending down to hug him.

My mom went to give Elnando a hug as he said, "Hi, Mrs. Belezzi."

"I'm glad you could make it, Elnando."

"Hey, Caleb," Elnando said.

"Hi, Elnando!"

We followed my mom and Caleb through the kitchen and out to the backyard. It was a muggy day, and the trees were already showing their orange and red leaves for Indian summer."

A huge white tent was set up in the backyard, with metal chairs and tables both inside and outside the tent. Although my family could easily afford to have had the event catered, my mom, Nonna and Mema insisted that they make all the food, for not only this occasion but every occasion. "We are Italian and hospitality and good food is what we stand for, and nobody makes food like your mother and me," my Nonna often said. I was Italian, courtesy of both sides of my family, although my dad's side was full-blooded with the darker features, my mom's were all Mediterranean blonde, Italian mixed in with a little French. My mom's parents, Mema and Grandpa, lived nearby and were lovable yet quieter, simpler folks compared to my other grandparents. My mom was closer to them than any of their other three children who now lived in different parts of the country.

Both sides celebrated good food and family, often mixing together at many of our holiday functions, which were mostly hosted at our house. Besides my mom, Mema and Nonna were the greatest women I have ever known. They were exquisite beauties, who were always classy and kind. Nonna and Poppy now lived in Florida during the winter months. You always knew when my cool-as-a-cat Poppy was around by the stale smell of cigar smoke that permeated the air, as he often sat lounging in a chair slowly puffing away in his own little world. He was once the driving force behind Belezzi Builders, its founder who guided my dad through the ropes. I often heard stories of how my dad was at construction sites wearing a hard hat before he could even walk. My dad was my Poppy's only son, and the baby of the family. They were extremely close, and my dad took right after him with his charming personality. My Aunt Gina, my dad's older sister, was sweet, skinny, with long, curly jet black hair that she often straightened. She lived in Long Island with my Uncle Chris, a quiet reserved corporate type and my two cousins, Gabby who just turned eight, and Monica, who was now becoming a teenager, in a large stucco home that was built especially for them by my dad and Poppy. Uncle Chris worked in finance and did very well, allowing my Aunt Gina the luxury of being a stay-at-home mom.

Soon, the rest of my dad's employees started to arrive. Some of them I knew, such as Jack and Dolores who had been with my dad's company since the beginning, and some I barely recognized.

My dad came over and greeted us. He kindly shook Elnando's hand, and said, "Glad you could make it. There are bottles of water and soda in the cooler. Melanie, make him feel comfortable."

"Thanks, Dad," I said, giving him a hug.

Elnando and I both grabbed bottled water out of the cooler.

My mom and Caleb came over to us, as Elnando and I found our own private area under the tent while everyone else mingled. "Would the two of you mind helping Nonna and Poppy? They just arrived and could use a hand."

"Not at all," Elnando responded.

"Good, you get to meet my Nonna and Poppy," I said, as we walked to the driveway to meet them. They opened their trunk to boxes filled with trays of piping hot food. The aroma of sweet sausage and peppers and baked ziti made my mouth water.

I hugged them both. "Nonna and Poppy, this is my friend, Elnando. He is also a dancer at Fillmore," I said smiling.

"I think we need to see the two of you break out in a little dance," Poppy said, while doing a comical imitation of Gene Kelly.

I started to laugh. "We'll save that for our winter showcase."

"Nice to meet you, son," he said, extending his hand to Elnando.

"It's good to meet you," Elnando responded warmly.

"It's nice to finally meet you, Elnando," Nonna said.

"Thank you," Elnando said, nodding his head.

We grabbed the boxes and carried them in. Poppy made a mad dash for the backyard, as Mom arranged them on the counter and Nonna and Dolores, Dad's talkative employee, helped keep Caleb occupied and out of Mom's hair by asking him a ton of questions.

At once, my Aunt Gina, Uncle Chris and their two daughters walked in along with my Mema and Grandpa, who were armed with bags of food. I grabbed the bags from them, put them on the counter and introduced all of them to Elnando. They were all warm and gregarious toward him. Gabby, the younger of my two nieces, asked if she could go on the trampoline with Caleb, and if Monica could watch them.

I looked at Monica who stood texting, oblivious to those around them.

She continued texting as my Nonna yelled over to her and demanded a hug.

"I think Elnando and I will take you two out."

Gabby walked over to Caleb and sweetly said, "Caleb, follow me. Melanie and her friend are going to take us out back to go jump on the trampoline."

Caleb asked, "Melanie, are you going to jump, too?"

"Caleb, I'm pretty sore. I've got to rest my body this weekend, but Elnando and I are going to watch the two of you."

"Okay."

We watched Caleb and Gabby bounce up and down; giggling with every fall they took. As we watched them,

121

Elnando and I observed everyone at the party from a distance. I stared at them as if watching a silent movie. Everyone seemed to be having a good time. In the corner of my eye, I noticed a very attractive girl in her late twenties. Her motions were animated as she flipped her hair and smiled suggestively next to my dad at the beer cooler; their distance apart was uncomfortable, and my dad seemed awkward in her presence.

I opened the protective mesh on the trampoline and peeked in. Caleb and Gabby took a final bounce and lay exhausted and out of breath.

"You guys are tired already?" I kidded.

Elnando chimed in, "I'm tired already."

"All right, Elnando! Let's go see if the food's ready. Gabby, can you guide Caleb to the edge and I'll help him down?"

"Here, Caleb," Gabby said, grabbing his hand. "I'm going to walk you to the edge and Melanie's going to catch you."

"Gabby, would you like to play with my trucks in the dirt?"

Gabby looked over at me for mercy, but then smiled and said, "I would love to."

"Gabby, the birthday boy is all yours. Elnando and I are going to see if the food is ready."

As we walked over, my Poppy stood at command with his cigar in one hand and beer in the other.

My dad laughed and said, "Quiet, everyone! Big Steven wants to make a toast."

With his hands shaking, he said, "I want to thank all of you for coming out to my son's casa today to celebrate my grandson's birthday. Steven has told me about all the incredible projects all of you have been involved with, and I

122

have to say, I couldn't be prouder of my son and the company that he continues to lead successfully, despite this horrible economy. I thank you all from the bottom of my heart for your dedication to my son and his company. Salute!"

Everyone chanted, "Salute." I glanced over at Elnando, as he stood stone-faced, watching everyone clink their drinks together.

"Relax, Elnando," I whispered.

He whispered back, "I would like to see how they would act if someone told them that they were going to have their precious mansions torn down and that there was nothing they could do about it."

"Elnando, I'm sorry my dad's a part of this. There is nothing I can do," I said, watching my dad walk toward the house, hoping he did not see the look of anger on Elnando's face.

Elnando turned toward me. "How about you imagine for a moment that the government, along with several other groups, had plans to tear down your home, and all your neighbors' and you had no say in it. Your neighbors who are the same color as you and share the same core beliefs, and are the people you trust."

"Yes, Elnando, I see your point! It's also the same people in your neighborhood that drove you to join a gang, and possibly commit murder. Maybe splitting them up really isn't such a bad idea!"

A surge of anger came over Elnando as he walked toward the house.

My mom looked over at me as she passed around a tray of spanikopia. I mouthed, "Don't ask."

I followed Elnando as he stormed into my house. As we approached the kitchen, we heard giggling and the words, "Is this what it's like to live like Mrs. Belezzi?"

Chapter 25

Lauren

"You're finally back. I thought I was never going to see you today," I said, walking into Steven's office.

Everyone left for the day and I finally had my chance to be alone with him.

"Lauren, we need to talk," Steven said, sounding exhausted.

"What's going on, Mr. Belezzi?" I asked trying to be funny.

He put his face in his hands. "We've got to end this. Once and for all, we have to end this thing between us."

"What's this thing?" I said, taking a seat in front of his desk.

"You know what I mean. Look, I can't be doing this to MaryAnn anymore. I love my wife."

I laughed. "Oh, you didn't love her while you were with me?"

"Lauren, try to understand. It's not right what we're doing. You're young, smart, and beautiful. You can have any man you want."

"I know all that," I said, getting up and leaning on the desk, "Admit it, we have so much fun together, and you like the mystery of us sneaking around."

"Lauren, it may be fun at that moment, but it's not meant to last. I have a family who I love."

"Don't you love me?"

"Lauren, I don't really know how I feel about you."

"Then why do you keep showing up at my door?"

Steven stared at the floor. "I don't know. I don't know anything anymore. But, I really think its best that you stop working here."

"You're firing me? I can't believe this! You're actually firing me."

"I will give you some money to hold you over the next few months and a glowing recommendation."

"I bet you will." I pulled a cigarette out of my purse and lit up.

"Lauren, please don't smoke in here."

"Fuck you!"

"I'm really sorry. I'm sorry about everything. I should never have done this to you, my wife, everyone. I really don't know what I'm going to do now."

I shook my head and grinned. "What are you going to do? Steven, you're going to go home to your sweet suburban wife, your little disabled boy, and your little girl, the ballerina, and live happily ever after. That's what you're going to do!"

"I truly feel bad about everything I did."

I blew out some smoke. "At least you enjoyed it!"

"It was like getting drunk, Lauren. It's great while it's happening, but you don't feel all that great the next day."

"I must have made a real alcoholic out of you."

We sat silent as I continued to smoke. "Do you want me to go over anything with you before I leave?"

"No, I'll figure it out."

Steven unlocked his drawer, pulled out his checkbook, and started writing.

"Take this," he said.

I went to grab the check and we both held on to it.

"I'm really sorry, Lauren."

"Don't be! You'll be back."

Chapter 26

Melanie

I had a few hours between classes, and I decided to give Dad a visit. I called him earlier in the day and he said he would be in the office all day catching up on things that put him behind when he was on-site, that it would be great to see me, and wondered if everything was all right. I told him we'll talk when I get there. I sensed a feeling of nervousness in my otherwise calm Dad's voice as he hung up.

When I arrived at the office, Dolores greeted me and, of course, mentioned how it was a shame we had to leave so soon before the cake and gifts were opened. I lied to her like I did to my parents and Caleb, and told her how we had to get back to school in order to have some time to rehearse, that it was first come, first served in the rehearsal studio. Although the truth was, Elnando had a bug up his ass and it was best that we leave immediately. Also, I was pissed and wanted to know what was up with "that girl" and her sly comment I overheard her say in my dad's presence as we entered the kitchen. I looked around the office and was glad that SHE wasn't around.

Dad came out and greeted me, and directed me to his office. "Good to see you, sweetheart. Do you have time to go out for lunch?"

"No, I don't have that much time. Dad, there's something I need to talk to you about," I said, taking a seat in front of him, and wanting to get right to the point. It had been weighing on me about talking to my father, and I wanted to get it done and over with.

My father twitched in his chair, "What's going on?"

"I need your help. It's Elnando."

"Melanie, if this is about the company tearing down his home, it's just about settled."

"It's not about that, Dad. He's in trouble and I want you to help him."

"What kind of trouble?"

"About four years ago, when he was around thirteen-years-old, he was involved in a crime, and somebody got hurt."

"How hurt?"

"They died."

My father let out a loud sigh. "This is the gentleman you're involved with, Melanie? You can have any man and you pick this one? C'mon, Melanie."

"I take it you're not going to help me."

"No, I'm not going to help him! Let me guess! He's in a gang."

"Dad, it's complicated. He's at Fillmore now. He's a good guy. He was young. He feels guilty. He's thinking of going to the police. He's not even sure if it was his bullet that killed the person. I thought maybe you could get him a lawyer or something."

"This is unbelievable, Melanie! I can't believe I'm hearing this from you! Your Mom and I worried about you living here in the city. We were afraid of the people you might encounter walking the streets, not the people you would meet at Fillmore."

"Dad, I love him," I said as I started to tear up.

"These aren't the people we associate with, Melanie. It's your first year of college, and you should be focusing on your dancing."

"I am."

"You shouldn't be dealing with this nonsense. You worked way too hard."

"Dad, the young girl who works here for you, she followed you around Caleb's party like a lovesick puppy dog. I overheard her making some remark about what it's like to live like mom. Should you be associating with people like that, let alone having them work for your company?"

He looked at me, shocked not only at the words I was saying, but that I was actually talking to him in such a manner.

It broke my heart to hurt my dad with my words.

I got up and walked toward the door. "Thanks for your help, Dad."

Chapter 27

Lauren

I emerged from the hot shower. It was soothing and relaxing, just what I needed. I draped my fluffy white bathrobe around me and wrapped a towel around my head. I was in for the night. A hurricane had been predicted, and although my parents begged that I go with them to visit my aunt upstate, I was feeling low and thought it was best to wait it out in my own home. I doubted anything would actually come of the storm and the truth was I didn't care. I was in no mood now to go out, and I was sure I would be in no mood later tonight, plus all the watering holes were being boarded up. Everyone either left town or was like me, a prisoner by choice in their own home.

I started a pot of tea and turned on the news. Report after report of the disastrous weather ahead of us played on. My laptop was charging and candles were on the table. I was at least prepared if "Sandy" should make an appearance. The teakettle whistled. I returned to the kitchen and turned off the stove. As I was about to prepare my tea, the doorbell rang. My heart fluttered.

Please, God! Let it be Steven.

I removed the turban from my head, ran my fingers through my damp hair, and threw the towel on the couch. I looked through the peephole. It was Steven! I smiled at him. "Come in," I said, unlocking the door. He was clean-shaven and dressed casually in jeans and a long-sleeve cotton gray shirt. He seemed unhappy, and worn out.

Before I could say a word, he said, "Lauren, I'm just here to make sure you're all right."

Interrupting him, I blurted, "I told you that you would be back."

"It's not like that, Lauren."

"Like what, Steven? You just happened to be in Williamsburg and you thought you would stop by before a hurricane hits to check on my well-being? You gave me the talk. You fired me! Remember? I am fine! Does that make you happy? You can leave now," I said, grabbing the door knob.

Steven grabbed my arm. "As much as I still want you, we can't ever be together."

I let go of his grip and took a seat on my couch. "Why exactly are you here?"

Steven took a seat in the chair across from me. "I don't know what the fuck I'm doing," he said, clearly frustrated.

I sat silently studying him. He looked so pained. I wanted so desperately to be in his arms, but there seemed to be a hidden line separating us, both emotionally and physically.

Steven looked down at the floor as he spoke, "I love MaryAnn so much, and I love our house, our children, and the life we've built together. She's an incredible woman but, when I'm with her, I want to escape with you."

We sat for a moment without words. Then I got up and knelt before him and put my hands on his lap. "Then escape with me, be with me, or let's just keep doing what we've been doing. We have so much fun when we're together."

"When I broke it off with you at the office, it was because I didn't want to hurt my wife or family anymore. Lauren, I didn't want to hurt you anymore either. But, there is something I have come to realize. I may keep showing up at your door, but you're not the type of woman I could ever be with long term, whether I was with MaryAnn or not. You are what you are, Lauren."

I backed away from him. "What is that supposed to mean?"

"This is what you do."

"You mean sleep with married men?"

"Yes."

I grinned and shook my head. "And, aren't you a married man?"

"This isn't me. This isn't what I do."

"You seem to being doing it very well."

"But I'm not this type of person."

"You could have fooled me."

"Lauren, you're going to move on with your life, and although you're beautiful and could have any guy you want, the person you're with really won't matter too much, as long as it works for you, and how ever long it works for you. Am I right?"

"That's it! You have me all figured out! You obviously don't know how I feel about you!"

"It doesn't matter, because that is the type of woman you are."

"You're a bastard, Steven, a real bastard!"

Steven got up to leave. I pounded his chest with my fists, as I started to tear up. "Why did you come back here? Why?" He grabbed my wrists and then we fell into each other's arms.

Steven let go, put his hands on my face and softly kissed my lips. "Goodbye, Lauren."

"This is really it?"

He didn't say a word and walked out the door.

As much as he broke my heart, I knew deep down inside that I would always be a part of Steven's life. Forever!

Chapter 28

MaryAnn

I walked out back and carefully stacked the patio chairs into our shed. I wanted desperately to move the tables that scattered our backyard, but I knew I was not physically strong enough. Steven insisted they would be safe, and that it would do nothing but cause him backache if he tried to move them.

An evacuation was declared for both New York and New Jersey, due to the threat of severe hurricane-type conditions that were due to ravage the entire Northeast. Steven insisted it was just a scare tactic, and that Irene was harmless and Sandy would be, too. I questioned him as I peered at the ominous sky, as the wind chimes that hung clumsily from the deck danced slowly in the air playing a mystical tune. A shiver ran down my spine as I looked from a distance at the sprawling acres of land that surrounded us. It was the calm before the storm, and the uncertainty of what may occur, left me with a feeling of anxiety that could be cut with a knife. Where was Steven? Why did he leave the house so early this morning? He should be home by now. I worried about his commute home and about the safety of Melanie. Being stubborn like her father, she insisted that it will probably be nothing, and that she needed to be there for her roommate, Ming-Na. I suggested that Ming-Na come home with her, too, but she laughed and said, "Now that wouldn't be any fun."

Barkley's excessive, loud barking rang through to the outside of the house. *It must be Steven, Thank God!*

I tightly closed the patio doors and proceeded inside.

Caleb yelled, "Barkley, be quiet. It's only Daddy. Stop barking!" He had his Braille toys scattered across the corner section of the living room. For a child whose blindness limits his range of space, he sure could make a mess.

Steven walked in and my heart skipped a beat. I felt like he had just returned home from war. He was safe and hopefully he would be in my arms tonight.

Caleb rose from the floor and jumped up and down at Steven's arrival. Steven swung him around, kissing him, until Caleb proclaimed that he was making him dizzy.

"Steven, I think we should leave."

"We aren't going anywhere," he said, walking over to the fire pit. "I built this place with my own two hands, and it wasn't built with Popsicle sticks. Stop worrying! Irene didn't blow our house down and neither will Sandy," he said, lighting the fire pit.

Suddenly, our Adirondack antler chandelier that hung above the center of the dining room table flickered. Sandy had finally caught Steven's attention.

I looked at Steven and back at the chandelier. "I think that's a sign."

"We're fine! Right, Caleb?" Steven asked in Caleb's direction.

"We're fine, Daddy," Caleb said, enthralled in his toys with Barkley lying by his side.

Steven sat back on the leather coach and put his feet up on the hassock. "Relax, MaryAnn. Go get yourself a nice glass of wine and while you are at it, you can pour me a glass, too."

I silently agreed and walked through to the kitchen. Steven's idea wasn't bad, and it would clearly help take the edge off. I poured two generous glasses of Pinot Noir. As I walked back to the great room, I heard the wind howl and, out of the corner of my eye, I noticed the drooping branches of the weeping willow outside our back window sway in repeated beats to the sound of the wind.

Steven and I sat side by side, and after our first glass, I thought it would only make sense to bring out the whole bottle and make a night of it. As Steven sat comfortably, I walked back and retrieved the wine bottle and a sleeve of crackers for Caleb. I decided to leave the crackers on the side table, not wanting to interrupt Caleb's quiet play. I poured Steven another glass. "It's not too late. We can stay with your parents or mine. They both got hotel rooms."

"MaryAnn, let's just relax. Cheers," Steven said, clinking his glass against mine. "We have a top-of-the-line generator that automatically flips on. We should be good."

Caleb stood up. "Can I go to my room and listen to some music?"

"Sure. Would you like a snack first?"

"I'm not very hungry."

Barkley followed us as we made our way to Caleb's bedroom.

"What type of music do you feel like listening to?"

"I want to listen to some of Melanie's CDs."

I laughed. "Now I don't think Melanie would appreciate that. How 'bout the Bieber?"

Caleb nodded his head and sang the chorus from the hit song "Baby."

"I take it, that's a yes!"

Caleb loved Justin Bieber's music and especially that song since it came out over two years ago. Caleb had a love for music, and I had planned on getting him piano lessons in the future. For now, I thought our plate was filled with enough activities. I'm glad I had pursued the horseback riding lessons for him. I believed it was definitely a wise choice. He loved it and it was extremely therapeutic for him. Thankfully, Caleb also enjoyed playgroup with other blind children at the community center and attending the Center for the Blind preschool. He loved being in the company of other children just like him. Although it was fun for him, it could also be challenging at times as they prepared to transition him into their School for the Blind next fall.

Caleb jumped onto his bed, as I put on his favorite Justin Bieber CD. Caleb and I rocked back and forth as every song that talked about teen love played on.

The songs started to sound the same to me after awhile, and I decided to join Steven again. I kissed Caleb's forehead and told him if he needed us, to just say so, we'll hear it over the monitor.

~ ~ ~

Steven looked half-dozed, with his feet on the hassock, watching the movie *Fast and Furious* on HBO.

I cuddled up next to him and whispered, "Being housebound may not be such a bad idea, and I bought lots of groceries." I patted Steven's knee. "I miss you, Steven. I really miss having you around lately."

Steven yawned and stretched. "I miss you, too. Everything seems to happening at once; a lot of projects are taking off," he said, rubbing his eyes.

"I understand, and I'm proud of you. You work hard to give us everything we have."

Steven suddenly looked flush. "MaryAnn, I'm sorry."

"Sorry about what? Being at the office so much?" I grabbed his hand. "If business wasn't crazy busy, then trust me both you and I would really be sorry." I chuckled. "More wine?" I asked, grabbing the bottle off the side table.

"Sure."

"I think I'm going to let you get me drunk and take advantage of me tonight." I laughed.

Steven didn't answer. I thought he would have been a little bit more enthusiastic about my suggestion. He put his arm around me and stared at the fire, as the burning wood crackled and popped. I laid my head on Steven's chest and shared the hassock with him as we watched the rest of the movie in silence.

"Would you like a sandwich? I bought lots of cold cuts," I asked, as the movie ended, feeling a rush of dizziness as I sat up.

"Did you buy roast beef?"

"Yes, I did."

"In that case, I will have a roast beef sandwich with extra mayo please, and don't forget the salt and pepper."

"I'll get right on it."

I regained my equilibrium and walked to the kitchen. I took out the cold cuts, turkey for Caleb and me, and roast beef for Steven. It was thin and rare, just the way he liked it. I cut the crust off of Caleb's sandwich and lathered lots of mayo on Steven's, along with several shakes of the salt and pepper. I put some rippled chips on the side of our plates and chips on the inside of Caleb's sandwich. He liked the taste it gave the sandwich as well as the crunch.

I served Steven with a smile, and proceeded to go upstairs and get Caleb.

I walked in as Caleb was bouncing Thumper, his stuffed bunny, to the beat of the music.

I laughed as Caleb turned in the direction of my sound.

"Mommy, you scared me!"

"I'm sorry. I will knock next time. I made you a turkey sandwich."

Caleb stood up clumsily on his bed. I grabbed him in my arms and attacked him with kisses.

"I love you, Caleb."

"I love you too, Mommy."

"Let's go eat our turkey sandwiches," I said, putting him down.

As we walked through the great room, Steven was munching away. "Caleb and I are going to eat in the kitchen."

Caleb yelled, "We'll be out soon, Daddy."

"You promise?"

"I promise."

I put Caleb on the stool and we ate our sandwich and chips. I looked out the patio doors as the sun set and an eerie darkness started to invade the sky. The wind suddenly started to pick up speed, making a burring hum.

"Mommy, what's that noise?"

"It's just the wind, honey."

"It sounds angry."

I looked out as a light drizzle started to come down.

I think Sandy is going to be one angry bitch.

I looked over at Caleb. "How's your sandwich?"

"It's good."

Caleb finished and I cleaned up the kitchen.

I grabbed him off the stool. "Let's go join Daddy."

I walked with Caleb to his play corner. He immediately started playing with his sensory toys and trucks.

Steven was clicking the remote, as station after station gave reports and warnings of the storm.

I sat next to him. "Steven, this doesn't look good," I said as the television reception went on and off.

"I told you, MaryAnn, we're going to be fine."

I couldn't sit still. I got up and lit the scented candles on the dining room table and on the hutch in the great room, just in case we should lose power.

As the reception on the TV went on and off, Steven finally settled on one station, and within minutes the news reported that a state of emergency was declared and that no one was to leave their home.

It was too late, too late to leave, and hell has no fury like Sandy.

I peered out the window; leaves blew ferociously from the shaking trees.

The next few hours, Steven sat listening to the same endless reports of bad weather as Caleb played with his toys.

It was finally eight o'clock, time for Caleb's story and bedtime. Caleb was exhausted and kissed Steven goodnight. Without argument he followed me up to his bedroom. Barkley followed along in back of us and got comfortable at the end of Caleb's bed. Caleb and I sat side by side on his bed as I started to read one of his favorite books, *Miss Spider's Tea Party*, and, although being blind and never having seen any insects in the book, or anything else for that matter, he truly enjoyed the poetic rhythms and the different voices I gave each of the characters.

We said our prayers, and I asked Caleb if he had any special prayers. He responded, "For everyone to stay safe."

I kissed his forehead and tucked him under the covers.

"Goodnight, Caleb."

"Goodnight, Mommy! You forgot to warn me."

"Warn you?" I asked, confused.

"Not to let the bed bugs bite."

I smiled and tickled his side. He laughed.

"You're right! Don't let the bedbugs bite!"

I stared at him as I turned off the light.

Please God, keep my family safe, I prayed.

I grabbed my cell phone out of my sweater pocket and texted Melanie, as I stood outside Caleb's door. "Are you all right? I love you, Mom XXOO"

Within seconds she responded, "I'm fine. I'm hangin' with Ming-Na, at Elnando's dorm room. Darnel is here too, with his new boyfriend, Michael. We're having a good time. Don't worry! I love you more!" XXXOOO"

I walked back down to join Steven. He was staring out the window. As I approached him, he turned to me and said, "We'll just have to make the best of this. We should check on Melanie."

"I just heard from her. She's fine."

"MaryAnn, there is something I need to tell you."

"What?" I asked, taking a seat on the couch.

Steven stood in front of me. "Melanie came and visited me at the office last week."

"I didn't know that."

"This guy she's with…"

"Elnando."

"He's no good. He's been involved in some messed-up stuff in the past and she wants me to help him."

"What! What kind of stuff?"

"He's part of some sort of gang, and when he was around thirteen-years-old he was involved in a shooting in which the bullet from his gun may have killed someone. Now, he wants to come clean."

I gasped, feeling a sick feeling come over me. "He may have killed someone! He's in a gang! I can't believe this! Oh my God, Steven! I can't believe you are telling me this! What did you say to her?"

141

"She wanted me to find him a lawyer. I told her no. MaryAnn, this guy is some passing fling for her. She has worked way too hard. She doesn't need this. We don't need this."

"Steven, our daughter is in love. I don't understand why she didn't tell me. I don't understand why you didn't tell me," I said, shocked at what he revealed to me.

"I'm telling you now."

"You know what I mean, Steven. We don't keep secrets!"

Suddenly, a hostile wind pounded the house as all the lights flickered.

Chapter 29

Melanie

"Oh, look at him go!" I shouted, and cheered as Darnel jumped onto his bed. He put his collar up and danced to the Soulja Boy song, "Pretty Boy Swag," as Elnando, Ming-Na, and I sat comfortably on the floor with our sweatpants and slippers on.

Michael, Darnel's newest addition: a clean-cut-looking acting major, who hailed from Italy, dressed in Ralph Lauren from head to toe, also sat alongside us. Michael was incredibly handsome, with olive-colored skin and deep set, dark brown eyes. He spoke with an Italian accent and his charming, irresistible manner could make both men and women fall head-over-heels in love with him.

We surrounded ourselves with cans of Natty-Ice, bags of carrot and celery sticks, sliced apples, pretzels, and a jar of crunchy peanut butter. Darnel and Elnando went out earlier and bought the snacks and the beer with their fake IDs, along with a couple of boxes of miniature chocolate chip muffins, a half-gallon of orange juice, and bottles of water.

Darnel jumped down and joined us on the floor as the rest of the Soulja Boy's CD played on. "Come on Sandy Baby, bring it on," Darnel shouted. With that being said, we all raised and clinked our cans.

An emergency evacuation was declared for the city, but we all made a pact that we would stay together, knowing that Ming-Na and Michael didn't have family in the area, and none of us felt like dragging them home to ours. Mayor Bloomberg announced school closings for the rest of the week, and we all decided to make the most of it. The past few days had been extremely intense for all of us, and we all needed a break, not only mentally but physically.

It felt good to hang out, and the buzz from the beer was making me forget all of Elnando's troubles and my aches and pains as well.

Darnel dug deep into the peanut butter with his celery stick and asked with a smirk, "Mel, you didn't want to go home to Elnando's place for the weekend?"

Elnando looked at me and said, "He's such an asshole."

Darnel laughed as he continued digging into the peanut butter.

"I actually was going to have Melanie meet my mama and some people very close to me this weekend, but it looks like Sandy may have made other plans for us."

"Sure, you were!" Darnel kidded.

I whispered animatedly, "I don't remember any of this. I think he's lying."

"Seriously, babe, I was going to bring you to my neighborhood..."

Darnel cleared his throat and interrupted, "You mean hood."

"Yes, I was going to bring Melanie to my hood."

Suddenly, the pulsating wind made a pounding crash into the window.

Ming-Na yelled, "What the hell?"

Darnel got up and lit some candles. "We just need a little ambiance, folks... And, who wants to play some Uno?" he asked, grabbing the cards off his dresser.

I yelled, "I do," and reached over and grabbed Ming-Na's arm, "Don't you, too, Ming-Na?"

"Sure!" She laughed and mimicked my, "I do!"

Elnando asked, "How 'bout Pictionary? We have it."

Darnel laughed. "Of course, you want to play Pictionary. You're an artist."

I looked over at Elnando and asked, "You can draw, too?"

"What can I say; I'm a man of many talents."

Feeling tipsy and good, I reached over and kissed him. "Don't I know!"

Darnel got up and announced "Ming-Na, Michael, have you played Pictionary before?"

They both answered "Yes" in unison.

Darnel grabbed the game, a note pad, and a black Sharpie marker. Ming-Na was the first person to draw. At this point, everyone was feeling a little buzzed and all the rules and the time limit went down the toilet. Ming-Na, tried her best to draw, *The Sound of Music.* We all laughed hysterically, as none of us even came close to figuring it out, even though she drew an ear and music notes.

After that, it was my turn with "Rock-A-Bye Baby," and I thought my image of a rock, a hand waving, and a stick figure with a big head were sure giveaways. None of them could guess it for the life of them.

After a few rounds, Michael announced in his Italian accent, "I'm going to head back. I'm starting to feel quite tired."

Darnel looked at Michael with a flirty grin. "Your roommate went home to Yonkers, right?"

Michael answered, "He did."

Darnel grabbed his beer. "Bye, kids! Behave yourselves!"

We all laughed.

Michael waved goodbye to all of us, and in broken English said, "It was very nice meeting all of you."

We all responded, "You, too!"

Ming-Na stretched on the floor. "I'm tired, too. I'm going to be heading back."

I asked, "Why don't we stay here? You can sleep in Darnel's bed."

"No, that's all right. I want to sleep in my own bed tonight."

I turned to Elnando. "Elnando, I'm leaving. You get to have this whole place to yourself tonight."

Elnando asked, "Are you sure you don't want to stay here tonight, Ming-Na?"

"I'm sure. Thank you, Elnando. Melanie, why don't you stay?"

"No way, I'm not leaving you alone tonight."

Ming-Na smiled. "Mel, please, I really don't mind. It will give me a chance to sleep in tomorrow morning without anyone interrupting me."

I kidded, "Are you saying I interrupt you in the morning?"

"I'm saying, stay the night." Ming-Na came over and gave me a hug.

"Ming-Na, if you change your mind, just come back here."

"Or you can go join Darnel and Michael," Elnando quipped.

"Thanks! I'll text you in the morning, but not too early."

"Bye, Mel. Bye, Elnando."

We both said, "Bye," as Elnando picked up the beer and munchies off the floor. I got cozy on his bed, and turned on the television and clicked through the channels, each one giving reports of the incoming doom that was upon us.

Elnando grabbed the remote out of my hand. "I'm sick of hearing about this." He went over to his CD player and turned it on.

The R&B sounds of John Legend pulsated through the speakers as Elnando came over and lay upon me. He kissed me gently as he worked his way down.

We molded our bodies together not only in lust, but as two people who truly needed each other. I whispered, "Elnando, I don't want to lose you."

Elnando pushed the top of my hair back and looked straight into my eyes as I repeated, "Elnando, I don't want to lose you. I don't want to lose you, ever."

He laid his head into the side of my neck as we squeezed our bodies close.

Elnando whispered, "Mel, let's…"

Then he suddenly stopped, frozen, he looked at me and said, "Let's enjoy this moment."

Chapter 30

Steven

MaryAnn, Caleb and I became prisoners in our own home. All the warnings regarding Sandy were correct. Sandy was as pungent and brutal as expected. The generator that I spent thousands of dollars on was doing its job, but MaryAnn still insisted on bringing up candles and a lantern just in case. MaryAnn put a candle on each of our side tables and dressers, giving the room a warm glow. At around midnight, Caleb woke up because of the sound of the whirling wind. MaryAnn cuddled him in his bed as he fell back to sleep.

When she returned, I held on to her for dear life. The ticking sounds of the pouring rain hitting our patio tin roof, along with the sound of the gusty strong winds, amplified in our large bedroom. I felt like we were going to be lifted off the ground at any minute. I knew at this moment, that it was MaryAnn I wanted in my arms. This is where I needed to be and she was the only woman I truly loved. I envisioned Lauren as well, but the excitement of her faded as feelings of guilt berated me. I started to kiss MaryAnn. Our bodies entangled, as if we were fighting off the madness erupting outside our bedroom window.

Suddenly, we were interrupted by a loud banging crash. It sounded like it came from the downstairs. Caleb yelled, "Mommy!" MaryAnn slipped on her bathrobe and ran to his bedroom. I clumsily put on my boxers and dashed down the stairs.

I walked apprehensively through the great room, the sound of wind and rain grew stronger with each step I took. As I swung the door open to our kitchen, I couldn't believe my eyes. The hanging pots and pans rattled, as rain poured in.

Shard glass was everywhere, as our 200-year-old tulip poplar tree collapsed through our back, bay window, destroying our kitchen.

MaryAnn came up beside me with Caleb in her arms. "Oh my God!" she screamed.

I put my arms around her and Caleb, and said, "I think we need to leave now."

Part 2

The Second Act

"What lies behind you and what lies in
front of you, pales in comparison to what
lies inside of you."
~ Ralph Waldo Emerson

Chapter 31

Lauren

I could hear the wind hurling as I sat curled up in a fetal position in my papasan chair. The chair was usually hidden in the corner with loads of clothes thrown on top of it, ones that needed to be put away, or the outfit that I decided to change out of immediately after putting it on, because it wasn't quite right for the day or occasion. Tonight the clean clothes were hastily pushed to the floor.

I put on my baby blue fleece pajamas with floating clouds and gold stars that I usually wore when I was stuck in bed fighting some sort of ailment. Every year on Christmas Eve since we were young, my mother would give me and Stefani what she called "Christmas jammies" to wear to bed. It was a tradition that she continued even when Stefani and I moved out on our own. The pajamas felt warm and cozy, reminding me of the fun times my family and I had shared during the holidays.

Feeling scared and alone, I held tight to my chest, the soft pink afghan that my grandma knit for me as a young girl. I watched, frozen with fear, as the flame flickered on the autumn-spice-scented candle that I lit earlier when the power went out. Feeling trapped in the midst of what seemed like an apocalypse, I desperately wanted someone with me, anyone. Sandy was real. It wasn't a hoax set up by government officials. Sandy was pounding my bedroom window with both fists, like the devil himself.

Cuddled in my own paralysis, I started to think about my life. *Was Steven right about me? Will I always be a person who just thinks about herself? Who was he to judge me? But was he right?*

These questions continued to haunt me as I fell in and out of consciousness.

I could readily admit that I was selfish and spoiled. It's my nature, and being adopted added to it. I was given everything I wanted; I lacked for nothing. Being beautiful played to my advantage as well. I was accepted by the popular crowd in high school I believe, because of my good looks. Junior college was like play time for me. I met a lot of guys at late-night parties, and by that time they were highly inebriated, but I didn't care. I wanted to have just as much fun as they did. All in all, if I wanted a guy, I knew I could have him no matter what. It made no difference to me if he had a girlfriend or was married. I figured if they were that committed, then they shouldn't be lured by me so easily. How long can I continue playing this game? Intellectually, I knew I was hurting people. Many of the men I was with had girlfriends, who they were truly committed to, or wives and children. I helped these men deceive these women for my own selfish lusts and desires. I never considered anything like this ever happening to me, simply because I thought I was too beautiful and compliant, and that I was everything a man could need.

As I drifted further into sleep, it seemed as if the devil or maybe it was God himself, escaped through the window and decided to torment me with questions. If that was so true then, where are they all now? I garbled my answers. *They're not here, they're not here.* And, Steven, above any of them, where is he? *He's at home with his beautiful family. That's where he is. Steven is at his home with his beautiful family and that is where he will always be!*

Suddenly I sat up, jolted out of my semi-consciousness by a deafening boom outside my bedroom window. I cradled my knees and prayed for the first time in a

152

long time, *God please! Please be with me! At this moment, you are the only man I need!*

Chapter 32

Elnando

I stepped outside the campus and lit my cigarette. I couldn't believe my eyes. Although it had been days since Sandy first hit, it looked like a war zone. Garbage scattered the city streets like confetti. I hadn't heard from my mama or Birdie. They decided to stay put in Spanish Harlem. I was anxious for their safety, and I couldn't get any reception on my cell phone. In frustration, I started walking with no destination in mind. I finally had clearance and tried calling, only to get the recorded "This number is not in service" runaround. I noticed only 2 bars left on my phone. *"Great!"* As soon as I turned the corner, I noticed makeshift charging centers setup outside neighboring bars and brownstones. Crowds of people gathered around them, and I was in no mood to be in the company of others, especially anyone as equally frustrated as me. Melanie, Ming-Na and Darnel were rehearsing in the crowded studios. I knew being crammed in with all of the other dancers, vying for space, would do me little good. I told Melanie and the others that I would try to practice later in the day. Mentally, that was my plan in hope that fewer people would be there later, and that I would be feeling in better spirits by then. Although classes were cancelled for the rest of the week, the dorm reps informed us the school could not give us a clear answer as to when they would be resuming.

The holiday production was to be cast this week. The whole freshman dance department seemed anxious, as this was the first big production for us. I was very proud of Melanie. It was noticeable how much she had grown as a dancer in the few short months we had been at Fillmore. She

154

seemed to be pushing herself beyond her limits, especially with the added weight I put on her shoulders.

A taxi traveling at a snail's pace came up beside me. I flagged it down and walked over to it. It came to a cautionary stop.

"You feel like taking a trip to Spanish Harlem?" I asked the driver through his open window.

"It may take a while," he said, and I couldn't tell if he was exhausted or frustrated at my request.

"No problem," I said, jumping in the backseat.

~~~

The drive was slow and cumbersome as predicted, with all the road closures and alternative routes the cabbie had to take. The drive seemed even longer as we drove in utter silence. The only sounds made were the shrill pitches from the radio as he played with the dials, in hopes of finding a station.

Water and debris filled the streets of Spanish Harlem. Finally, the silence was broken.

"How far do you have to go?" the cabbie asked as he tried to find a clearing.

"This is good," I answered. I figured it would be easier for me to meddle my way through this, than him with his cab.

I paid the driver with my credit card, and said, "Be safe," as I stepped out.

"You, too," he said as he observed the area around him.

I watched him pull out and sighed, knowing the next three blocks were treacherous. Very few people were out, and the ones I saw acted like amateur filmmakers, recording what they saw as they stood in front of the flooded basketball courts and fallen trees.

155

As I drew closer to my home, I couldn't believe how much destruction was done to the empty lot next to it. It was a dump before and now it was over-flooded with branches and debris. It looked uninhabitable, even for the homeless who sometimes set up camp there. If Melanie's dad was to come here today, the look on his face would be priceless.

As I walked into the lobby, I noticed there was light. I was relieved to see that they still had power. I took the stairs to the sixth floor. The raucous noise that usually can be heard through the walls seemed noisier than ever, as a tangy smell of dirty diapers lingered in the air.

For once, I wished my mom was away working on the cruise line, rather than being home having to deal with the hardships of the city. I knocked on the door. "Mama, it's me."

She opened the door, and we hugged each other tightly.

"Oh Elnando, you're okay! I was so worried about you."

"Mama, I'm fine. I tried calling you, and you don't text."

"I know, I know, but you're safe. You shouldn't have come here. How did you get here?"

"By taxi," I said, taking a seat on her sofa.

"Can I get you anything? Have you eaten?"

"Mama, I'm fine. Sit down."

She sat across from me and smiled. "Tell me, how is that fancy school of yours? Did they lose power?"

"It's going really well. I really love it, and yes, we lost power, too!"

"Oh, no, but I'm so happy to hear you're enjoying school."

"When do I get to see you dance? And more importantly, when do I get to meet this wonderful girl you've been telling me about?"

"Soon, we have a winter dance showcase coming up, but hopefully you'll meet her before then. I had plans of introducing you this weekend, but..."

"I understand! Everything is so topsy-turvy right now."

"Mama, when do you leave for your next cruise?"

My mama looked at me and laughed. "My next cruise, you mean when do I deport?"

I smiled at her. "Mama, when are you taking off?"

"I'll be leaving a week from tomorrow."

"Then, I'm glad I stopped by. Mama, there's something I want to talk to you about."

"What's going on?"

"I wanted to thank you for everything you have done for me. I know when I was younger I was a handful. I'm sorry."

"You went through a difficult stage. What teenage boy doesn't? And you had lost your papa. But, you are extraordinary. You pulled through and discovered a passion hidden within you. We should all be so lucky. You have nothing to be ashamed of."

"Mama, but I do! There's…"

"Stop! You can't look back. Remember that Bible story Birdie always talked to you and Jewel about, something about if you look back, you'll turn into a pillar of salt? You don't want to turn into a pillar of salt, do you?"

"No, that wouldn't be a good thing. What's going on around here? I know you and Birdie have to move soon."

"Don't worry about it. It's all talk."

"If it does happen, where will you go?"

"Don't worry about it."

"Mama, I'm worried about you. Where will you go?"

"Don't worry about me. I'm sometimes gone for months at a time. Maybe I'll become a stowaway. No worries, I'll be all right. I'll always be all right. I will find something. You don't have to worry about me. You just worry about school."

"I do worry about you and Birdie and..."

"Elnando," she interrupted. "The only thing you need to worry about is getting through school. Everything else is going to be fine. Trust me."

"I do worry about you."

"I know you do, but don't. I'm so proud of you, do you know that?"

I looked down humbly and nodded my head.

"You worked hard. You're in a school that only a few have the luxury of getting in to."

I smiled at her.

"You beat the odds."

If she only knew!

"Thank you, Mama. Have you heard from Birdie? I would like to stop in and see her."

"I've checked on her. She's fine, but I'm sure she would be delighted if you dropped in and said, 'Hello.'"

"I think I will," I said, getting up.

"You're leaving already? You just got here."

"I can't stay, but I'll go check on Birdie really quick, and Jewel. It's going to take me a while to get back."

"If you need to stay here, you can. Remember, this is your home."

"I know. I love you, Mama."

"I love you, too."

~~~

My mama's heart would be broken if she knew what I did. Reality was hitting me in the face; I was not only putting my life in jeopardy if I decided to come clean, but I would also be jeopardizing the lives of everyone I love. If it came out that I went to the police, retaliation was imminent. Why was my conscience eating at me so much?

I decided to head up to Jewel's apartment, before visiting Birdie. I knocked on his door, but no one answered, not even his mom.

Where could they be?

I took the stairs and headed back down to Birdie's. I knocked and she yelled, "Who's there?"

"It's me, Elnando."

She opened the door. "What on earth are you doing here?"

"I came to check on you," I said, giving her a hug.

"You're crazy coming here today! How in God's name did you get here?"

"I took a cab."

"Come, let me get you something," she said, leading me to her tiny kitchenette.

As soon as I took a seat at her kitchen table, I felt at home.

"What can I get you?"

"Nothing, I just wanted to check on everyone."

Birdie proceeded to take out her percolator and start a pot of coffee. Then she unwrapped half of a coffee cake and cut me a huge slab. I grew up eating slices of what I refer to as her *famous* coffee cake, at this very table. Glazed with vanilla icing, her homemade coffee cake is, still to this day, one of my favorite treats.

"We're all right. But Jewel, that's a different story. You need to talk to Jewel. Lately, it seems like he's been up to no good. He still hasn't found himself a job and I'm starting to get worried about him."

"I stopped by his place, but no one was there."

The coffee finished percolating. Birdie poured two cups of coffee. Handing one to me, she said, "Just the way you like it, light on the cream and filled with sugar."

Birdie blew on her steaming coffee, "I haven't heard from Anita. But, Jewel is probably running around somewhere, who knows where. Enough about him! Tell me, how is school?"

"It's great!"

"I'm so happy to hear that. My Elnando is at Fillmore. It truly is a dream come true."

"You got me there."

"You got you there!"

"You and Joe, I can't thank you enough," I said, looking into Birdie's tired eyes.

"You thanked us by being a good boy."

"You know, Birdie, I wasn't always a good boy."

"I know that, but you were just a kid. Like all the rest, you were heavily influenced by the filth that is trying to destroy the young and bring down not only this neighborhood, but our people."

"I was still involved with them for awhile when I first met you and Joe," I said, my words starting to tremble.

"I know you were, and like I said, you were just a kid," she said, putting her hand over mine.

"I was involved in some terrible things."

She sipped her coffee and looked solemnly at me. "I'm sure you were."

"I want to come clean."

She put down her coffee cup. She gently squeezed my hand "Elnando, it's done. Whatever it is, let it go. Give it to God. Enjoy your life."

I nodded, as Birdie let go of my hand, and quickly changed the subject. "Now when am I going to meet this wonderful girl I heard you're dating?"

"Soon, like I was telling my mama, I had planned on bringing her here this weekend, but Mother Nature had other plans. Hopefully you'll meet her before our winter showcase."

"Your first performance at Fillmore, that's going to be something else!"

"You better be there!"

"I will! I have to ask you, has your mama mentioned to you that this place may be torn down?"

"I was going to ask you about that."

Without mentioning my girlfriend is the builder's daughter.

"They're thinking of putting some fancy condos here. Are they *outta* their minds? Where do they expect all of us to go? Frankly, I don't see it happening."

"If it does, do you know where you'll go?"

She smiled. "I think I'll stay with you at Fillmore."

"I would love that."

"I don't know where I'll go, but I'll find something."

"You know I'm here for you. By the way, how is everything at the studio?"

"Well, I'm not there too often anymore. I'm no spring chicken. The rest of the crew is doing a great job with the young kids, but one thing is certain, there's no one there quite like you."

"Thank you, Birdie. I'm glad you're all right."

"I'm really glad you stopped by, even though I wish you didn't come here with everything going on. It's good to see you."

161

"It's good to see you, too! I have to be heading out now."

Leading me to the door, she said, "You take good care of yourself."

"I will," I answered, giving her a hug.

I walked out of my home. Crowds of people were gathering, many more than *the wanna-be* film crews who were there when I first arrived.

I smelled charcoal grilling and heard Jewel's voice. He was standing at a portable grill flipping burgers.

"Jewel," I said, going over to him.

"Look, who's here," he said, giving me a manly hug.

"You all right, man?" I asked.

"Yeah, I'm good."

Jewel turned to one of the men surrounding him. None of them looked familiar to me. "You want to take over?" he asked, handing them the spatula.

He wiped his hands on his pants. "You want one?" he asked, pulling out a cigarette and walking away from the crowd.

"No thanks."

"Good, these things ain't cheap. What brings you out in this apocalypse?"

"I came to check on my mom, Birdie, and all of you."

"Well, that was awfully swell of you," Jewel chided.

"So, how *you doin'*?" I asked.

"I'm hangin' in there."

"Birdie is worried about you."

"Birdie needs to just worry about Birdie."

"She loves you, you know."

Jewel didn't answer, and I just kept following his lead.

"When you going to get serious, Jewel?"

"C'mon, man! Leave me alone."

"I have to tell you, I'm worried about you. I've been thinking about some of the things we did together."

"Why *you goin'* there?"

Remember that shootout? That has been weighing on my conscience lately. I keep thinking, what if it was you or I whose bullet killed that kid? I think a lot about coming clean about it."

Jewel angrily threw his cigarette and lunged at me, pinning me against the wall of a closed-up bodega. He grabbed my collar tightly and with a horrified look in his eye asked, "Are you fuckin' crazy?"

The look in his eye left me feeling helpless. I didn't want to fight back. I couldn't even say a word.

After a few seconds, he let go.

I continued with my back against the wall, as Jewel crouched down next to me with his head in his hands.

Chapter 33

Lauren

Sandy did a number on my neighborhood in Brooklyn, and Steven did a number on me. Both Brooklyn and I were damaged; we were a mess, in need of deep repair. I wondered if Steven's office regained power and if he was there. I could make an impromptu personal visit and say I wanted to pick up some personal belongings I left behind, even though the only thing I left behind was a free healthy-living calendar I got from my pharmacist, that I scribbled on and marked for site visits that I was to accompany Steven on.

It had been a few weeks since both Sandy and Steven came at me like a tidal wave disrupting my life. I desperately wanted to get the hell out of Brooklyn. The subways were finally in full swing again, which made my decision all the more easier. *I can call the office to see if they are even open,* but the thought of Dolores answering made my stomach turn. It was already mid-afternoon, and I figured if Steven wasn't there, I could always head over to a bar and call Katt and Tiffany to meet me.

I gave a final look in the mirror. I looked hot. I had on my favorite pair of tight blue jeans, a black cami with a long sleeve maroon satin blouse, and my comfy black Uggs.

I arrived at his suite. The lights were on, but the office was somberly quiet. Dolores wasn't at the greeter's desk. *Thank God,* I thought, as I walked past all the cubicles until I arrived at Steven's office. No one seemed to notice me walk by and I was glad. I only wanted to see Steven and not have to deal with any office theatrics.

I gently knocked on Steven's door.

"Come on in," he answered.

His jaw dropped, as I took a seat in front of him. I looked at him, feeling myself melt like ice by his presence.

I was quickly brought back to reality when he asked, "What are you doing here?"

"I was in the neighborhood and I..."

Steven interrupted, "Did you NOT remember the talk we had?"

"I'm sorry. I missed you."

"Lauren, you can't be showing up here anymore. We can't see each other ever again. I thought I made that clear!"

"Yes, you made it clear. Don't you miss me?"

"Lauren, stop!"

"You know, I never asked you. What did you tell your little family here about my leaving?"

"I told them you found other employment, and that they needed you to start right away. Why?"

"I really don't give a shit! I was just curious."

I figured Steven probably told them I left on my own, just to protect himself. Although Steven and I were incredibly secretive around the others and everyone thought of Steven as a stand-up guy, I really wasn't sure if the rumor mill, run by Dolores, even suspected that there was anything between us.

"You never answered my question. Do you miss me?"

"It doesn't matter, Lauren. We can't see each other ever again!"

"If you're so sure that you never want to see me again, then I will make it easier for both me and you. I'll leave New York and go to L.A. I'll stay at my sister's place for awhile. I can get the same thrill from L.A. as I can here. Hopefully, in due time, I'll forget any feelings I had for you."

"You will, Lauren. You will move on."

"Will you?"

"I definitely want to."

165

I arose from my seat. "I guess I'll be heading out then."

Steven got up, walked me to the door and opened it for me. I stood close to him, slyly smiled and inched forward to kiss him. He turned around and walked away.

~~~

As I walked away from Steven's office I heard whistling, and I knew Jack was near. Thankfully, I made it to the greeter's desk without Jack, or anyone else who ventured into work that day, seeing me. A faint feeling suddenly overwhelmed me as I staggered to the public restroom on that floor. I was glad no one was in there. I splashed cold water on my face and let it slowly drip down. I leaned my elbows on the clammy, white porcelain sink and hunched forward. Feeling weak in the knees, I stared at the stranger before me. This is me, I reminded myself. What stood before me was defeat and despair, two things I was unfamiliar with.

The bathroom door flew open as a portly-looking old woman in a business suit shuffled in. I quickly regained my composure. Ignoring her smile, I headed out.

~~~

I breathed in the crisp air, and I wanted to get lost in the hustle and bustle of New Yorkers and the eccentric tourists who flocked the streets. My mind was on cruise control, as I found my way to Bryant Park. I sent Katt a message, "Is it too early for a drink?" She replied, "Is it ever?" I knew Tiffany wouldn't be able to join us; she was busy playing catch up in her role as an assistant to the assistant editor at one of the city's biggest literary agencies.

Being one of a handful of secretaries at an exclusive law firm, Katt didn't think twice about leaving when the clock struck five. I questioned her once how she kept such good hours in such a high powering office. She replied, "Trust me!

166

No one will give me any trouble. I'm the lowest on the totem pole, but I'm in most demand amongst the lawyers." Knowing this, I texted her that I was heading back to Brooklyn, and to meet me at Smitty's ASAP!

~~~

Smitty's was in Williamsburg, not far from my apartment, and had since reopened since Sandy hit. I wanted to be close to home, and I figured Katt could spend the night at my place if she wanted.

The bar was rustic, with a familiar cozy feel to it. It was well known for their good food, as well as their spirits. I took a seat at a back corner booth. I watched as the place started to fill up with locals, many of them familiar to me. I wasn't in the mood for conversation, just Rum and Coke and Katt's listening ear. Forty-five minutes and three Rum and Cokes later, Katt arrived. She squeezed next to me in the booth and put her arms around me.

"Hey, baby girl!"

I was feeling tipsy, but not my normal feel-good, more of a party kind of tipsy. The Rum and Coke was a relief for the pain I was feeling inside.

"Are you okay?" she asked, pulling away. Ugh," I said, putting my head down.

"Oh no," Katt said, moving across from me. "What is it?"

"Steven. He wants nothing to do with me."

"Do you think it's because he's m-a-r-r-i-e-d?" Katt asked, accenting the word "married."

"I guess." I smiled at Katt. I knew her and her comedic sarcasm would make me feel better. "Katt, I'm thinking of staying with my sister in Los Angeles for a while."

Katt glared at me. "Is it because of Steven?"

"Yes, and I no longer have a job."

"Tell the prick to give you more money!"

"It's not the money. I think I need a fresh start, an escape from here."

"Lauren, this is a big city. There are a lot of places you can escape to."

"You're probably right."

"I am right! You need to get your groove back on. You need your *mojo* back!"

I laughed.

"Look over there! There are some hot looking guys waiting to buy us drinks."

In the middle of the bar were three thirty-something-year-old men. They were dressed casually, in the same manner as many of the men I encountered through Steven's company.

Katt announced, "I'm going over there…"

"Katt," I interrupted her as she walked away.

From the distance, I watched her swivel her hips and flirtatiously slither her way to the middle of them. A moment later, she looked in my direction, holding up a large mug overflowing with beer, and with a huge smile, she pointed to it. Then she waved me on, and mouthed the words, "Get over here."

I slowly got up and joined her. I was already tipsy, and I could tell Katt was getting there. Being one of the few single ladies in the pub, I should have been in my glory. The men were easy on the eyes, and I'm sure Katt and I could have our pick, but tonight I felt different. I didn't want to party. I wanted to be loved, and I only wanted to be loved by Steven.

Chapter 34

Melanie

"Nice isolation, Melanie! You're looking mighty fine out there!" Olivia's constant barrage of comments was starting to sound like white noise, as I concentrated on every move I made. There was no room for error, and like all the dancers, I desperately wanted one of the main roles in the winter showcase.

When the music finally came to an end, we all stood in position. Olivia smiled proudly and told us all to take a minute break. "I mean a minute, as in, as of now you have 59 seconds, so move it," she said in her usual demanding tone.

All of the dancers rushed to their corners and grabbed their water bottles and towels. Then we all took a seat on the floor in front of Olivia, who sat like a high princess in her wooden chair. Like obedient school children sitting on a carpet after recess, we all sat exhausted, ready to take a nap, but anxious for our teacher to speak.

"As you all know, our winter showcase is going to be Fokine's masterful piece, *The Firebird*. Thankfully for all of you, this ballet requires a huge cast. Some of you will be playing the part of wives, Indians, attendants, cavaliers, pages, and even monsters, and we will have some seniors fill in as extras on the final celebration scene, which will be stunning to say the least.

"This is a ballet based on a Russian folktale and it is filled with love and magic, so your physical expression will be just as important as your technique. Now that you know what the winter showcase is, I know you will all be googling *The Firebird* as soon as you leave here."

We all chuckled as Olivia continued, "In a nutshell, this ballet is about a journey of Prince Ivan, the story's hero, who enters the magical world of Kashchei the Immortal. While wandering in this unforeseen territory, he sees the Firebird and captures her. She pleads for her life and agrees to help Prince Ivan in exchange for freedom. Prince Ivan then comes across thirteen maidens, and he falls madly in love with one of them, the beautiful Tsarevna, with whom Prince Ivan shares a very romantic kiss."

Suddenly, a few of the dancers yelled, "Woo!"

Olivia shook her head and smiled. "Prince Ivan confronts the evil Kashchei to ask for Tsarevna's hand in marriage. The two argue, and Kashchei sends his magical creatures after Ivan. The Firebird, being true to her word, intervenes. This is where the magic and energy of the dance really picks up! The Firebird casts a spell on the creatures and sends them into an upbeat dance. In the end, the Firebird reveals to Ivan the secret to Kashchei's immortality, and Ivan gets the girl. Like all good fairy tales, they all live happily ever after."

Darnel yelled, "Yeah, Baby!" We all laughed, including Olivia.

Olivia continued, "I have been convening with the seniors who observed you over the past few days. We have come to a decision about what role each of you will be playing. I will post it today, sometime after 5:00 p.m., in front of the amphitheatre doors. All of you are making continual strides, and I want you to keep reaching further, even if you are not rewarded one of the main roles."

She paused for a second and looked across at all of us. "You are now dismissed. Enjoy the rest of your afternoon!"

I gathered up my duffel bag. Elnando met me at the door, sweating and anxious. He said, "Let's get out of here."

We didn't say a word to each other as we walked out of the studio. We were physically spent and emotionally drained by the intensity of training the past few days.

I broke the ice, and smiled at him. "You looked good out there."

He smiled back. "You didn't even notice me. You were focusing on yourself."

"That's not true! I snuck a peek now and then. You danced really well, and you were the hottest guy out there!"

"Geez thanks. You looked pretty good out there, too!"

I teased him, "You forgot something."

"What?"

"You forgot to mention, 'and the hottest chick.'"

He smiled. "Well, that's a given!"

I felt grubby, and I couldn't wait to shower. "I think I'm going to head back to my dorm and shower, and then if you want, we can meet at the cafeteria and get something to eat."

"That sounds like a plan."

"I'll text you when I'm ready."

Elnando leaned over and kissed me casually on the lips. "You really did look good out there, Mel."

"Thanks. Time will tell."

Elnando grabbed my hand, "I don't want you to be upset if you don't get one of the leads."

"Are you saying that as a reassurance, or you don't believe I'm capable?"

"Stop it, Melanie! You're an incredible dancer. Everyone here is, or else we wouldn't be here." He put his arm around my waist, pulled me close and whispered, "I've

171

said it to you before and I'll say it again, you're a beautiful dancer and a beautiful woman. Believe that!"

I leaned my head on his shoulder. "I'll try. The competition here is fierce, Elnando."

"It is, because this is Fillmore. We're the best of the best!"

"You're the best of the best Elnando," I turned and hugged him. "I'm scared to death of losing you. I've been thinking non-stop about everything and…"

"Stop," he said, interrupting me. He grabbed my face in his hands, and smiled. "Listen, I feel really disgusting right now, and you smell really bad!"

I giggled. "I do not!"

"Melanie, go take your shower, relax a bit, and we'll meet up later to check the list. We will talk after we see the posting. My mind is really on that right now."

"I understand."

Elnando softly touched my face. "I don't want to ever lose you either, baby."

We each went in our own direction, and in my heart there was something I knew I wanted more than ever—for Elnando to feel free, without ever going to the police.

Chapter 35

MaryAnn

"Really, Steven, this could be worse! Most people lost everything, including life. It's only our kitchen. It's not the end of the world! Not to mention, we own a construction company, and we have insurance!" I said, as I fluffed the accent pillows on the vintage lace bedspread that overlaid the bed in Steven's parents' guestroom. My in-laws graciously offered their home to us, after the destruction to ours. Our plan was to stay for a week, as Steven mustered out his crew to get our home back together.

Steven sat defeated in the beige-colored Queen Ann chair that nestled in the corner of the spacious guestroom, as I picked up his clothes that he haphazardly threw on the floor.

"This couldn't have happened at a worse time."

"What would have been a better time for you? When we were all gathered around the nook eating breakfast on Saturday morning? Really, what would be a better time for you to be inconvenienced?"

"MaryAnn, you don't understand. Everything that I had scheduled has to be rescheduled. It's not just Belezzi Builders that handles a project, its unions, government officials—it's an army. Now, because of everything that is going on in the city, we aren't going to be able to move forward on a lot of projects until early spring. This is going to put off the demolition of the Spanish Harlem project, and who knows when we can start building there. This hold-up is going to give the people there more time to think, more time to get restless, and more rallies that someone from our company has to attend. It's all bullshit and I'm tired, and living back at my parents' home, if only for a few weeks, is anything but a joy!"

"Think for a moment how inconvenienced you would feel if you had to leave your home, because it was being demolished for the sake of high-rise condos."

"Really, MaryAnn, we are offering them settlements. They will probably never have it so good."

"I'm sure you'll be getting lots of thank you letters in the mail."

"MaryAnn, I don't need this. I'm just the guy who owns the building company, like I said, 'It's an army that works on these jobs."

I stopped puttering and stood in front of Steven, looked him straight in his eyes and said, "And it may be an army that will bring them down!"

Chapter 36

Melanie

"Oh my God, I can't believe it! I'm the Firebird and you're the Prince. Look, Elnando," I said pointing to the list. "Ming-Na is one of the princesses, and Darnel got the role of the evil one. This is too good to be true!"

"Shhh, I see," Elnando whispered, keeping his cool.

Most of the freshman dance department was huddled in front of the cast list posted on the door of the amphitheatre. Although we were all competing for lead parts, all of us developed a deep camaraderie through the endless hours we danced together. I appreciated Elnando reminding me to curb my enthusiasm, knowing how I would feel had I not been chosen for a lead role, and the heartache that everyone whose name was not posted on top of the list must be feeling.

As we walked away from the amphitheatre, we ran into Darnel. Elnando quickly grabbed my arm as I was about to spit out the words, 'Guess whose playing the evil Kashchai?' Elnando whispered, "Let him enjoy the moment."

Darnel asked, "What's the verdict?"

Elnando kept walking, pulling me along with him. "You have to find out for yourself, man."

"Thanks, you two! I'm probably playing the tree."

I laughed and followed Elnando's lead.

As soon as we hit the bottom of the narrow stairs of the amphitheatre, I couldn't resist the urge to leap for joy. I spun and leaped as if I was in a competition, but with the joy of already knowing that I had won. I beat out all the beautiful dancers who danced by my side, and Elnando was going to play the prince, the main character, and Darnel, the antagonist of the play. *What a perfect pairing!*

Suddenly my thoughts turned to Ming-Na, who was going to check the list after her Art History class. *I hope that she will be happy playing a princess. I think she will make a beautiful princess.*

I twirled into Elnando's arms, "We did it!"

"I know! We have a lot of hard work ahead of us," he said, swaying me back and forth.

I turned around and faced him. "Just think! You get to kiss the beautiful princess, played by Anastasia, straight from Sweden."

Elnando teased, "Is somebody jealous?"

"Please! She doesn't even speak English."

"But the question is, is she a good kisser?"

I smiled, shook my head, and punched him in the arm.

"Hey, watch it! I need this arm to grab you with."

"It will be fun having you chase after me."

"Melanie, you're a real firecracker, I mean firebird," Elnando said as he took a seat at a bench facing one of the man-made ponds on campus.

I sat close to him and put my head on his shoulder. "Elnando, now can we talk about what's really important?"

Elnando grabbed my hand. "Yeah, we need to talk. I've been doing a lot of thinking. I don't want to hurt you Mel, or my mom, or anyone else for that matter. I've decided I'm not going to go to the police."

I let out a sigh of relief.

Elnando said solemnly, "I just have to learn to put everything behind me. I went as far as I could away from that lifestyle. Going to the police, I realize, will do nothing except cause heartache for everyone around me, and these people I belong to are mad *motherfuckers*. They will go after everything I love, including you, Melanie."

I felt weak in the knees as he said those words.

"Elnando, you belong to me now, not them."

"Unfortunately, Melanie, once you're a Latin Knight, they own you, and there's only one way out."

I shuddered, knowing what Elnando was referring to, death.

Chapter 37

MaryAnn

Something was going on with Steven. Was he going through a mid-life crisis? Was it Melanie being at college in the city and dating a guy he wasn't that keen on? Was it the stress of impending work projects? Could it be as simple as having to deal with getting the kitchen and back of our house put back together? Or, was it none of the above? Steven was all over the place the last few months, working out early in the morning, putting on a little bit more cologne than usual and wearing nicer looking clothes to the office.

Lately though, the working out had ceased, along with the gleam in his eyes. Whenever I looked over at him, he seemed withdrawn, both in and outside of the bedroom.

My cell phone vibrated. It was Melanie. "Mom, I got one of the lead roles in the winter showcase!" she exclaimed.

I was overjoyed at hearing those words. I wish she could have told me in person, so I could have squeezed her tight. "That is incredible news. I am so happy for you! What kind of part do you have?"

"I am a firebird, who changes the fate of a prince, played by no other than my Elnando. Can you believe it, Mom?"

"Yes, of course. You're an incredible dancer Melanie! Speaking of Elnando, your father told me you spoke with him and…"

"Mom, I don't want to talk about it. I want you to know everything is all right now. Please don't dampen my mood."

I had been waiting to talk to Melanie in person about what Steven told me. Realizing on the phone that speaking to her now may be the only time because of her crazy schedule. I wanted to share with her my concerns, especially about being with someone with so much baggage for such a young age.

"Fine, we'll talk about it next time you're home."

"Mom, there's nothing to talk about. Please be happy for me. Everything is good. Actually, it's great! Will you do me a favor? I'm heading to my next class and I have classes the rest of the night, will you tell Dad the news?"

"I will, and Melanie, I really am happy for you."

"I know you are, Mom."

Maybe this news will put a smile on Steven's face!

I decided to call Steven on his cell phone and tell him the news. It went straight to his voicemail. I thought, this news deserves an interruption, and decided to call the office to see if he was there.

Dolores, his matronly receptionist answered, "Hi, Mrs. Belezzi. Mr. Belezzi is not here. I'm not really sure where he is. I want to thank you again for having all of us at your home. That party for Caleb was beautiful."

"Thank you so much, Dolores. That reminds me why I was putting off mailing the thank you notes. I need the new girl's address, the one who started in the spring. I forget her name."

"Oh, you must mean Lauren. You know, she no longer works here, but let me check her file, just a moment while I find her address for you."

All of a sudden I felt a knot in my stomach, remembering Caleb's party and how at a distance I noticed her following Steven around like a lovesick teenager.

Dolores returned to the line. "Thanks for holding, Mrs. Belezzi. I found her address."

179

I could barely hold the pen as Dolores rattled off her address.

"Dolores, why doesn't she work for Steven anymore?" I asked, knowing Dolores would provide me with full details of why she chose to leave, who her new employer is, and even her favorite color."

"Mrs. Belezzi, I really don't know. Maybe Mr. Belezzi could fill you in."

"Thank you, Dolores."

"Take care of yourself, Mrs. Belezzi."

I knew right then and there the missing piece was this young woman and her relationship to Steven, whatever it may be. My gut was telling me something, along with Dolores' lack of words. Dolores was never hush-hush about anything, from the few times I saw her each year. I learned from her that Jack loved to gamble, bet on the horses, and even had a bookie; that Burt, who worked on proposals, was incredibly cheap and his wife's supposedly homemade Christmas cookies were really Stella D'oro, straight from the grocery store; and that Marjorie, who used to take care of billing and moved south, was sky-high in debt, and that their college daughter liked to use heroin.

Dolores' lack of gossip was telling me something! I looked down at the address. I had time to kill before I needed to pick up Caleb.

Hmm, this is insane! What am I going to do? Knock on her door, tell her I just happened to be in Brooklyn, give her a thank you card, and ask her why she left the company, and if by chance she happens to be fucking my husband?

Suddenly, the very thought made me feel nauseous, and guilty at the same time. Steven would never cheat on me. I shouldn't even think such things, but the feeling kept gnawing at me. She is so young, barely through her twenties.

Am I being completely irrational? I could only hope!

~~~

What the hell are you doing? You're acting insane. This is ridiculous, I kept saying to myself, as I continued to drive. I felt like I was on a mission, *but what kind of mission?* I thought. My feelings brought me here. I wasn't being rational. I should just talk to Steven, but lately Steven wasn't being the man I knew and loved.

My navigator led me through the streets of Williamsburg, which were still in disrepair from Sandy's destruction. I found a parking spot close by, just a few feet away from her apartment. I parallel parked.

"I should have at least brought her thank you card." I chuckled sarcastically.

Suddenly, the young woman I remember from our party emerged from the stairs. She wasn't made up and was dressed casually in gray yoga pants and a pink hoodie. Her shiny brown hair was parted on top and hung loosely over her shoulders. From my distance, I noticed her eyes—they were filled with sadness.

I felt like a cross between a stalker and a cop on a stakeout, as I watched her take a seat on her stoop and light her cigarette. Between puffs, she put her head down. My motherly instincts were kicking in. She looked like a fragile child, not the young woman that I thought was chasing after my husband. I had an unexpected desire to run over and put my arms around her, and ask her if everything was all right.

After a few minutes of watching her sulk, I thought: *This is ridiculous. What am I doing here?"* I put my car in reverse. I dismissed everything I had previously thought and swore to myself that no one would ever know what I just did. I glanced out my rearview mirror, and as I was pulling away, I noticed in my side mirror another figure walk out of her apartment. I looked over and my heart sank. In the corner of my eye, I saw Steven.

Chapter 38

Steven

I turned toward the sound of burning rubber; it was a gray Lexus, just like MaryAnn's. As it sped by, I saw MaryAnn. We looked straight into each other's eyes.

I was in a state of shock. I could not believe I just saw MaryAnn! I grabbed the railing, as panic pulsated through my body.

"That was my wife," I said barely audible, trying to catch my breath.

"That was your wife?" Lauren asked, questioning what I just said.

"Oh my God, that was MaryAnn!" I said, feeling out of sorts and not knowing what to do next.

"What the fuck?" Lauren questioned. "What was she doing here?"

"The question is, what am I doing here?"

Lauren sat staring at the ground. "What are you going to do?"

"I'm fucked. I'm truly fucked." I leaned over the railing on the top step. I felt nauseous, as dry heaves and anxiety paralyzed me.

Lauren looked up at me. "Just stay."

I squatted to my knees. "Are you serious? Are you fucking serious?" I got in Lauren's face. "Do you know what is happening? I'm going to lose my wife. I'm going to lose everything now! Don't you get it?"

Lauren's eyes bugged out as a look of terror shot across her face.

Catching my breath, I slowly sat down next to her. Feeling sheer panic, I collapsed with my head to my knees.

"I'm scared," I said as Lauren just stared fearfully straight ahead.

"I have to see MaryAnn. I have to go home," I said getting up.

Lauren continued to stare into space, and in a robotic tone said, "You took the train here. Your car is in the city. Are you going to be all right getting back?"

"I'm leaving, Lauren."

Lauren shot up and grabbed my arm. "I'm really getting out of here, Steven. I don't know exactly when, but I'm leaving. I'm really leaving."

"Good," I said, as I walked down the steps.

~~~

I took a seat at the counter of an old run-down coffee shop called Sonny's Place. It was a few blocks away from Lauren's apartment. I needed to think. What was I going to tell MaryAnn? The more I thought about MaryAnn, the angrier I got at Lauren. Why did she send me that text, "Meet me at my apartment ASAP, I need to speak to you." I was done with Lauren, although I still thought of her, as guilt continued to plague me with what I had done to my wife and family.

Filled with fear of what Lauren needed to speak to me about, I got there as fast as I could. Thoughts lingered in my mind, *Oh my God! She's pregnant (even though we always used protection), or she's going to blackmail me by revealing our affair to someone at the office or worse yet, to MaryAnn.*

When I arrived, Lauren's big emergency was she needed some extra money, because she basically had gone through all the money I had given her, because she still hadn't found a job, and because she wasn't sure when she was going to move to L.A.

I screamed at her, "What the fuck? You sent me all the way here for that? Did you even look for a job? Go apply for unemployment, or for God's sake, just leave!" I angrily reached into my wallet and threw two fifty-dollar bills at her."

Bending down like a desperate stripper, she grabbed the money off the floor and placed it neatly on her coffee table. She looked up at me and smiled. "You feel like having some fun?"

"You really are some kind of whore, Lauren."

Lauren just stared at me shocked, as tears welled up in her eyes. She stormed out of her apartment.

Breaking me free from my thoughts, and returning to my cruel reality, an old Italian waitress, with a harsh Brooklyn accent, held a pot of steaming coffee in front of me, "Coffee?" she asked.

I just nodded.

"You look like you could use a cup." Seeing her smile through her tough exterior comforted me, if only for a moment.

"You okay?" she asked as she poured the coffee.

"No, I screwed up," I answered solemnly.

"We all screw up," she said as she walked toward the unkempt old man who sat a couple of seats down from me. He looked like a regular; he stayed transfixed on his spread-out cards as he continued to play his own private game of solitaire.

I aimlessly put the sugar and creamers into my cup, barely taking the time to stir it. I slowly took a sip and wondered how long I could sit here.

What am I going to say? What if she doesn't forgive me? So many thoughts ricocheted through my mind as I sat paralyzed with fear. *I never knew or appreciated how good I had it. I had it all—perfect wife, perfect job, children whom I adored. I wish I could take back everything I did. God, please let MaryAnn forgive me!* I prayed.

I took out my cell phone. *Should I call her and make sure she is all right?* I put myself in her shoes. She must be devastated. I just stared at the phone. I couldn't even muster the strength to push the buttons, as anxiety overtook me.

"More coffee?" the old waitress asked.

Barely able to speak, I said, "You can top it."

Looking down at my cup, she slowly poured the coffee. Then she glanced up, and our eyes met. "You sure you don't want a bite to eat?"

"Coffee is fine."

"Suit yourself!" she said and turned away.

"I may be here awhile," I mumbled.

Not knowing if she heard me or not, she answered, "Good thing we're open 24 hours."

I smiled as best I could in her direction.

I glanced at the unkempt old man. How I wish I could trade places with him right now. To sit aimlessly, as if there's not a care in the world! That would be something I could only long for at this moment.

I caught a glimpse of the old waitress's name tag, as she bent over to partake in the old man's game. Her name was Stella, and she reminded me a lot of my great Aunt Mary, who died a few years back. With brassy silver hair, bright red lipstick and sparkly earrings, she seemed feisty and colorful, like my great aunt, who lit up the room whenever she entered.

Stella smacked her hand on the counter and stood up. "Next time you're here, I want your hand in some Gin Rummy." The old man smiled, and even with his toothless grin, he seemed to have things going better for him than me.

I took out my wallet and placed a $20 bill on the counter. Stella came over, "Don't you want the bill?"

"No need."

"You want some change?"

My whole life is about to change, I thought.

"Nope, keep it!"

"Where are you off to?"

I was a little taken aback by her question. Her concern felt as familiar to me as my great aunt's loving barrage of questions she threw at me at every family event.

"I'm heading back to Jersey."

"Is that your home?"

"I'm not so sure anymore"

"I here *ya*! Sandy did some devastation there."

"It was actually me who did the devastating."

Stella picked up my cup and saucer, and put it in a black bucket that sat on the counter behind her. When she turned around, she stood before me with her arms folded. "I'm sure your mess will be easier to clean up than Sandy's."

"I'm not so sure."

Stella grabbed a dingy white rag from under the counter and wiped the counter as I got up. "My grandmother used to say, nothing is ever ruined. It just needs a little reorganizing and a little rerouting, and a whole lot of faith!"

Feeling hopeless, I responded, "I'll remember that."

She smiled. "You need a cab, or anything?"

"I left my car in the city."

"Hmm," she answered, as if she was pondering what I just told her, and then yelled across the diner, "Vinnie, hurry up with your coffee. This gentleman needs to get home, right away!"

Chapter 39

MaryAnn

I swerved the car to the right. I wasn't thinking or following any type of direction. I was a rollercoaster of emotions. I made another sharp turn and blew through an intersection, amazingly there was no car around, and I wondered if there was a stop sign at the previous corner. After driving like a mad woman through several city blocks, a moment of clarity came over me. *MaryAnn, collect yourself before you kill someone or yourself.* As I came upon the next intersection I saw an empty lot. I pulled in next to the marquee, which read, Lennie's Garage, with the bottom half of the second "n" missing. The place looked abandoned with boarded-up windows; it was a perfect place for me to park and get control of myself. I slammed my fists on the steering wheel and wailed.

Nausea overcame me and I opened my driver's door. I jerked my body forward and took in the fresh air, as shivers ran down my spine. On impulse, I threw up! As I stared at the puddle before me and wiped the milky spit from my face with my sleeve, I noticed a young couple walking their dog on the cracked concrete sidewalk in front of the lot. The couple sported similar style blue jeans and leather jackets, walking an adorable pit bull with a spiked leather collar. The dog looked too sweet for spikes and reminded me of the dog in *The Little Rascals*. The couple looked content, and their body language told me they were in love, and in no rush to get anywhere.

To be young, fashionable and free! Actually, I would long to be anyone right now other than me.

Staring at me as he continued to walk, the young man yelled, "Lady, you all right?" I felt helpless as I signaled my hand up, and mouthed the words, "I'm fine."

I closed the door and noticed the time on my dashboard. *Oh, my God! Caleb! I completely forgot about him!* I would never make it to his school in time, and I was in no shape or form to be in front of anyone, even if most of the people there were blind. I quickly called my mom. I needed her to not only pick Caleb up from school, but keep him for the weekend. We just moved back into our house days earlier. The windows were replaced, but the kitchen and back side were still in disarray. I needed to confront Steven, if he had the guts to come home.

Thankfully, she answered and I quickly explained to her, as my voice cracked through every word, that she needed to get Caleb from school and keep him for the weekend. When she wanted details, I abruptly cut her off, and explained everyone is safe, but Steven and I have some things we need to work out. I will call Caleb later, and he needs clothes, and—*then I lost it*! As the tears fell from my face and I started to hyperventilate, my mother calmly reassured me that everything will be all right, not to worry about clothes or anything else that Mema and Grandpa are overdue for a dinner date at the mall with Caleb, and after dinner they'll do some clothes shopping. Hearing her calming words of reassurance made me desperately want to be in her arms right now.

"Please just take care of yourself, MaryAnn, and call me later."

"I will. Thank you, Mom."

"I love you, honey."

"I love you, too."

I rubbed my eyes and turned on the ignition. I needed to go home!

Chapter 40

Elnando

"All of you are champions. Remember that!" I said, looking at the group of inner-city youngsters who were about to experience their first taste of dance. The kids were a mix of Hispanic and Black, and their ages ranged from 9 to 13 years old. They were an enthusiastic group made up of different shapes and sizes, with varied fitness levels. Most of them hailed from the projects in Spanish Harlem, while some were from projects in different boroughs and had come to the program through word of mouth.

We began with a basic warm-up, a series of lunges, neck isolations, heel raises, and leg and hip swings, and I explained the importance of doing it before every dance class. I demonstrated how to do a simple ballet chassé, and they mimicked me, chasing one foot to another. They had rhythm, some more than others, but all of them were happy just to be here. I played Miley Cyrus's "Party in the USA" and taught them some more introductory moves. The group laughed when I flailed my arms and animatedly swiveled my hips to the chorus of the song. The group was loosened up and I enjoyed showing them the most important thing about dance—getting lost in the moment and enjoying one's self.

They were now ready for a combination of beginner contemporary dance moves. Through a series of plies, relevays, torso spirals and contractions, they danced with confidence to Adele's song, "Chasing Pavements." They especially liked executing the sidefall from a standing position during the chorus, which explains Adele's struggle in deciding whether or not she should pursue a relationship with the man of her dreams.

When I first heard that song, I was reminded of the dreams I had when I was a teenager in Joe's contemporary dance class. I realized I had talent, but my gift was not only a blessing but a curse to those who didn't share in my dream. I knew I had to keep my hand in the gang life. Although it was low key because of all the time I spent in the studio under Joe and Birdie's watchful eye. I struggled, asking myself, is this worth it? The harassment from the gang and other teenagers in the neighborhood, the wear and tear on the body, not to mention the small chance of actually making it professionally. All of these concerns overwhelmed me, even at such a young age. In the end, I decided to *chase pavement* and I'm glad I did. It ultimately saved me from a life of destruction, and through dance I found Melanie.

After 45 minutes of constant movement and sweat pouring from every part of their bodies, I saw something in their expressions and the way they were now carrying themselves that I didn't see before. I saw hope, and with this, I believed this group could do anything!

When they finished, I had them take a seat on the floor. They sat like obedient school children, waiting to be rewarded.

"I thank all of you for coming! I was once just like you, and I started in this very program at fourteen-years-old, a lot older than when most professional dancers begin dancing. Dancing became my life. I stuck with it, and I am now a first year student at Fillmore. How many of you have heard of Fillmore?" About half of them raised their hands.

"For those of you who have never heard of Fillmore, it is one of the finest schools of dance, not only in this country but in the whole world. It is located right in the heart of Manhattan. I am a first year student there now, and if all of you keep working hard, you have a shot at going there, too! I really hope all of you continue to come each week. I will be stopping in periodically to check on all of you. Marcy will be back next week, and I cannot wait to tell her what a talented group you all are."

With that being said, the front door flew open! It was Jewel. He was carrying a tool box, and he looked like he was on a mission.

Jewel looked over at me and, without saying a word, walked toward the back room where students weren't allowed.

I announced that before we leave, we need to give ourselves a round of applause! I yelled, "Woo-hoo," as they clapped and laughed. They were dismissed, and every single one of them went on their own into the big city, without an adult present.

I toweled myself down and took a gulp of my water. Jewel wasn't right, and I had a bad feeling about approaching him.

I walked into the back room. Jewel was bent over an old milk crate, with a wrench in his hand. Looking like a skilled surgeon, he worked steadily on the wobbly door knob.

"How's it going?" I asked, taking a seat on another milk crate across from him. The tarnished purple milk crates were like antique furnishings in the studio. I remembered Jewel and I stacking the two of them, and plowing down into the other, the few times Birdie and Joe weren't watching us. As much as I loved dance, some of my most cherished memories at the studio were hanging in the back room with Jewel while Birdie and Joe taught classes. We were the only kids allowed back there, because most of the time Joe and Birdie took care of us while our moms worked. We would raid the mini-fridge, which usually was filled with fresh apples and pears. Often the other instructors would surprise us with treats, like chocolate chip cookies and glazed doughnuts. The studio was our second home. Jewel and I had our secret meetings on these very milk crates, comparing scores of 1 through 10 of who the hottest dancers were, and who most likely could be cast as Peter Pan.

The studio became an innocent escape, more so for me than Jewel, who still hung out with the gang members whenever he got a chance. Jewel was a pretty good dancer, but he never developed a passion for it, like I did. I believed it was mostly because he was afraid of what the other boys in the neighborhood would think or say about him. Jewel messed with me a lot about being a dancer, but in the end we were cool and I always knew he had my back. Birdie and Joe tried their best to keep Jewel busy and out of trouble, by having him sweep and mop the studio and take the trash out at night. Like myself, he adored Birdie and Joe. Joe became the father he never had, and Joe became the father I needed once my papa died. He brought us to Shea Stadium, bought us baseball cards, and threw a baseball with us every now and then. Joe had a strong presence, and Jewel never razzed him about being a dancer.

"I'm hanging in there. I've been lookin' for a job," Jewel said as he tightened the bolt on the knob. "How the hell did they manage this one?"

I laughed. "I think they break things just so you can come over and fix them."

Jewel chuckled.

"It's good that you're looking for a job."

"Yeah, it's real good that I'm unemployed."

Except for odd jobs in the studio, drug dealing, and running for the Latin Knights, he's never had a "real" job.

"At least you're looking. What else is going on?"

"Shontee is cracking down on some things."

194

Shontee was in his late thirties, and one of the major players in the Latin Knights. He rose up when I started getting heavily into dance. I never really knew him, but have heard stories through Jewel of what he was capable of. He would think nothing of killing a person, in the same manner as one would kill a fly.

"What sort of things?"

"Territory and shit like that."

I shook my head, knowing drug territory was not to be played with, and this could bring on war.

Jewel jerked the doorknob back and forth. "Fixed," he announced.

"It's good you can do this kind of stuff."

Jewel laughed and chided, "You going to give me a standing ovation?"

"No, just a round of applause," I said, clapping.

Jewel smiled, which I was glad to see. "You're an asshole."

"It's always good to see you, man!"

"You stoppin' by your Mama's and Birdie's?"

"No I *gots* to get back. This was a last minute thing. Marcy couldn't make it."

"Marcy, Hmm, is she the one with the nice ass?"

"If you mean the nice, big bulbous ass, you are correct!"

"You know, we miss having you around, Elnando."

"I know, but I have to admit I love seeing my mama, you, and Birdie, but there's a whole other world outside Spanish Harlem. I'm glad I made it out of here."

Jewel packed up his tools and got up. "No one ever leaves Spanish Harlem."

"You're probably right."

Jewel punched my shoulder as he opened the door, "Don't forget to lock up and…"

"What else?" I asked, thinking he was going to ask me to do something like take out the bathroom trash.

"Elnando, don't ever forget where you came from!"

Chapter 41

Steven

I parked in front of the house. It seemed like such a long distance to the front door. I stood for a minute, looking at the house. I had never been so afraid to enter my own home or see my wife. I looked up, searching for God or some sign of peace. I noticed the crescent shaped moon. I wanted to escape there and plead with God to erase everything that I had done during the past few months.

As I slowly made my way to the front door, I heard Barkley's familiar barking. I put my key in and unlocked the deadbolt and the front door. MaryAnn hadn't changed the locks. Maybe she took off. I couldn't tell because she parks her car in the garage. The lights were off throughout the house. It was still early enough for Caleb to be awake, and I didn't hear his enthusiastic, "Daddy," as I entered the house. I walked up the stairs to our bedroom. One dim light was on, and MaryAnn was lying on her side, holding tissues in her hand while facing the wall.

I stood with my hand on the cold wooden door molding. "MaryAnn, I am so sorry. Please forgive me. I'm so sorry," I whispered.

MaryAnn continued facing the wall, as she sniffled. "Get out. Get out! Now!"

"MaryAnn, let me explain," I said, walking toward the bed.

MaryAnn turned abruptly around and sat up. Clutching her pillow, she said with a vengeance, "I hate you. I fucking hate you! I want you out of here! Now! Go back to your little whore."

"Please, MaryAnn, let me explain."

197

"Explain? Yes, please explain!" Through sobs MaryAnn asked, "Did you sleep with her?"

My eyes started to well up. I couldn't get the words out.

"Well, did you?"

"Yes," I said, barely getting the words out.

"That's all I needed to know! Now get out! Get the hell out of here now!" MaryAnn said, while grabbing the portable metal alarm clock off the bedside table and hurling it at me.

As it hit me in the chest, I said, "I am so sorry."

I walked over to the bed and knelt in front of it.

"I am so sorry. You need to forgive me. I never meant to hurt you! Never!"

"You are not the man I thought you were, Steven. I don't even know you anymore. Did you ever think about what your son or daughter would think? How about your parents or mine? You disgust me! I want you out of here. You're pathetic. I hate you! I hate you so much!"

I couldn't even look her in the eyes. I dug my head into the bed and muttered, "I'm sorry. I'm truly sorry."

"Good! Now get out!" MaryAnn said, kicking me in the head. Her light kicks became pounding kicks. I got up and grabbed MaryAnn's shoulders and started shaking them. "I am so sorry. I am so, so sorry," I said, as I crashed into her arms and cried inconsolably.

Chapter 42

Melanie

"I can't do this anymore, Elnando. I'm tired," I said as I spun into his arms.

"You can. Let's go," he said as he continued with the routine.

"You're not listening to me. I said, 'I'm tired.'"

"Fine," Elnando said as he walked over to the boom box and turned the music off.

I yelled over to him, "Elnando, enough is enough! We've been dancing for over seven hours. We haven't eaten..."

"That's the life of a dancer, Sweetheart," Elnando interrupted me while peering through some CDs which lay upon the speaker.

I sighed and grabbed my water bottle off the floor near the back corner.

"You know that," Elnando said, looking over at me as I gulped my water and took big breaths.

"Trust me, I know that," I said, catching my breath. "We need to get away from here. This is insane."

Elnando started laughing as he continued to look through the CDs.

"Can we please go somewhere, anywhere? We have a three-day weekend," I begged.

"Where would you like to go? I have no money."

"I'm not asking you to spend your money."

"Good, 'cuz I got none." He chuckled.

Elnando walked by me and grabbed his duffel bag. "You realize it's only 1:00 in the afternoon?"

"Yes, and we've been in this studio since 6:00 this morning, vacation has already officially begun, and guess what? I need one! No one is going to be around. Ming-Na is going to visit her best friend at college somewhere near here, and Darnel and Michael have some big romantic plans. I texted my mom and she said she's real busy and dealing with a lot of who knows what right now. And my dad, he hasn't returned any of my calls or texts; who knows what he's up to."

"You still got your daddy's credit card."

"Why? Wait a minute—I never told you I had my dad's credit card."

He laughed. "All rich white chicks have their daddy's credit card."

I smirked at him. "That's not nice, but you're probably right."

Elnando toweled himself down. "If you really want to get away, I have a cousin who lives in Schenectady. He's the head chef at a café near there. We can go visit him."

"Where the hell's Schenectady?" I asked, barely able to pronounce it.

"It's upstate, near Albany. It's about three to three and a half hours away."

"That's really not what I had in mind. How about we go visit your mom? I'm dying to meet her, and Birdie, and your partner in crime."

"You mean Jewel? That wasn't nice. We're a day late; my mama is headed toward the big seas. But, I promise you, you will meet all of them real soon, if they're all still living in the same place. That is if your daddy doesn't tear it down."

"Please, Elnando, not now. I'm exhausted."

"Fine, then we'll just go spend his money! Go shower, pack casually for the weekend, and I'll let you sleep on the bus."

"We're taking a bus?"

Elnando quipped, "You're right! It's your daddy's money. I'll check the train schedule, and text my cousin. You go ahead! I want to check out some songs I found, and hopefully we can leave in the next few hours."

"Fine, but don't take too long!" I said, as I walked out the door. "*Shentaddy,* here we come!"

"Schenectady, Mel! It's Schenectady," Elnando yelled back.

"You know I don't speak Spanish," I teased him.

~~~

The train ride was incredibly relaxing. I slept the whole time, while Elnando listened to music that he downloaded. We pulled into an old train station, nothing like Penn or Grand Central. It had a much calmer feel, along with a quarter of the people. I stretched my legs, grabbed my duffel bag, and followed Elnando's lead. The main drag looked like a mini New York City avenue, minus the street vendors and hustle and bustle.

"So, this is Schenectady," I said, sarcastically looking around.

"Come on, I want to show you something," Elnando said, grabbing my hand, pushing me further along to whatever it was that was exciting him. As we crossed the street passing several store fronts and coffee houses, a large old-fashioned marquee which read "Proctors" stood out front and center in the middle of the street. The billboard below it read *Wicked,* November 7-25.

"Are you going to buy us tickets?" I joked as I followed Elnando into the lobby of the theatre.

201

"Yeah, with my good looks and charm."

"It may work."

Walking in I understood why Elnando was so enthusiastic. The historic architecture was beautiful. There were several boutiques in the concourse that displayed vinyl 45's and *I Love Lucy* and *Wizard of Oz* memorabilia inside their copper-framed glass windows.

"This happens to be one of my favorite theatres. When I was a kid, before dance entered my life, I would visit my cousin Angel, and Sal, his older brother. My aunt brought us to children's shows here. I have many good memories of this place. It reminds me a lot of Shubert's."

"It is absolutely beautiful," I said as we walked through the red carpeted foyer. I looked up, entranced by the two marble staircases which led to the balcony."

Without any interference from the various staffers walking by, Elnando opened the door to the theatre. It was a sight to behold, with gold-leaf detailing and a huge gold and black chandelier hanging in the center, surrounded by several smaller fixtures, as heavy velvet ropes hung from the stage.

"Elnando, it's hard to believe we are going to school so we can perform in places like this," I said, looking up in awe at the stage.

"Sweetheart, you and I are going to be in even bigger venues than this!"

I looked around, mesmerized by the quiet theatre. "My only hope is that we're together," I said, turning toward Elnando.

"We will always be together, but in reality, the chance of us getting jobs in the same company or city is pretty slim, you know that. Let's not think about that now."

I couldn't answer him. I just stared ahead.

Everything I work so hard for comes out on a stage as wondrous and beautiful as this.

Elnando then led me to another smaller theatre that was on the other side of Proctors.

"This is the GE Theatre; this was an add-on. It was pretty new when my aunt started taking us here. This is where most of the events were that Angel and I went to. I went to a really cool science show here, showing neurons and shit like that."

"Hmm, inspiring," I said, smiling at him.

Elnando smirked and shook his head. "I'm starving! I say we go drop off our stuff, and get a bite to eat."

"Now where are we headed?" I asked as we walked out of the theatre.

"My cousin's place."

"How far is that?"

"Right there!" Elnando said, pointing across the street.

"Where?" I asked, confused.

"Right above that pizzeria, and my aunt and cousins lived for awhile above that Burrito Bar over there," Elnando said, pointing his finger across the street.

Elnando's family, they live nothing like mine, I thought as I looked across.

I came from money, because of the hard work and long hours that both my poppy and father put into the company that was once my poppy's and is now my dad's. They were both an example of what it means to be honest and hard working, and although we lived in Franklin Lakes my family acted like any typical Italian family. My mother and father never put on any airs, and our home was always a welcoming place for dancers from other parts of the state to stay when they came to the studio I attended for advanced dance training and seminars. It is because of dance that I had met people from all walks of life, some whose parents were both doctors, to an equal number with welfare moms, doing whatever they had to do so their child could dance. The world of dance really opened up the whole wide world to me that I otherwise would be limited to in prestigious Franklin Lakes. Knowing that Elnando's family lived in city flats above window shops was no surprise to me, nor did it make me think any less of them. I knew his family came from a long line of hard workers and I knew in my heart how lucky and fortunate all of my family and I were to have and enjoy the best of everything.

As we crossed the street and walked closer to the flat, the aroma of pizza was mouth-watering, especially since the only thing I had eaten so far today was a protein bar, and I was famished.

"We'll drop off our stuff quick, and head over to my cousin's restaurant."

"Where's that?"

"Not far from here, in Schenectady, well kind of, Niskayuna."

"Huh! What's up with the names? How far is that?" I asked.

"It's not too far, and my cousin said his girlfriend would drive us over."

"It's a car ride! Then before we head up, can we please grab a slice of pizza?"

"I thought we would eat at my cousin's restaurant."

"We can eat there, too. I'm starving," I pleaded.

"Come on, I'll treat you to a slice."

We ordered two large cheese slices, and a Diet Coke for me and a regular Coke for Elnando. We devoured it and then walked up the stairs to his cousin's flat.

Elnando knocked, and I was immediately startled by the ferocious barking coming from the inside of the apartment.

"Does your cousin's girlfriend know we're coming?"

"Yeah," he answered, as the door slightly opened. A tiny woman in her early twenties with long shiny brown hair and big green cat-like eyes welcomed us.

"You must be Angel's cousin. Come on in, and have a seat. I'm Deena," she said, giving a light back kick to the dog. "Shut up Crator! He'll be fine. He just likes to give people warnings."

I walked in, staying close by Elnando's side. The tiny apartment was more like a studio. Everything appeared within eyeshot, a papasan chair, an old futon, TV, small stove, refrigerator, microware, and in the back, a tiny corner section and a doorway that led to what I presumed was the bedroom.

She was right. The tan, muscular pit bull dropped to the floor and immediately became unfazed by our presence.

"I appreciate you having us, especially so last minute. We needed to get out of the city for a few days," Elnando said, taking a seat on the old futon, as I sat next to him.

"No problem," she answered sweetly. "What is your name again?"

"I'm sorry, I'm Elnando, and this is my girlfriend, Melanie."

"It's nice to finally meet the two of you. You're the dancers."

"Yes, we dance, but nothing like Angel," he said with a chuckle.

"Yep, nobody does the salsa like Angel," she quipped.

"Can I get the two of you anything to drink?"

I answered. "No thanks. We hit the pizza place before we headed up here."

"I hit that place before I head up here, too. Unfortunately, way too often! Since I moved in six months ago and fifteen pounds later, I've come to realize, never move in with a guy who lives above a pizza joint."

"It could be worse," Elnando said.

"Huh?" she asked.

"You could live above a bakery."

We all laughed.

"I suppose I should get back to work. You two are sitting on your bed. There's beer in the 'fridge and snacks in the cupboards. Help yourself! Angel is at the restaurant. He'll probably be there the rest of the night. If you want, I can give you a lift over there, whenever you like."

"That would be great," Elnando and I said almost in unison.

"I have a huge midterm coming up, so I will be working on my computer in the little tiny alcove back there, but please feel free to make yourself at home."

"What are you going to school for?" I asked.

"I'm finishing my last year at Union. I'm a finance major."

"Wow," I said.

"Why is the question, why-oh-why did I ever choose finance?"

I smiled at her, loving her friendliness and generosity.

~~~

Elnando and I got comfortable, as much as we could on the old futon, and decided to forgo the beers, not wanting to dig into their supply. Elnando lightly dozed off, while I quietly flipped through the channels.

After about 40 minutes, Deena came over and asked, "You guys didn't get yourselves anything. Don't be shy."

"We're fine. Thank you," I said as Elnando laid his head upon my shoulder.

"Do you want me to get it for you?"

"No really, we're good. Thank you so much for letting us stay here. We really appreciate it."

"No problem. Whenever you're ready, I'll drive you over to see Angel."

"I'm ready, but I don't know about sleeping beauty here."

"Ah, let him sleep. He probably needs it."

"What? What's going on?" Elnando asked, startled.

"Nothing, go back to sleep," I said, smiling and rolling my eyes.

"No, I'm up now," Elnando said as he took his head off my shoulder and stretched.

"I can drive you two over now if you want."

Elnando yawned and said, "Are you going to hang out with us? We'd love to treat you to a margarita."

"Oh, that sure sounds good, but I'll pass. I think I'll drop you guys off and head back here, where it's nice and quiet. I have a lot of work to get done."

~~~

We walked a few blocks and hopped into Deena's run-down orange Nissan. Within minutes, we were on quaint Union Street, filled with what appeared to be independently owned shops. Deena explained that her college, Union College, which was very historic and prestigious, was only minutes away, which explained to me why almost every shop on the street had "Union" in its title.

Deena parallel parked on a side road just a few blocks away from the cafe.

We walked the ramp into Tesoro's. The café was in an old Victorian house, with lots of big windows and a South

207

American ambiance. A middle-aged woman, with an infectious personality, greeted Deena. She warmly introduced herself to Elnando and me as Gloria, the owner. Gloria immediately got Angel, who came over and gregariously introduced himself to me, and gave Elnando a huge manly hug. Angel had the same genuine kindness about him as Elnando. He was small in stature with shiny brown hair, olive skin, and dark brown eyes. For being a chef, he was impressively dressed in a long sleeve white coat and pin-striped white pants, which had barely any noticeable stains.

I couldn't help but wonder if he had gotten mixed up with the wrong crowd as a teenager, and if he shared the same skeletons in his closet as Elnando.

Angel walked us over to a small side table in the very back corner. He and Elnando made small talk about how the family was doing, and what's new in their lives. Then he got up and announced to us, "Anything you want is on the house. I have to get back to work, but I will be back later to do some Salsa," he said, doing a 1-2-3 step.

Elnando shook Angel's hand and exclaimed, "Man, we picked a good night to be here!"

"You know it! I'll catch you two later," he said, pointing with both hands at the two of us.

"It was nice meeting you, Melanie."

"It was nice meeting you, too!"

I turned to Elnando and said, "Your cousin seems very nice."

"Its 'cuz he is."

"Salsa, Elnando! We can never escape dance."

He smiled. "I guess not!"

A small petite waitress, with sparkling blue eyes and a big toothy smile, took our order and lit the small glass orange votive on our table. Elnando ordered the Cubano Panini and a Coke, and I ordered a cup of Southwest Chicken Chowder and a Mocha Latté.

As I sat eating my meal with Elnando, I felt at home, even though we were miles away from the city, a ballet barre, or Jersey. The small café began to fill up with up with couples, young and old, and small groups of girls around my age looking for a fun girls' night out. I noticed that many of the older couples were Hispanic, but overall there was a nice mix of different nationalities.

The young waitress who took our order was joined by a young man who sported a dirty white apron, and they began to push the front tables to the side of the café. Suddenly, an older Hispanic male, who seemed to be bursting with energy, took to the center of the café with a wireless 'mic in hand, and as the lights dimmed announced, "Hello, everyone! Look at this beautiful crowd! We are so happy to have you join us tonight because it's..."

As he placed the 'mic out to the crowd, what I suspect to be the regulars yelled, "Salsa Night!"

He continued. "That's right! We have good food, good drinks and, of course, good music."

Suddenly, a full spectrum light lit up the center wall as the high-pitched percussion sound of a bongo was hit.

The happy announcer yelled, "Everyone please give a warm welcome to, the Algato All-Star Band."

The crowd cheered wildly as the five-piece band, which consisted of middle-aged Hispanic men, each wearing a red Panama fedora hat with a black band, silky royal blue neatly-pressed dress shirts, with thin shiny yellow ties and tan slacks. They smiled at the crowd with the enthusiasm of veteran rock stars. Their instruments consisted of a conga, small piano, guitar, a trumpet and the fifth instrument, two wooden sticks that were being hit together, which Elnando explained to me was called a clave. Elnando proudly continued to inform me that the clave is the main instrument providing the essential groove of a salsa song.

People began leaving their tables, as the music played on. A short, cute, wrinkly, bald Hispanic man, who appeared to be in his late seventies, came over to our table and said, "Come up and join us. I'll teach you how to Salsa," as he comically wiggled his hips.

Elnando and I both laughed.

"Go ahead, Melanie, but be warned, this lady has two left feet," Elnando kidded.

"Thanks, Elnando," I said as the older gentleman led me away.

The older gentleman, who introduced himself as Denny, lit up the dance floor as the fast-paced big-band sound blared throughout the café.

I looked over at Elnando and signaled for him to come join us. As soon as Elnando hit the dance floor, all the women, both young and old, gathered around him. Denny looked shocked at Elnando's smooth moves and didn't seem to mind at all that Elnando now owned the dance floor. A woman in her late seventies, with short gray hair, a floor-length lavender dress and clunky satin high-heeled gray shoes, danced around Elnando and was overtly swooned by Elnando's presence. Elnando smiled sweetly at me and extended his hand to her. She animatedly fanned herself and proudly accepted. As he spun her around and twirled her back and forth into his strong arms, the rest of us on the dance floor stepped aside. Denny led everyone in loud cheers. Angel came out and stood by my side and said, "This guy doesn't miss a beat."

"No, he doesn't," I answered.

"He seems really happy."

"I hope so."

"He is going to give Miss Delilah Fudwell a heart attack!"

"I hope not!"

The music came to a stop and Elnando knelt down and kissed the old woman's hand. She blushed and waltzed away from the dance floor. Elnando grinned and walked over to us.

Soon Denny and the old woman Elnando wooed joined us.

Denny patted Elnando on the back. "Thank you for showing my Delilah here a good time. You got a heck of a lot of good moves, young man!"

Elnando laughed. "Thank you!"

Delilah went over, gave Elnando a hug, and smiled brightly. "You can dance with me anytime."

Denny bent over and whispered loud enough for all of us to hear. "Thanks again, son. Maybe I'll get a little action tonight!"

We all laughed as they walked away.

Elnando took a seat, smiled, and said, "I'm beat."

Angel replied, "I hear *ya!* I'm done for the night. I say we sneak out of here, before Miss Fudwell comes back and insists you take her home."

~~~

We arrived back at Angel and Deena's apartment. Crator gave his warning as Deena greeted us. We took a seat on the futon and Deena insisted we have a drink. "Whatever Angel has in the 'fridge is yours for the taking."

"Except! Only kidding! Really, help yourself," Angel said, getting comfortable in the papasan chair across from us.

Elnando, went to the 'fridge and grabbed a can of Natty Ice. "What do you want, Melanie?" he asked.

"Water is fine."

"No *natty* for you?" Deena asked, curling up with Angel on the chair.

"I think I better stick with water tonight," I said smiling at her.

Elnando came over and gave both Deena and Angel a can of Natty Ice. "We don't like to drink alone."

He gave me my water, as Angel and Deena popped open their cans. Angel made a toast, "To my little cousin, Elnando! You came a long way baby, and I couldn't be prouder and happier for you."

Elnando raised his can. "Hey, you didn't do too bad, either, a big time chef, hot girl!"

Deena chuckled. "You know it, baby!"

We all got up and clinked our drinks.

Elnando said, "Angel, I think it's time for some poker. I may be broke but *I gots* to win me some money."

I asked, "What about us? Can Deena and I play?"

"Sure," Elnando responded. "We'll just make it strip."

~~~

Deena and I decided to keep our shirts on and ended up watching an *A Haunting* marathon, while Elnando and Angel became enthralled in several games of poker, with short stacks of dollar bills being exchanged.

I explained to Deena how Elnando and I met at the audition for Fillmore and that he was my first "real" boyfriend.

"That's so cute! Angel and I met at the café he works at. I used to work there, too. Now, thanks to my parents' generosity, I no longer have to work and I can just focus on my studies. But, since I moved in with Angel, my parents are *pissed*, even though Angel is paying all the rent, and my parents' money is basically going toward my tuition, food, and my little shitbox of a car and, of course, alcohol." She chuckled.

Deena twisted her hair to one side and fiddled with the ends. "I just think they dislike Angel, 'cuz he's Hispanic and grew up in Amsterdam."

"Amsterdam? That's like, on the other side of the world!"

Deena laughed. "No silly! Amsterdam, the city! It's not too far from here. He moved to Schenectady when he started high school."

Again, more crazy names! Deena's comment made me wonder if the real reason my dad didn't care for Elnando was because Elnando was Hispanic. I've never heard my dad or anyone else in my family utter a racial slur, but who knows! Maybe deep down inside, my dad was a racist. Although, I suspect Elnando's past gang involvement and the fact that Elnando grew up in the very housing project that his company plans on tearing down, had a great deal to do with it.

Deena sighed. "Angel's family loves me, and it stinks that his mom and brother moved to Miami. I really hope that someday my mom and dad will accept Angel. It seems like every time I talk to them, they ask me if I'm still serious about that Hispanic fellow. I tell them yes, and remind them that he's Catholic, too!"

~ ~ ~

By around 2:00 am, Deena and I had seen every haunting imaginable. Elnando and Angel had called it a night, with Angel finishing the game by pushing all his ones over to Elnando.

"Keep it, and remember me when you're rich and famous," Angel exclaimed.

When Deena and Angel finished in the bathroom, Elnando and I got ready for bed. We turned off all the lights and television. After watching hours and hours of *A Haunting* marathon, I was glad to have Elnando by my side. As we snuggled close together on the tiny uncomfortable futon, I turned to Elnando and asked, "Wouldn't it be cool to have a simple life like this?"

"No, we would be bored to death," Elnando said, thrusting his body over mine.

"We would have stability, and it would guarantee that we would be together forever!"

"There are no guarantees in life."

"I'm glad, Elnando, that you decided not to go to the police."

Elnando abruptly got off of me and asked, "Why did you bring that up?"

"You seem to be really content right now."

"Goodnight, Melanie," Elnando said, turning and facing the opposite direction.

Chapter 43

Lauren

My sister Stefani seemed harried as she led me out of the airport. She explained that it would take her hours in L.A. traffic to drop me off and return to her job as a production assistant on the CBS Studio Center lot. Time was money, and both of them were *awasting*. Even Stefani's appearance looked rushed, unlike the chic made-up chick who normally hits the clubs with me when she is home. Her appearance was more like a frustrated soccer mom. Her shoulder-length blonde locks were now pulled back in a ponytail with a baseball cap, and what strands were showing were in desperate need of a dye job. The fashionista look that she usually sported in spiked heels was now replaced with black spandex capris, a mint green nylon T-shirt, and fluorescent green sketchers. Even the Japanese freedom tattoo on her right wrist looked washed out.

When we arrived at her new apartment, she pulled into her garage like a bat out of hell. She grabbed one of my suitcases and I grabbed the other. Stefani moved like the speed of light, and I was barely able to keep up with her on an average day, and now, with jet lag and Stefani on a mission, I was at least five steps behind her. We came upon Apartment 2B. She quickly opened the door and plopped down my heavy suitcase and said apologetically, "Welcome to my new apartment. I really have to go. This is my spare key. It's yours now. There is a small bedroom in the back; it has a pull-out sofa and a dresser. I think you'll like it. There are a few bottles of water in the 'fridge and a bunch of take-out menus in the drawer under the kitchen counter. Help yourself and make yourself at home. I have no idea how late I will be.

I am so sorry I can't stay with you and help you unpack, but..."

"No need to explain. I understand," I said, giving her a quick hug.

She hurriedly walked out. With her hand still on the door knob, she suddenly turned around and in a small voice said, "Lauren, I really am glad you're here."

"Yeah, me too," I said, lying to both my sister and myself.

I dragged my suitcases one at a time to her back bedroom. The bedroom was painted in paisley purple. Against the wall, stood a tall wooden bookshelf filled with relationship and "how to get what you want in life" self-help books. I couldn't believe Stefani actually had these books. I never knew of a time when Stefani or I didn't get what we wanted. Then I corrected myself—Steven! I wanted Steven, and when he kept returning to me, I thought I had him, hook, line and sinker. Now I was thousands of miles away, without him or any man for that matter. I emptied my suitcases and gently folded my clothes into her antique dresser. She was right I did like the bedroom. I looked around at the photographs that hung on the bedroom wall. I would guess Stefani took all of them. She was extremely creative. The still photos were all black and white, mostly of plants that I couldn't name.

I felt the hot sun peek through the open shades of the bedroom window. I was thirsty and alone. I wanted someone to talk to. I took my own guided tour of her tiny apartment. Not a thing was out of place. I suspected the place looked untouched because it was unlived in. Stefani often said work was her life, and when she went home, it was just to rest her head for the night. I made my way to her kitchen area. It reminded me of the little play kitchen Stefani and I had as kids that our father put together inside a huge pantry in our old house. Stefani's kitchen contained what seemed to be half an oven, a small refrigerator, and a table for two. I believed Stefani spent more time in our make-believe kitchen than she ever would in the kitchen she has now. In the back of the kitchen were sliding glass doors with the blinds fully open revealing the pool area. I grabbed a bottle of water out of the 'fridge. I opened it and took a big gulp. I walked over to the doors and gently pulled the blinds aside. I unlocked the doors, and with all my might I tried to open the glass door. After several tries it finally budged.

As I walked out onto the balcony, the smell of coconut oil hit me. I breathed it in along with the warm air and looked up at the squealing seagulls as they played a round of chase in the bright blue sky. So this is where I am going to call home. It is much better than my digs in Brooklyn. I looked down at a sea of women with copper tans and fake tits. *This place could be Silicon Valley!* I laughed to myself.

It was mid-afternoon. Why aren't these women at work, as if I was one to talk? And where are all the men? Sunny skies, hot bodies, and from what I had heard in the past from Stefani, the drugs *are aflying.* No wonder she moved here.

I walked back in and grabbed my hot pink bikini that I had neatly tucked into the bottom drawer of my new dresser. I slid it on and turned sideways in the mirror attached to the door. I gazed side to side at my reflection. *I look good and my tits are the real thing,* I thought, cupping them into my hands. I bent down and grabbed my cell phone out of the denim shorts that I had thrown on the floor. I snapped a mirrored shot of myself. I should send this to Steven; see if he gets this at home! Frustrated, I closed my phone and threw it on the bedroom floor. I need to get out of here!

217

Where does Stefani keep her towels, perhaps the bathroom? Nope, not a towel to be found in her bathroom! *You've got to be kidding me.* Outside the bathroom I opened a door to a closet the size of a broom closet. I finally found towels. Unfortunately none of them were beach towels, and they were all the same ugly color, navy green. I hastily grabbed a large bath towel, and knew it would be too much of a mission to even look for suntan lotion. *Fuck it,* I said to myself as I walked out the apartment door.

I found an empty white sling-back chaise lounge a distance away from the other sun worshippers who surrounded the pool. The puke-colored towel only covered part of the lounge chair, and the sun was scorching my body as it beat against it. I guess this is not going to be a relaxing time for me, no long beach towel, and I left my phone and sun glasses in the apartment. Then it hit me! That is also where my key is, in my denim shorts on the floor in the apartment, of course!

Great, I said to myself, flipping the top part of my towel over my head. My body was boiling as well as my emotions!

Suddenly, a miracle was sent my way! A tall dark-haired suntanned muscular guy in his early thirties, holding his cell phone and a clipboard, walked in my direction and sat down in the chaise next to me. He seemed casual and immediately began texting, not seeming to notice me or my frustration.

When he was finished, he finally stared in my direction. I sat up and cradled my face in my hands and sighed.

He laughed. "You okay over there?"

"I'm fine," I said, too angry to even flirt with this gorgeous guy.

"My name is Glen," he said, extending his hand.

Gorgeous Glen, I thought.

"I'm Lauren."

"You new here?"

"Kind of, I'm staying with my sister Stefani."

"Stefani, Stefani," he said, trying to remember her. "Stefani, yeah Stefani, 2B, right?"

"Yeah, the bitch in apartment 2B."

"No, she's not a bitch at all," he said seriously.

I laughed. "I was kidding. You know the show; *Don't Trust the B.... in Apartment 23.*"

He looked at me, puzzled.

"Forget it! I take it you don't watch television much."

"Not much television, but I am in the film industry. I will check that show out though."

"Forget it! It's cancelled."

He chuckled. "That's Hollywood...There's a little sidewalk café just a block away. I could really go for something to eat. Would you like to join me?"

"I guess! Right now I could really go for a nice ice cold beer."

"Well, they don't serve alcohol there, but my apartment is right down the hall from your sister's, and my 'fridge is fully stocked."

"Sure, why not!"

I followed this gorgeous stranger up to his apartment. It was the same setup as Stefani's. It was the typical bachelor pad—messy, dishes next to the sink, shirts laid over the kitchen chairs.

"Have a seat," he said, as he walked over to his small 'fridge.

He tossed me a Bud Light and I caught it, popped it open and smiled at him as he joined me on the sofa. He grabbed something off the side table. It was a small glass mirror, filled with coke.

Gorgeous Glen leaned over and snorted a line. He put his head back and said, "Aah...your turn."

I took my hit and felt an ecstasy I hadn't felt since I was with Steven.

After several lines, and without invitation, I followed him to his bedroom. Feeling stoned, *Gorgeous Glen* seemed even more irresistible to me. We each took off our own clothes. He reached over to his bedside table and grabbed a condom. With his teeth he quickly ripped it open and threw the empty wrapper. Naked, incoherent, and rock hard, he lay back. I climbed aboard. The sex was intense, and suddenly I felt far removed from everything, almost giddy as I bounced up and down.

I blurted out, "You're in the film industry! I *wanna* be a star!"

He climaxed, and pushed me off.

"Can I be in your next movie?" I asked, lying to his side.

"Sure, you can."

Feeling even sillier, I asked, "What kind of films do you make?"

As he jumped off the bed, he answered, "Porn."

Chapter 44

MaryAnn

It was a few weeks away from Thanksgiving, and my dashboard thermometer read 58 degrees, a record high this time of year in the Northeast, but it felt good to rid myself of my bulky coat and walk freely out into the bright sunshine with only a light sweater.

I arrived at Caleb's school and walked into his classroom. One of his aides, fresh out of college, was sitting at a small table in a child's chair cutting out textile fabric. Upon noticing me, she stopped and pointed her scissors to the back window. "They're out back."

"Thank you. It's a beautiful day out," I said, hearing the echoes of cheers and laughter.

She flashed me a fake smile and continued with her cutting.

I walked out the back door to the playground. A line of rope was placed around the field with a long sock hanging on a pole at each base. They were playing kickball, one of Caleb's favorite games. Unlike the intensity at Melanie's dance competitions, Caleb's games were pure joy to watch. You could feel each child's sense of accomplishment as they made it to each base. It was heartfelt to watch as every aide, counselor, teacher, and child cheered when the ball was kicked, and the silly banter of the counselors bidding against each other while aiding their student in trying to steal a base.

I leaned over and put my fingers into the brackets of the cold metal fence. I was the first parent to arrive, and I was glad to avoid the awkward small talk that we often engaged in and just focus on Caleb. The wind suddenly started to pick up, and in the distance I heard the back door of the school shut as a strong gust of wind came across the playground. As I turned toward the sound I saw Steven casually walking toward my direction. The only time Steven ever picked Caleb up from school was on the rare occasions I had an appointment.

My heart sank. I wasn't ready to talk to him, nonetheless see him. Since finding out my husband was an adulterer, I refused to answer any of his texts, which pretty much all said, "Can we talk?" In a heated moment of rage and anger, I resisted and left one voice message for Steven, incisively telling him, "I will handle Caleb and Melanie, my way. You did enough damage." Surprisingly, he listened.

I never lied to Caleb or Melanie, but I was still numb from shock at what Steven did to me, our family and our marriage. I sat with Caleb when he returned from my parents after that dreadful night. I gently explained to him that an emergency came up and Daddy had to do business out of town, and he was very sorry he couldn't kiss him goodbye, but he will call us as soon as he gets the chance. I had planned on telling Melanie in the same manner when she returned from her weekend away, but the time never seemed right. She had been dancing around the clock preparing for her winter showcase, and barely had time to answer my texts, so a heart-to-heart was out of the question. In a way, this gave me some relief. Melanie didn't need this weight on her shoulders. She had enough stress, and taking on her parents' mess should not be one of them.

I stared straight ahead, as Caleb's team played the field.

Steven stood by my side and solemnly said, "Hi."

I ignored him.

"Please, can we talk? Are you ever going to talk to me?"

I turned around and faced him. "Yeah, when we sign the divorce papers!"

Steven didn't respond. I could see the pain in his eyes. He leaned over and grasped the fence. In defeat, he looked down.

I had been grieving the past week and a half. I hadn't thought rationally or even thought of divorce, or what was to come next for Steven and me. The word divorce was as shocking for me to say, as I'm sure it was for Steven to hear.

Caleb's team was up. After the first two players struck out, it was Caleb's turn to lead the way. As the slow-moving large rubber ball rolled toward him, he kicked it with all his might. Both teams cheered. I yelled, "Go, Caleb." With assistance, he ran in the direction of first base, and using the rope as his guide, he made it to each base, yanking on the dangling sock. With the help and encouragement of all the staff and his classmates, he continued to run home, as his teacher shouted, "Slide, Caleb." And hearing those words, Caleb slid into home base. Caleb's teacher yelled, "Home run!" Not only did Caleb's team cheer, but the children on the outfield did as well.

I glanced over at Steven. He was trying not to appear distraught, as he cheered for show.

After the game, one of Caleb's aides escorted him in our direction. "Daddy," Caleb shouted, letting go of the aide's arm and running toward Steven.

Steven bent down, as Caleb fell into his arms.

"I missed you, Daddy."

"I missed you, too! You are quite the champion out there," Steven said, hugging him.

"I scored a home run!"

"I know. That was pretty awesome. How did you know I was here?"

"I smelled your cologne," Caleb said, still in his arms.

As hurt and confused as I was, deep down inside I also missed Steven and the smell of his cologne.

Steven rubbed Caleb's messy hair away from his face and said, "Caleb, it's a really warm day out. What do we usually do when it's warm out?"

Excitedly he responded, "Get ice cream!"

"That's right!" Steven said, picking him up into his arms.

"But, it's not summertime."

Steven kissed Caleb's cheek. "I know, but it's a beautiful day, the kind of day that calls for ice cream," Steven said, putting him down.

I can't believe Steven went ahead and made plans for Caleb, without consulting with me! He probably figured I would have ignored him. He would have been right!

"Is that you, Mommy?"

"It's me," I said, walking toward him and giving him a hug. "Good job out there. You scored a home run, wow!"

"I kicked the ball hard!" He said, grabbing my hand. "C'mon Mommy, we're going to get some ice cream!"

Chapter 45

Elnando

I glanced over at Melanie as she tried on hats at the new upscale boutique. The store was one of the many new small businesses opening up throughout Spanish Harlem. I couldn't believe she was mine. She was as sweet as she was beautiful. Her wavy long golden blonde hair, pulled back on top with both sides in a braid, reminded me of a princess, and her big brown eyes had a tint of mischief in them. After being with Melanie, I knew what John Meyer meant when he wrote the song "Body is a Wonderland." Melanie was petite in size, but wasn't built like the typical skin-and-bones dancer. She had meat on her bones, and in just the right places. She looked tastefully gorgeous today, with her tight blue jeans, long leather coat, aqua blue collared shirt and matching ruffled scarf.

Trying on a big yellow hat with a large rim, she turned around from the table top mirror and gave me a silly wink. "What do you think?"

"It's definitely you! Are you planning on moving south or joining a Baptist church?"

She laughed. "Maybe both!"

"Are you ready yet?" I asked as she continued to pick up another hat.

"I suppose."

We walked a few blocks, when Melanie asked, "Are you sure a loaf of bread is enough? Can we stop and get her some flowers, too?"

"This is plenty," I said, holding on to the long loaf of Italian bread we picked up earlier from Betty's Bakery and Breads, which was a few blocks down from our school. I knew it would be a perfect addition to anything Birdie, my mom, or Anita would put together, and ever since my papa died, my mama hated flowers. He used to bring them to her and now she says they remind her of death.

"Yes, this is great," I said, hitting her gently on the head with the loaf of bread. I didn't want to explain to her my mama's dislike of flowers and I was anxious for my mama, Birdie, and Anita and possibly Jewel to meet her. I knew they would love her. I was glad to have Melanie for dinner the day before Thanksgiving, and call it a, "pre-Thanksgiving." My family's custom wasn't to celebrate Thanksgiving, but on that day we gathered together with family and friends and shared a large meal. This worked out great for Melanie. Now, we could spend the actual Thanksgiving day with her family.

As we walked past several brownstones and renovated buildings, Melanie remarked, "There is so much culture here, the boutiques, the cafés. Harlem is not such a bad place!"

"Not so much anymore, because THEY keep tearing down every high-rise housing project, so when people come to Spanish Harlem, they don't have to see the poverty and despair," I said, approaching my home.

"When you say THEY, do you mean my father?"

"I mean the city, government. If you want to add your father in the mix, go ahead."

Melanie stopped me short, "Are your mom, Birdie, and the rest of your neighbors going to resent me?"

"They don't know anything about your dad's business, but all's they got to do is look over there," I said, comically pointing to the vacant lot next door with the sign Belezzi Builders, that was scrolled over with graffiti.

Melanie sighed. "Great," as we approached my home.

I smiled at her. "Don't worry! They'll never make the connection."

We entered the lobby. I was shocked to see so many people gathered, many of them holding picket signs.

Melanie turned to me and sarcastically asked, "Did you plan this?"

"No, but let's see what's going on," I answered, grabbing her hand and walking over toward the large group.

A middle-aged black man in a dapper pin-striped suit addressed the crowd. As the crowd silenced, he introduced himself as Councilman Larry Media, and spoke firmly, "I will not let them take your home away!"

With that being said, they all applauded. Then someone yelled out, "I heard a rumor come April that *they gonna* turn off the power and shut off the water!"

He eloquently responded, "It's just a scare tactic. Pay it no mind. Legally, they can't do it. My team and I will challenge everyone trying to tear this place down, but I need all of you to keep your voices heard, and be the strong advocates Harlem needs."

Suddenly, a voice broke out, "I hope you're right! I don't have the cash to move. I can't afford the utility bills for a new apartment, which are covered here by HUD. On top of that, I can't afford no 'fridge to put in a new place."

Melanie stood stunned. I grabbed her hand. "Let's go! They're waiting for us."

~~~

The elevator was dark and smelled like fried chicken and cat piss. I usually took the stairs, but I was hungry and anxious to see everyone, and have them meet Melanie. It shook as it ascended to each floor, and the lights went on and off. I saw the fear in Melanie's eyes.

The sounds of the projects welcomed us as we exited the elevator, crying children, loud bass music, and muffled yells. Melanie was silent as she followed me to my mom's apartment. At first knock, my mama answered. She looked beautiful, even in her old tattered apron that covered her whenever she made a big meal. Her jet black hair was sleekly styled, and she had a great tan from just returning from her job on the cruise line.

"Hello, darling," my mama said, greeting me and giving me a huge hug.

I walked in as Melanie followed. My mama extended the same welcoming greeting to Melanie. "Melanie, I finally get to meet you. You're so beautiful. My Elnando has told me so much about you."

The fear finally left Melanie's face, as she hugged my mama and said, "It's so nice to finally meet you."

I gave my mama the bread as Birdie and Anita, Jewel's mother, walked into the room. They both greeted Melanie and me with open arms. Anita still looked the same, with her short black hair, which was styled the same exact way since I met her when I was around four years old. Her dark olive skin showed little signs of aging except for a few wrinkles, which, I believe, were courtesy of her son, Jewel.

The house smelled of turkey, as my mouth watered. My mama asked, "Are you two hungry?"

"We're starving," I answered as Melanie smiled.

Two large card tables were pushed together and placed between the tiny kitchen and adjoining living room. The table was set with the red clay dishes that my mama always used out for special occasions, a yellow colored embroidered tablecloth and blue linen napkins. Mr. and Mrs. Turkey salt and pepper shakers sat in the center of the table, which I'm sure my mama bought from the neighborhood Dollar Tree, her favorite store.

Melanie asked, "Can I help in any way?"

Mama smiled and said, "We got it covered. You help yourself to something to drink. Soda, wine and a pitcher of water are on the counter."

I poured Melanie and me two cold glasses of water. We took a seat at the table, as Birdie and Anita helped my mom finish up the final preparations. I noticed an extra place setting. "Is Jewel coming?"

Anita turned from the stove. Rolling her eyes, she said, "I told him the time, but one never knows."

Birdie shook her head disapprovingly as she carried a casserole dish filled with Cuban rice and black beans, over to the table.

"Can I help?" Melanie asked again.

I patted Melanie's knee under the table. "Do you see any room for us? They got it covered."

Melanie leaned over to me, "In our kitchen, you're helping."

I laughed. "We'll see."

As the table filled with cranberries, stuffing seasoned with adobo chorizo and green pepper, Anita's homemade tortillas, and our sliced Italian bread, my mama announced, "It's Turkey Time." In the center of the table she placed an antique platter filled with sliced turkey, marinated with sour oranges and garlic.

Melanie stared wide-eyed at the food. "I wasn't sure what to expect, but everything looks absolutely delicious." She chuckled. "I'm sorry, I brought Italian bread."

We all laughed.

My mama said, "No worries! We love Italian bread, and you're Italian. I know this is a different take on what you're used to."

Melanie smiled shyly and nodded her head. My mama reached for my hand, and announced, "Let's say grace." I grabbed Melanie's hand as Birdie grabbed her other. Suddenly, a knock was heard. Anita announced, "It's probably Juliano."

My mama yelled, "Who is it?"

"Jewel," he yelled.

"Come in," my mama yelled back.

As Jewel entered, my mama said, "Just in time. We were just about to give thanks."

Jewel took a seat at the empty place setting and held on to Birdie's and my mama's hands, as my mama prayed. "Thank you, Lord, for gathering us all here safely today. We thank you for family, this good food and the roof over our heads. We ask for your blessing in Jesus' name. Amen!"

"Amen!" we all exclaimed.

Jewel looked good. He was clean shaven, and wore tan pants and a buttoned-down white cotton shirt, a stretch from the usual street clothes I was used to seeing him in.

As we started to dig in, I introduced Jewel to Melanie. He slyly smiled at me, as if to say, *"You done good."*

Jewel was unusually quiet throughout the meal as Melanie made small talk with my mama, Anita, and Birdie. Melanie couldn't answer fast enough as Birdie bombarded her with questions about her dance training.

When dinner was finished, Melanie took it upon herself to help clear the table. Jewel announced, "I'm heading out for a bit."

Anita questioned him, "Where you going?"

"If you really want to know, I'm going to smoke a cigarette."

Birdie chimed in, "Smoking ain't good for you. You're a young man. You need to keep your lungs clean."

I chuckled to myself. *If she only knew what he usually smoked.*

I couldn't believe my eyes as I looked over at Melanie. I wanted to pinch myself. This is my girl—beautiful, classy, sweet, and comes from a rich family, who knows everything about me and is in my home in Spanish Harlem. I slept with many of the neighborhood girls, many right in this project, but none of them were good enough to bring home to Mama. Melanie looked up and smiled, releasing me from my thoughts.

As Jewel walked out the door, I said, "I'm going to join him."

Birdie piped in, "Don't tell me you smoke, too?"

I chuckled and gave Birdie a quick peck on the cheek. "You think I *wanna* damage this great physique?"

Birdie giggled and whipped my behind with her dish towel.

"Ouch! I'll be back in a minute," I said, looking over at Melanie.

I opened the door. "Hey, wait up," I yelled over to Jewel as he walked down the hall.

I caught up to him. "*Where you off to?*" I asked as we entered the elevator.

"I said I was going to have a smoke."

We stood in silence as a couple of young boys stood next to us.

We got out and walked through the lobby into the fresh air.

Jewel took out his cigarette and lit it up.

I stepped a few feet away from the smoke and said, "Glad you made it today."

Between his puffs, he answered, "You're glad I made it? You're the one who's not around anymore!"

"I know, Jewel. Like I've said before, things are changing."

He ignored me and continued smoking while watching every person who walked by us like a hawk.

"Listen, why don't you head back with me and Melanie? You can stay at my dorm. My roommate is at his boyfriend's place for the next few days."

Jewel chuckled.

"I want you to see my school. We can hang out tonight and watch the parade tomorrow morning, like we did when we were kids. I don't have to be at Melanie's parents' house 'til around 4:00. How 'bout it?"

"Elnando, like you said! Things are different. We're not kids anymore."

"I know we're not, but you'll always be like a brother to me."

Jewel smiled, and threw his cigarette out on the ground, and stepped on it. "That school's making you sweet."

"Sweet! That reminds me, dessert is waiting for us! Are you coming back with us?"

"Not tonight."

"Why?"

"I got plans, some other time."

"What plans?"

"Let's go, Elnando. Melanie is probably wondering *where your at.*"

We took the smelly elevator up, and I was glad there were no people in it to add to the smell.

We walked in as Melanie was sitting in the living room looking at old photo albums.

She looked up and smiled. "What a cute baby you were, Elnando."

Jewel chided, "Any pictures in there of him pretending he was in 'N Sync?"

I elbowed him, "There are probably 'pics of both of us pretending we were in 'N Sync. You remember the moves? C'mon, show 'em."

Jewel busted out in a move and sang, "Bye, Bye, Bye."

We all laughed.

Jewel stood on his toes and pointed down at me, "Damn, I have better moves than you AND Justin Timberlake."

Birdie added, "It's a shame! You should have listened to me and Joe, and danced. You always had such good rhythm."

Anita responded, "It's a sore subject, Birdie. Juliano is still finding his way."

Jewel looked at us, "And now, I'm going to find my way out the door!"

Anita looked at him with concern. "We haven't even had dessert yet."

Jewel answered, rubbing his stomach, "I don't think my stomach could handle dessert, right now."

I whispered to him, "Why don't you stay, man?"

"I *gots* to go," he said as he walked to his mom and Birdie, and gave both of them a kiss on the cheek.

My mama hugged him and said, "Don't be such a stranger."

Jewel smiled. "I won't."

In a gentleman-like manner he shook Melanie's hand and said, "It was great meeting you!"

She answered, "It was nice meeting you, too!"

Jewel walked over to me, and we gave each other our signature handshake as he said, "Catch you later."

"Is everything all right?" I asked, leaning into him.

"Yeah, I just want everyone to have some alone time with you and your girl."

"You sure?"

"Like I said, I'll catch you later." He turned and started to walk away and then turned around abruptly and said, "Elnando, *you done good!*"

"Thanks," I answered.

As he walked out, my mama brought down another photo album from her corner bookshelf.

I protested, "Please, Mama, no more! Melanie has seen enough."

"No, no, I want to see them."

My mama protested, "See, Elnando, she wants to see them, plus this one is of your Papa."

My heart sank. As Anita and Birdie walked over to the kitchen area, I followed them.

Anita asked, "You hungry for some pumpkin empanadas?"

"I am always hungry for pumpkin empanadas."

Birdie answered, "I made them. They just need frying."

"I'll do it," I said, trying to avoid sitting next to Melanie and my mom as they talked about my papa. "You, ladies, go sit. You did enough."

Anita answered, "Birdie's going to fry them while I put on some tea."

"You two go relax. Get out of my kitchen," I said, looking around the tiny area.

Birdie answered, "If you insist, they're in the 'fridge."

I took the large platter filled with Birdie's pumpkin empanadas, her signature dish when she and Joe joined us every Thanksgiving, out of the 'fridge.

I doused the large frying pan with oil. I put the flame on low and gently dropped the pastries filled with pumpkin. I quickly grabbed my mom's yellow teapot with daisies all over it, and filled it with hot water, and placed it on the stove. I turned each of the empanadas slowly, as the sweet smell began filling the air.

My mama yelled, "They smell real good, Elnando. Melanie, we have Birdie's pumpkin empanadas for dessert. They are a tradition for us. They are a little bit different than the pumpkin pie you are probably used to. They are pumpkin filled in a delectable crust."

Melanie answered, "They smell delicious."

Mama chuckled. "I also made an apple pie, just in case."

"I'm sure I'll love them!"

As the oil sizzled in the pan, I overheard my mama showing Melanie pictures that I was already familiar with—my papa when he arrived in this country from Cuba and him in his uniform at his job as a waiter at the Windows of the World restaurant that was in the World Trade Center.

I didn't want to see them. I only wanted to see my papa. I was still angry at God for taking him out of my life. My papa was the world to me, and my anger seemed not at any particular group, but at God for allowing 9/11 to happen.

Birdie walked over as the teapot whistled and asked, "You okay?"

"Yeah, the empanadas are just about done, and no worries! I didn't burn them."

"That's not what I was asking about," she whispered.

I ripped off a piece of paper towel from the rack and slid it over the platter.

"I hate when she talks about him," I said in barely a whisper.

"Why?"

"Why?" I repeated, as I put the hot empanadas on the paper towel. "Because he's not here, he was taken from us. It pisses me off. That's why. And, why did He let it happen?"

Birdie started to gently take out my mother's dainty antique Spanish orange and blue designed teacups, with a matching sugar bowl and creamer. With great care, she put them on the bright orange coffee tray that was a fixture on the counter. She turned to me and said, "God didn't let it happen."

I rolled my eyes as I wiped off my hands on the dishtowel hanging crookedly from the stove. "He didn't stop it."

Birdie faced me, as she continued to whisper, "He is not to blame, but to run to. Remember that, Elnando," she said, walking out of the kitchen area. She announced, "We have tea ready, and Melanie, you can have coffee, if you like, from the new-age coffee maker."

Melanie laughed. "Tea is fine."

Birdie returned, forgetting she filled the creamer with whole milk, something I'm sure Melanie rarely has, in addition to the many other foods with a different twist on them that she tried today.

My mama came in, grabbed the stack of dessert plates and smiled at me. Then she returned and grabbed the utensils out of the drawer and the deep-dish apple pie from the 'fridge. "Elnando, grab the container of Cool Whip in the 'fridge, please."

I brought it out and walked back. Deciding on coffee, I put my K-Cup into the Keurig coffee maker. I was glad I convinced my mom to splurge and buy it a year ago.

My mom served up a generous serving of empanadas to each of us, and announced, "Who would like some apple pie?"

Anita answered, "Rosalie, I think we need to get through this first."

Melanie kindly smiled as she prepared her tea, and a huge smile came across her face as she tried the empanada. "This is so good," she exclaimed.

Birdie answered, "Thank you."

I chuckled. "It sure beats regular pumpkin pie, doesn't it, Melanie?"

"It certainly does," she said as she dug in.

My mama announced, "Melanie, it has been such a pleasure meeting you. I'm glad you got to see where we all raised Elnando. I don't know if Elnando mentioned it to you, but Christmas will probably be the last holiday we have here. It's looking more and more like our home is going to be torn down."

Melanie cleared her throat and said, "I'm so sorry to hear that."

"As you can see, this is no place fancy, and no place where I would want you and Elnando to settle if you ever got married, but it's our home. Many friends have been made between these walls. We built our lives here, and through the years, drugs and gangs have tried to destroy it, but we stayed because money-wise, it worked for the few of us who held on together. Now they want to tear it down and build condos that none of us can afford."

Solemnly I said, "Mama, you can afford it."

She answered, "Don't be talking nonsense, Elnando. The money I got from your papa's death is blood money, and much of it has gone to Fillmore."

"I understand, Mama."

"The money is for the future for all of us sitting here at this table."

"Mama, it is the future."

"What I'm saying Elnando, your papa's money is not to be used to live in some fancy schmanzy place. We're doing fine, living just the way we are."

We were all silent. After a few seconds Birdie broke the ice, "Melanie, how 'bout I pack you up some empanadas for you family."

My mama added, "They raised such a beautiful daughter; I'm sure they are very sweet people. You should definitely bring them some; and before we are forced to move, I insist they join us for dinner."

Chapter 46

Melanie

Beneath the blue skies, I looked down at all the chaos in the streets. "Oh look, it's Hello Kitty," I yelled to Elnando.

"Meow," Elnando said as he came over to me. He animatedly nibbled on my neck, swooped my legs over and sat next to me in the wide window sill.

Thanks to Michael, Darnel's boyfriend, we had perfect seats for the Macy's Thanksgiving Day Parade. A friend of Michael's lives in a high-rise on 6th Avenue on the 8th floor, and was away for Thanksgiving, so the place was ours. It had three huge oval bay windows overlooking the street, and was decorated with an artistic ambiance, with black and white photos scattered on the walls. The hardwood floors glistened, and perfectly cared-for plants in brightly colored ceramic pots filled the empty spaces. Michael said, in his broken English, that he met the owner, who was an investment banker, when he first came to the city, and that he was in his late fifties. I wondered about this friendship and would have loved to know more, but Darnel was always in his presence, and with his Italian accent it was difficult for Michael to even place a food order, let alone tell a whole story.

Darnel came over and looked out the wide bay window, with only a sheer valance on top, as a stream of marching bands and cheerleaders passed by. "Screw this! Let me know when you see Spiderman or Matt Lauer," he said, walking back to the chrome island that was centered between the living room and kitchen. Michael was sitting there on a stool, having no interest in the parade, drinking coffee, and munching on the bagels that Elnando and I brought as a courtesy for letting us use his friend's place. I offered the two of them to come to my parents' home for dinner. Darnel thanked me for the offer, but explained that he was bringing Michael to his hood to meet his family.

Darnel's family meeting Michael will probably be less awkward than my dad seeing Elnando again.

I also extended an invite to Ming-Na, but she just started seeing a violinist in the music department whose family is from Westchester. She is crazy about him, and he asked her to join him and his family for dinner.

"Oh, it's Buzz Lightyear," Elnando said. "Some of my favorite memories were the years my mom, Anita, Birdie, Jewel and I went to Times Square to watch the parade. We were all smushed together like sardines. We never could see anything, but we always liked the cool toys Birdie would buy us from the vendors."

I asked, "Does Birdie have kids?"

Elnando answered, "She has two daughters. They're a lot older than us. They used to dance, but now they're both married with children. One lives somewhere upstate. She visits Birdie pretty often, and the other one lives in the state of Washington. Her daughters were grown when Birdie moved into the project and opened the dance studio. Birdie was always an activist for the arts, I guess. She used to live in Queens."

"I really loved meeting her, your mom, Jewel and his mom. You have a really nice family."

"I was nervous about bringing you to my home, but, as my mama said, 'Christmas is probably the last holiday that we will celebrate there.' I'm really glad you got to see where I grew up and you don't judge me by it."

Pretending to push him out of the window sill to the fire escape below, I said, "Are you kidding me?"

240

Elnando pulled me into his arms. His cologne was turning me on, and he looked incredible in his zipped-up, gray pullover and tight blue jeans.

"I love you, Melanie."

"I love you, too!"

I leaned my head on Elnando's shoulder. "We couldn't ask for better weather. This parade is exactly what New York needed."

"New York is back!" Elnando exclaimed.

Suddenly, out of the blue, Michael asked, "El--*moo*, is that *El--moo?* It is! I like *El--moo!*"

Elnando and I turned around as Darnel and Michael were walking toward the uncovered bay window next to the window sill.

We all started laughing as Darnel said, "Yeah, he's pretty cool!"

~ ~ ~

I was excited to see my family. Although it was only a month since I had been home, it seemed like an eternity. The texts were few and far between, and the phone calls were sporadic and quick. I was relieved to hear that they were safe when Sandy hit, and that the only damage to our home was the kitchen area.

In my quiet moments when I thought of them, I always felt a little homesick. Classes, rehearsals, studies, and spending time with Elnando left me little free time. Since beginning at Fillmore, I had lost all contact with my friends from high school and Miss Elle's Dance Academy. Being at Fillmore was like being in a private island within the heart of New York. So much was expected of you there, and when you weren't in dance class, it seemed like everyone talked about dance class and everyone hung out with everyone from dance class. In addition to having Elnando by my side, Darnel

241

and Ming-Na helped ease the pressure of the demands placed on every dancer at Fillmore. Most of the freshman dance majors at Fillmore were between 17 and 19 years of age; many of us were years ahead maturity-wise. Most of us had been dancing since an early age, and when you have the talent, and it is recognized and nurtured like it was in my case, and like the many who now attend Fillmore, dance becomes your life.

My grade school years consisted of class, then three to four different dance classes at night after school, not to mention Saturdays, which were all-day dance affairs. Many weekends consisted of traveling to competitions, and they were intense. My friends were all dancers, with the exception of a few friends that I carried along from grade school, and my mom's friends became other dance moms. When I was twelve, Caleb was born unexpectedly. The other dance moms stepped up and helped by chaperoning me along with their daughters, while my mother and father dealt with what seemed like countless surgeries and learning how to raise a blind child.

A few of the competitive team dancers from Miss Elle's, who were a few years ahead of me, made it into Fillmore and are now in their junior or senior year. When I run into them on campus, it always feels like a reunion.

As sweat is emanating from every pore in our body, and every joint in our body is hurting, the aching pain we feel is not like that of a 17 year old, or probably that of a 35 year old, but from what I have been told, it's more like that of a 70 year old. We push our bodies to no extent, because we love dance, and even though the life of a dancer is only about ten years, most of us could never picture ourselves doing anything else. The fact that Elnando was a late bloomer at the ripe old age of fourteen amazes me.

242

I wouldn't change a thing about my childhood, but at times when I watch Caleb play in his little area it reminds me that I have no memories of playing. I remember Barbie dolls, but not playing with them. I don't ever remember being silly or getting dirty. I only remember dancing.

~~~

"We forgot the empanadas," I said to Elnando, as I rang the doorbell and proceeded to walk in.

Elnando smiled. "I'm sure they won't mind. But we got flowers, although they're looking a little wilted."

We bought the flowers from a vendor on the way to the parade, and by now they had lost their entire luster.

"Yeah, I think they have seen the light of a better day," I said, trying to talk over Barkley's excessive barking.

Barkley was especially happy to see us as he jumped on Elnando. "Hey, there," Elnando said, petting his head.

Caleb yelled from the corner rocking chair, where he sat with a Braille book on his lap. "It's Melanie!"

I walked over to him and gently gave him a kiss on the cheek. "Elnando is here, too!"

"I know!" he said.

"Caleb, Elnando wants to shake your hand. Is that all right? You remember him, don't you?"

Caleb reached out his tiny hand.

"Hi, Caleb!"

"Hi, Elnando!"

The house smelled delicious and I was starving, since the last thing I ate was an asiago bagel at around 9:00. I glanced over at the dining room table and I saw only four place settings. I was surprised my mom forgot to set a place setting for Elnando, and I wondered where Dad was. He's normally lounged out on the couch, watching football before and after Thanksgiving dinner.

"Caleb, are Mom and Dad in the kitchen?" I asked, leaning down next to him.

"Mommy's in the kitchen," Caleb said, as he continued to place both of his hands on his Braille book.

"Caleb, what book are you reading?"

"It's *Monet the Mouse loves Christmas*."

"Hmm," I said. "Is it all right if Elnando feels it? Elnando has never seen or felt a Braille book before."

"Okay," Caleb said, holding out the book.

Elnando took it from Caleb and stared at it as if he was looking at something in some kind of Morse code.

"Feel it, Elnando," I said.

Elnando lightly touched the raised bumps on the page.

I remarked, "Doesn't it feel cool?"

Elnando nodded his head.

"Caleb, I think you should read Elnando your book, you can show him how the raised dots mean letters and words."

I was used to Caleb being self-sufficient since he was a toddler. My mom pushed him and wanted him to be as independent as possible should he never see again, but seeing how comfortable and good he was at reading Braille at only five years of age amazed me!

Elnando handed the book to Caleb, and he looked as equally amazed at Caleb's confidence level and ability to read. Elnando nodded his head and smiled. It was amusing to me how people forgot Caleb was blind and cannot see their facial expressions.

"I'm going to go check on things in the kitchen." I pushed the wooden swivel door that led to the kitchen. I was surprised at the new look of the kitchen, knowing the damage Sandy had done. The bay window had been fully repaired with new crown molding, and the kitchen was now a light crème color compared to the cranberry color that I was used to. The hard wood flooring had been replaced with a darker oakwood. I knew once I heard our home was damaged, my dad would have his staff work on it ASAP. The remodeled kitchen looked better than before. I remember thinking how lucky we were, compared to so many other homes that were in Jersey. Also, the fact that my dad owned a building company made things a whole lot easier.

My mom's back was facing the sink as she spoke on her cell phone. "Fine, come. I want to make this clear to you; I'm doing this for them! No, I didn't tell them yet—my parents aren't coming for dessert. I told them not to! I don't even want to be in your presence. Why should they? You have ten minutes to get here, or we're starting without you," she said, slamming her cell phone shut.

I watched as my mom leaned against the sink, staring into space, as the uncarved turkey sat by her side.

I cautiously asked, "Mom, what's going on?"

The sound of my voice startled her. She turned around with tears in her eyes.

She didn't answer.

"Mom, what is going on?"

She took a seat on a stool at the kitchen island and put her head in her hands.

I sat next to her. "Why are you crying? Was that Dad you were speaking with?" I asked, confused.

"Yeah, it was your father. He moved out!"

"What?" I asked stunned. "What do you mean HE moved out?"

"About three weeks ago he moved out. He's staying at Nonna and Poppy's."

"You're kidding me! Why?"

"It's complex. Some things have changed in our relationship."

"What are you talking about, what things?"

"Things you don't need to know."

I couldn't believe what I just heard.

"Mom, I can't believe what you're saying."

My mom put her hand over mine, "I'm so sorry."

My shock started to turn to anger, "Why am I just hearing about this now?"

"Melanie, it's not something I could put in a text, and we hardly have time to speak. The weekend when everything went down, I had to come to grips with it before I could drag you into it. I didn't want to bother you. You have your winter showcase coming up, and I'm so proud of you!" she said, putting her hand on my shoulder.

Tears started to well up in my eyes. "Unacceptable, Mom, unacceptable! Does Caleb know about this?"

"I keep telling him Daddy has a lot of work to do out of the area. Melanie, I haven't yet figured things out."

"Does anyone else know?"

"I told Mema and Grandpa, and I told them not to come for dessert, that it would be too uncomfortable, and seeing as your dad is staying at Nonna and Poppy's, they know too. And I'm sure, because everyone is so worried about us, everyone else in the family knows, as well!"

"Great! Mom, what's going on? You and Dad are the perfect couple. This is insane! Is it me being away, or Caleb? What is it?"

"How can you even think anything like that? Some things have changed between your dad and I."

"Did Dad do something to hurt you?"

My mother's eyes stopped meeting mine, as the door flew open.

It was my dad. I looked over at him, like I had seen a ghost. Noticing the expression on my face, he came over and gently hugged me.

"Hi, Mel!" He looked at my mother, "Did you tell her?"

"Not everything," she said, with a sudden sternness to her voice.

"Let's all try to have a nice dinner," he said, leaning on the island.

"Fine," my mother said, getting up and going to the oven.

"Melanie, I'll help your mother. You go check on Caleb and rescue Elnando. He's going to be hearing that story in his sleep."

I couldn't even speak, let alone answer him, as I walked out of the kitchen.

I stood in the dining area as Caleb read *Monet the Mouse loves Christmas* to Elnando, for what I would suspect to be the tenth time. I tried to block out Caleb, and focus on trying to hear what was going on from the other side of the door. All I could hear was silence.

"Elnando, what would you like to drink?" I asked him, trying to keep my cool as he knelt next to the rocking chair as Caleb continued reading.

Elnando looked over at me. "Whatever you've got. Is everything all right?"

"Everything's fine. Did my dad say hello to you?"

"Yeah, but I don't think he wanted to interrupt the story."

I chuckled sarcastically. "I'm going to get us something to drink. And, an extra place setting," I murmured to myself.

As I walked back into the kitchen, there was complete silence as my Dad carved the turkey.

The food was lined up on the island, and I decided to follow my mom in silence, with dish after dish, to the dining room table before getting the drinks.

I returned to the kitchen, and turned to my dad. I looked at him with contempt and asked, "Dad, what do you want to drink?"

"Whatever everyone else is drinking," he answered.

I filled the glasses with ice, and poured four glasses of Ginger Ale, including one for my mom, and grabbed Caleb a juice box from the 'fridge. In a few trips everything was delivered to the table.

I pulled a fork and knife out of the antique silver box that was inside the large, Adirondack, carved wood cabinet that stood against the wall in the dining area. It was my unofficial job at all of the holiday parties to set the table, and I was glad to see an extra teal napkin on top of the extra tablecloths that were inside the cabinet as well.

The table looked picture perfect. The Lenox china with pale blue designs that we use at all special events was a special gift that my mom received as a bridal shower gift from my Mema. The silver which was passed down to my mom from her great grandmother had an intricate design and looked beautiful with the brown copper tablecloth. The teal napkins made the table look like an ad from the Macy's flyer.

Another noticeable difference was the missing wine glasses and bottle of Chardonnay that was a fixture at all of our holiday events.

My mom and dad walked out of the kitchen together. My mom was trying hard to look her Sunday best, while Dad and I looked like two wounded soldiers. As if nothing had just taken place, my mother walked over to Elnando and gave him a hug. "It's so nice to see you. I'm glad you can join us today."

Elnando picked up the bouquet of carnations from the coffee table that we brought for her. The already wilted flowers looked almost dead.

"I'm sorry I should have given these to you when I came in," Elnando said apologetically.

My mother smiled. "No problem! Thank you, that was very thoughtful of you. Let me just get a vase and put them in some water, and then we can have dinner."

As my mom retreated to the kitchen, there was an awkward silence. Dad gave Elnando a handshake and welcomed him, making small talk about tonight's game.

"Caleb, are you ready for dinner?" I asked him.

"I'm starving," he said, getting up and searching for his little "white cane" that was against the back side of the chair.

Caleb recently began using the cane. I knew my parents prolonged Caleb on relying on a cane for as long as possible, so that he could become proficient at focusing on his listening. Caleb seemed to handle it well and I was so proud of him!

Caleb made his way to the table, as Barkley strolled by his side. We all sat at the table, as mom returned with the flowers in a vase way too expensive for the $7.00 bouquet that we bought her. She put the vase on the table and joined us.

"Mom, everything looks delicious."

"Well, let's dig in," she announced.

Caleb announced. "We forgot to say grace."

My mom answered, "Caleb, why don't you say it?"

We all folded our hands and listened as Caleb said our family's grace in the best way he knew how.

249

"Mom, I'm going to help Caleb."

"No, you enjoy your meal."

"It's not a problem," I said, as Caleb squirmed in his seat.

I cut up his meat, which he was able to eat by himself, and then guided him with his potatoes and stuffing. I didn't even bother giving him the corn and green beans, knowing he wouldn't eat it.

My dad congratulated me on my role in the winter showcase and Elnando on getting the lead. He made small talk about how so many people are still recovering from Sandy, and that we were lucky that only our kitchen was damaged. He hoped the insurance company gives us some reimbursement, but it was all a waiting game.

Caleb couldn't take in the food as quickly as I was serving it to him, and he looked like a *mushmouth*, with mashed potatoes sticking to the corner of his lips.

With a mouthful of food, Caleb said, "Daddy, I'm glad you're back from work."

My father sweetly answered, "Caleb, I have to go away for a little longer, but maybe someday this week we can do something special."

"Like go to the Imagination Center?"

"That sounds like a plan," my dad answered.

The Imagination Center was an indoor gym with slides and ball pits, designed for children with disabilities and a staff trained to deal with special-needs children.

"Everything is so delicious," Elnando remarked.

"Thank you," my mother said, barely touching her plate.

When everyone was done, Elnando got up to help with the plates. My father left the table and put the game on.

As Elnando started clearing, my mother stopped him. "Go, relax. I've got this. Sit and enjoy the game."

Even in the midst of all the silent chaos, I couldn't help but laugh to myself at how cute Caleb looked with his gooey face.

His face needed cleaning. I went to the kitchen and grabbed the moist wipes that we always had on hand, because of Caleb. When I returned, Caleb was now running his fingers through the mashed potatoes, and throwing turkey meat on the floor for Barkley.

"No, Caleb! I'm going to wash your dirty face now," I said, trying hard to get off the now dried-on potatoes.

"You're too hard."

"You shouldn't be so messy. Now give me your hands."

He put out his hands, which were wet and sticky. "I'm going to have to use the whole package on these," I said, scrubbing his hands. I looked over at Elnando, who was watching the game in total silence with my father.

I lifted Caleb out of his seat. He found his way to his "white cane." *Mr. Independent*, I thought, as I watched him slowly maneuver his way to his play area. He leaned the cane down, and gently brought himself to the floor where bins of Braille books, blocks, and toys awaited him.

I followed my mom to the kitchen. "Mom, we need to talk!" I said, setting the dirty plates in the sink.

"Melanie, there is nothing to talk about," she said, putting the casserole dishes on the counter.

"What do you mean, there's nothing to talk about? Dad is sitting out there, like he's a stranger in his own house. What happened? I want to know now!"

"Nothing, we just need a break," she whispered.

I could feel myself getting heated up. "A break, you need a break? If you want a break, take separate vacations. Avoid each other for a few weeks. And, Dad staying at Nonna and Poppy's, all of this is ridiculous," I said, opening the dishwasher and turning the water on to prewash the dishes.

My mother flung a serving spoon from the counter into the sink. "What do you want me to say? You want the truth? Okay! Your father fucked his twenty-something assistant!"

"Dad, did what? I can't believe it!" I said, holding on to the counter top. I looked at the swivel door, knowing that the man I knew as my dad was a completely different person to me right now.

"Mom, I can't believe this! He's not leaving you for her or anything like that! Is he?"

"No," my mom said breathless.

"I can't believe this. I want to punch him right now! No, I want to kill him!"

My mom grabbed my arm. "Melanie, stop! He's hurting right now, too!"

"Oh really, he's going to hurt even more after I get through with him!"

"Melanie, no, you can't say anything. I shouldn't have even told you. This is between me and him."

I started to cry. "I can't believe Dad cheated on you, and with a twenty-something!"

My mom wrapped her arms around me and held me close. "I shouldn't have told you all of that."

"It was the girl at Caleb's party, wasn't it?"

My mom just shook her head. "How did you know?"

"I had a feeling. She's the only girl who works there, besides Dolores. I can't believe this!" As I pulled away, I said,

"Here, I was nervous about Elnando being here with Dad, because of Dad's company tearing down his home, and all that I told him about Elnando."

"I was going to talk to you about Elnando. Your father told me about your conversation..."

I interrupted her, "Mom, that's not important right now! Plus, Elnando is not going to the police. He's over it. Thank God, because my own father wouldn't even help him! I'm still a little pissed off about that."

"I really like him Melanie, but..."

"Mom, forget about it. Elnando loves me, and I love him."

She gently took her hand and brushed my hair back. Glancing at the door, she said, "At this moment, things are good for you. I am happy for you. Who am I to stop you, especially since the man he's sitting next to out there is your father."

I sniffled. "Can we have dessert now?"

My mom smiled softly. "Forget the dishes. Let's bring out the pies."

~ ~ ~

Mom and I brought out the plates, pies and whipped cream. My dad seemed to have loosened up, as he made obnoxious remarks at the ref's calls, with Elnando in agreement. Caleb seemed to be in a world of his own, as he built from what everyone could see except him, what looked to be a giant skyscraper made out of blocks.

My tears were gone, but I felt like the bottom had fallen out of me, and I knew I looked like I had been crying. I wasn't sure if Dad realized my mom had told me anything else, but I knew he wouldn't say anything in front of Elnando, and sure as hell, Elnando wasn't going to ask what's wrong in front of everybody.

My mom put on a pot of coffee and brought out a serving platter with mugs, sugar and creamer. When the coffee was brewed, I poured it into a carafe, as my mom grabbed a half-gallon of vanilla ice cream out of the freezer and a metal scooper.

My mom announced, "Dessert." All of us sat and ate together, ignoring the elephant in the room.

In addition to the pain I was feeling inside, I was apprehensive, knowing that my dad was going to drive us to the train station so we could return to the city. I wanted to let this all sink in before I got in the car with him and Elnando.

Should I tell him I know about the affair? I asked myself. I didn't know what to do.

As soon as dessert was over, I told my dad we needed to go back to school. I could tell Elnando wanted to finish watching the game, but I had to get out of there.

I kissed my mom and Caleb goodbye. My mom gave Elnando a hug goodbye as he thanked her for having him.

Elnando scooted down next to Caleb, and said "It was good seeing you, Caleb."

Not fazed at all by his leaving, Caleb said, "Bye."

My dad gave Caleb a hug, promising him that he would call him later, that he had some work he had to get done.

I bent down and messed Caleb's hair, startling him, "See you, *mushmouth*!" He responded, annoyed at what I had just done, "Bye, Melanie."

I hugged my mom tight and told her that we would talk later.

My dad gave her a weak smile and said, "Bye, MaryAnn." She ignored him.

~~~

The ten-minute car ride to the train station felt like two hours. During the drive he gave me his usual warnings about being careful on the subway, when there was so much more to be said.

He pulled into the parking lot of the train station. "Thank you very much, Mr. Belezzi," Elnando said, getting out of the backseat. I got out of the backseat and walked over to the driver's window. Dad rolled down the window.

"Thanks a lot, Dad."

"I love you, Melanie, I'm really sorry."

I leaned into the window. "I hope you realize Dad, when you cheat on your wife, you cheat on your family, too."

Chapter 47

MaryAnn

Everything seemed so surreal: Steven being here for dinner like some unwelcome guest, revealing to my seventeen-year-old daughter that her father is a cheater who moved out of her home, as well as letting the rest of the family know, lying to Caleb that his dad is on some work mission and is not able to be home much anymore. How long is all this going to last?

As much as I continued to feel angry at Steven and show it towards him, I was glad he came for dinner. I knew his presence meant a lot to Caleb and Melanie. Deep down inside, I still loved him in so many ways and probably always will, no matter what decision I make. So many questions lingered inside of me that needed to be put to rest. I never asked him, "Why?" Why did he have to hurt me that way? How do I know he won't do it again? And, did he stop the affair because he got caught? I knew we could never be the family we were, but wasn't that better than being a split-up family? And, if I still loved Steven, shouldn't I at least give it a fighting chance?

I sat drinking my glass of Chablis in front of the dancing fire, playing these questions over and over again in my head. I wasn't surprised when my parents showed up to check on me and Caleb. I told them earlier in the week that it would be too uncomfortable to have them around, especially if I should decide to tell Melanie what was going on. Thankfully, they listened, since Steven happened to be my surprise guest. I sighed a breath of relief when my parents asked if Caleb could spend the night. I needed to sort things out in my head, which felt like a hoarder's paradise. The more

I thought, the more jumbled things seemed, and the more ill I felt. Maybe I just needed to rest. I put my near-empty glass aside, and grabbed my favorite cozy blanket, with a moose design on it, off the top of the couch. I curled up and relaxed to the sound of the fire crackling. As my eyelids started to get heavier, I felt myself falling asleep. As I began to drift off, Barkley, who lay next to the fire, suddenly jerked and started barking. From a distance, I saw the front door slowly open, as Barkley ran over to it. I abruptly sat up as I heard Steven's voice calming him.

"What are you doing here?" I asked.

"This is still my home, isn't it?" Steven asked, walking toward me.

"Just get what you need and get out," I said, returning to my lying position.

"I don't need anything. Is Caleb in bed?"

"No, he's at my parents," I sat up again and covered my legs with the blanket. "Really, Steven, what do you want?"

"What I want is you, MaryAnn. I want you!"

"You should have thought of that when you were fucking your little whore! By the way, how is she?"

"I promise you, MaryAnn, I will never see or hear from her again."

"I never asked you; did it all end because you got caught?"

"MaryAnn, it was nothing."

"I'm hurting, and you're saying it was for nothing!"

"I can't explain it! I'm sorry. You're the only person who knows the real me. There is such an empty space in my heart without you," he said, kneeling before me.

I didn't answer and hugged my blanket in a ball, as I stared into Steven's brown eyes that were masked in pain.

"MaryAnn, I know you must hate me. I understand. I hate myself for what I did to you and our family. But, if I have to wait forever for you, I will. There's a big, empty space in my heart, and it can only be filled by you."

I sunk my head down into the scrunched-up blanket as tears slowly began to flow down my face.

Chapter 48

Lauren

"Roll cameras," the director said. Then a hippie in faded jeans, kinky black hair and a cheesy moustache, held out a clap board, and said "Scene 8, take 1, Sand Creek," and clapped the top down hard on his board. "Action, Amy," the director yelled. I sat next to Stefani, who had been sipping on the same Starbucks venti coffee for the last two hours, while holding on to her clipboard. If I was allowed to speak I would have loved to have asked her, "Is that a bottomless cup of coffee?" But no words could be spoken as the scenes were shot. Stefani was a Production Assistant, which is the lowest job on the totem pole, but one of the hardest working jobs at the CBS Studios lot. Her round-the-clock job, from what I could see, was to kiss the asses of the actors, directors, and anyone else affiliated with the show. She was a gopher who did whatever she was asked to do, and without question. Stefani loved her job. While at City College she majored in Communications and after several mundane jobs at small news stations throughout the east coast, she decided to head west, and took the first job she could find. Without a doubt, Stefani would move up. When she talked about her job, she never referred to herself as just a PA, but would proudly say how she had organized the director's notes and helped the Key Grip operators. What made me most proud of her was the fact that she wasn't afraid to get her hands dirty, and nothing could make her sweat.

The show was a one-hour mystery drama, called *Sand Creek*, which referred to an historic, made-up town in upstate New York where strange occurrences continually take place. Stefani was excited, as well as relieved that it got picked up by the networks for another season, and that she was guaranteed employment for another year. I thought the show was interesting in an eerie different sort of way, but I had only seen a few episodes, being that it aired on Friday nights at 9:00 pm and that was usually my *partay* time. Without a DVR to record it, I told Stefani I would have to wait for it to come out as a DVD boxed set.

The cast was incredibly kind and down to earth, but I was warned by my sister, that I was not allowed to go near them, or speak to them without being spoken to first. She explained that it was an unspoken rule on the set, that if you wanted to keep your job it was best to follow. The set was closed today; which meant no live audience. The director yelled, "Cut. Good job everyone. Go take a break!"

My sister turned to me, "Crafty Time."

"Huh?" I asked.

"It's time for us to take a break, let's go get some food," she said, getting up. I followed her to a large buffet set up with mini-sandwiches, a large fruit platter, veggie platter and my sister's favorite—hummus, in all different varieties, with a basket of pitas. At the end of the buffet, was a large cake stand with brownies, cookies, and croissants, while different flavored protein bars surrounded its base. I took a little of everything, having not had much good food or food at all since staying at Stefani's. My sister's plate was bare in comparison to mine, with only a pita and some hummus.

Stefani and I ate side by side in the same chairs from where we watched the scenes. When we were finished, I followed her around as she talked to, what she referred to as, the union workers, the electricians and sound techs. From the corner of my eye, I noticed a tall, well-built black man in his late thirties-early forties enter the set. Like a politician on a campaign, he made his rounds to each and every person on the set, greeting them with old-fashioned sincerity.

As he made his way to our area, I knew he looked familiar but I couldn't place him.

"It's so good to see you," Stefani said, giving him a hug, breaking what I thought would be the set's cardinal rule.

Finally it hit me! It was Kevin Tracy, the former NFL player, turned dancer on *Dancing with the Stars*, turned actor, turned headline maker for his crazy stints with underage girls, threatening behavior and drug use. He was on this show at the beginning, for about the first four episodes, the ones I happened to watch. He played a lead role as the small town's hard-ass, yet caring, high school football coach.

Frustrated and annoyed, the director announced through his bull horn, "Due to some technical problems, we will now resume in twenty minutes." We all glanced his way as he continued to yell, which could be heard without the bull horn, "People, get your shit together!"

"Oh no," Kevin said, smiling. "How are you doing?" he asked, addressing Stefani.

"I'm doing good. This is my sister, Lauren."

"Hi," he said, extending his hand to mine.

"She's staying with me for a while, and I thought I'd show her a little bit of Hollywood."

He chuckled. "Yeah, Hollywood, How *you* like it so far?"

"It's interesting."

He responded. "To say the least! Listen, I'm glad I caught you," he said looking at Stefani. "It's looks like I may be returning."

Stefani exclaimed, "You're kidding me! That's great!"

"They're going to try me out for a few episodes next season. I'm glad it got picked up for a second season. A lot of

261

shit went down for me, you know, but it will be good for me to be back. I'm going to need your help with some things."

"Whatever you need, I'm there. How are you doing? Really, I was worried about you."

"You know, truly, I'm doing all right. I know what's wrong with me now. I finally got some good counseling. I'm on some good meds now, and its not cocaine." He chuckled. "They gave my erratic behavior all these years a name, Bipolar. I'm bipolar. I take responsibility for a lot of the things I've done, but now it helps to know what led me to do them."

The director interrupted us. "Okay, people. Back to work. Places!"

Stefani gave him a quick hug. "I am so happy for you. We'll have to catch up some more later."

"Definitely, I have to meet with some of the writers. I'll *catch* you later."

Stefani grabbed my hand hurriedly.

"Stefani, what was that all about?"

"Shh! You heard the director. Places," she whispered, as we walked to our seats.

I sat watching take after take of the same scene. Hollywood wasn't at all glamorous, and I wouldn't admit it to Stefani but it was actually kind of boring. I found my mind wandering, and with an aching heart, I thought about Steven. I missed him so much. I also missed the city, Katt, Tiffany, and even the work aspect of the job I held at Steven's company. I couldn't believe I just met Kevin Tracy! He was incredible. He was even more gorgeous and down-to-earth in person. I wished I had thought to ask Stefani to take a picture with my phone of the two of us, even though it would have been breaking the rules.

I thought of how he admitted he was bipolar. I remembered learning about bipolar disorder in an Abnormal Psychology course I took in college. Thinking about what he said, I started to recall the many major ups and downs I experienced throughout my life. My moods were always all over the place. I thrived on adventure and chaos, and most of all attention. I thought most people wrote me off as spoiled and selfish, which of course I am. Nobody knew about the days I lay in bed until 3:00 in the afternoon, when I wasn't hung over, or what seemed like weeks on end that I felt ashamed, scared, and was just going through the motions, wanting to end it all.

"It's a wrap!" The director yelled, interrupting me from my thoughts.

Stefani turned to me. "You wait here. I'll be back in a few minutes. I'm just going to check to see if anyone needs anything before I leave."

"That's fine."

Patting my knee, Stefani said, "I know it's been a long day for you."

"No, this was fun." I lied.

~~~

The prima donnas' on the set sent Stefani to the convenient store, located on the lot. One of the teenage cast members needed tampons and the assistant director needed condoms. While I sat waiting for Stefani to return, one of the cast members, who Stefani referred to as a has-been actress from the eighties, whom I had never heard of or recognized, asked me to practice her lines with her. Before we started, Stefani informed me privately that she thought the actress couldn't read, and that she was possibly dyslexic. As I rehearsed with her, it was evident to me that the only thing wrong with her was that she was basically a bad actress.

263

~~~

When we finally headed back to Stefani's place, it was almost 8:00 pm. We had been at the studio for almost twelve hours. Now I understand why Stefani isn't home at all, and if this is how her life is going to continue, I would say it kind of sucks.

We made our way up to her second floor apartment. As Stefani fumbled around in her purse searching for her keys, I took a seat in one of the chairs near the side of her door. I sat breathing in the salty air, watching the palm trees sway in the wind. I felt tired and hungry.

"Hey, Glen," Stefani yelled, as she clumsily held her bulky purse up to her knee, staring at the found key as if it were a long lost child.

Gorgeous Glen was just about to turn the corner, as Stefani continued to yell, "Glen, I want you to meet my baby sister."

Gorgeous Glen looked around, and as if meeting me for the very first time asked, "What's up?"

"What's up," I repeated back barely audibly as *Gorgeous Glen* continued to walk toward his apartment.

"He's a little strange," Stefani whispered as she opened the door. I didn't dare tell her of our exchange, not that it would have surprised her.

We had left the central air on when we left early this morning. The apartment felt like an icebox, and I could feel the goose bumps rising on my arms.

I plopped on the couch as Stefani dropped her purse on the kitchen table and fumbled with her mail that I'm sure was weeks old.

My stomach was growling. I walked to the 'fridge. The only remnant that now remained in there was the rest of the pizza I ordered for myself yesterday, half a quart of

264

orange juice, 3 cans of Diet Coke, and 2 bottles of Sam Adams. I grabbed a bottle and opened it. "I have half of my pizza left. You want to split it?" I asked Stefani, who was now frantically texting.

"Sure," she answered, without even looking up. I threw my slice on a thin paper plate, and left the rest in the box for Stefani. I was starving. I didn't even bother heating it up. I wolfed down my pizza and guzzled my beer as Stefani continued to be on a mission, frantically texting to who knows who.

"I'm going to bed now," I said.

Stefani looked up and nodded her head.

~~~

I put on my yoga pants and a worn-out T-shirt that was a left-over from one of the guys from my many sleepovers.

It was almost 9:00 pm. The last time I had been to bed this early was about three years ago, when I had the flu. I felt restless and decided to see what Stefani was up to. I walked by her bedroom; the door was slightly open. I walked in and curled up next to her. She was on her cell phone laughing, as her beer and pizza sat untouched on her nightstand. As she continued to talk, I aimlessly watched *Dateline*, wishing I had seen it from the beginning.

"Did you have fun today?" she asked, turning off her phone.

"Yeah, thanks for taking me with you. I felt like it was "Bring your daughter to work day,"" I said, teasing her.

"I'm glad you came."

"Stefani, it was nice seeing where you work. I'm happy for you. You seem really happy."

"I am."

"I can't believe I met Kevin Tracy. I forgot he was on your show."

"Yep, and he's coming back."

"What's up with the two of you?"

"Nothing, we're just friends," she answered, grabbing her beer off the side table.

"So you've never..."

"I'm not answering you," she said, taking a swig of beer.

"It's just, you can have anybody you want, and you're just like me; you've gotten whatever it is you want. I just thought a hot guy..."

"Lauren, I'm not just like you. I just don't jump into things."

"I always thought you were...Maybe, I'm like Kevin Tracy. Maybe, I'm bipolar."

Stefani leaned over and put her cell phone on the bedside table. She leaned her head against the headboard. "I think maybe you are."

I felt an ache in my heart as she said those words. I sat up next to her. "Do you ever think about what happened to us at camp?"

"Huh? I haven't thought about that in a long time. We were so young, and we have to admit we were both in love with Rick. He was known throughout the camp as the "Hot Counselor.""

"Yeah, but he had sex with us. I didn't want that. He stole my virginity. He told me not to tell anyone. When I told you my secret, you said he did the same thing to you. We never told anyone our secret."

Stefani grabbed my hand. "We should have told someone. We weren't even teenagers. How could we have comprehended what a twenty-something was doing to us, and probably to so many more. I should have protected you. I'm sorry."

"It wasn't your fault. Maybe, that's why I'm such a hot mess," I said, leaning my head on her shoulder.

"You're not a mess. You're my sister," she said, wrapping her arms around me.

Chapter 49

Elnando

I made my way into position at center stage. As the music was cued, I became Prince Ivan. As Prince Ivan, I desperately wanted the firebird, and Melanie, playing the firebird, made the role even easier. There were three more weeks of rehearsals until show time. The winter showcase set the precedent for where we stood amongst the other dancers in our years to come at Fillmore. Everything was riding on this. The senior class choreographers put in their own spin, adding contemporary and even some forms of hip hop, to the classic ballet. I could tell Melanie's body was in it, but not her mind. The stress of her parents' marriage was weighing on her. She was off, her movements weren't exact, and the pressure from Olivia and the senior choreographers didn't help matters. Melanie was an excellent dancer, who gave every morsel of her being when she danced. I did not just have high hopes for Melanie, but Olivia did as well. With every turn or landing that wasn't perfectly correct, Olivia's cane came down, and the whole auditorium felt it like a jab to the heart.

"This is real life, people," Olivia screamed across the stage. "Get your game on, folks." I spun and leaped across the stage, making my way into the enchanted forest. As Prince Ivan I found myself suddenly swarmed by twelve beautiful princesses. And, art imitated real life—all twelve of them were knockouts. As they swung their smooth legs around me and pushed their breasts gently into me, each one of them was vying for my attention. The technical support team worked around us, rolling scenery in and out that they were considering using.

When the scene was complete, Olivia yelled sternly, "You're done, people. Get out. Next time you come to this stage, you better bring it!"

I let out a sigh of relief that we were done for the day. I looked over at Melanie who stood by the stage door. She shyly smiled, her eyes telling me, "Let's get the hell out of here."

Behind the orchestra pit, the wardrobe department sat with their clipboard. During the entire rehearsal, they could be seen writing notes regarding the costumes we were to wear. As the dancers and I exited stage right, one of the wardrobe mistresses yelled out a list of dancers, who they wanted to see about their wardrobe. I was glad to hear Darnel and Ming-Na's names called. I felt relief that they didn't need to see me or Melanie, and that we could escape without dragging Ming-Na and Darnel along with us.

~~~

I spent a few extra minutes in the shower. I stood under the nozzle as the hot water ran down my body. I ran my hands through my hair, taking in the moist heat, hoping it would make my aching joints feel a little better. When I came out of the shower, the bathroom was a sauna. Feeling exhausted and sore, I slowly dried myself off. I could barely bend my legs, and putting on my boxers was painstaking, and would probably be comical to anyone who was watching.

I knew Darnel would take off, after he took his shower. He wanted to catch up with some friends in the village, and I was relieved to have the room to myself. As I came out, I was surprised to see Melanie sprawled across my bed.

"Wow. You're here already."

"I knew Ming-Na would want to take her shower as soon as she got back, so I quickly took mine."

"I am beat. Olivia kicked our ass," I said, getting on the bed. Laying my head on the pillow, I pulled Melanie close into me.

"I just want to sleep," she said, putting her head on what space was left of my pillow.

"Then, we'll sleep," I said, stroking her hair and kissing her neck. It smelled like lilacs, and I could feel myself getting turned on.

Melanie turned toward me and wrapped her arms around me. "This isn't sleeping." She giggled.

"I know," I said, feeling a sharp pain in my lower back. "Guess what?"

"What?"

With every ache and pain in my body, I turned Melanie around and put her on top of me. "You're doing all the work."

She laughed. "This better be a drive-through, mister, because I'm sore as hell."

~~~

With a chuckle, I said, "Now we can sleep."

"Elnando, can you believe my dad cheated on my mom?"

With that being said, I knew any hope of sleep was out of the question. "No, I can't. Your mom, she's pretty hot."

"That's a good answer, I think."

"She's sort of a *MILF*!" I said, trying to be funny.

Melanie pulled the pillow out from under me and stuffed it over my head. "That, I don't need to hear!"

Sitting up, I said, "I'm only kidding, but yes, your Mom's hot. I don't know what to say."

I really wanted to say, your dad's a prick!

270

"I guess my dad's really a jerk. My mom's probably going to be a single parent, and if my brother doesn't find a donated cornea soon, that his body doesn't reject, he will be completely blind forever. Yep, my life sucks."

"Mel, I don't know what's going to happen to your brother, but let me tell you, he seems to have it more together than any of us. Your mom, she's a great woman. And your dad, he made a mistake. Look at the mistakes I made."

"You were barely a teenager."

"You know adults make mistakes, too."

"Remember Caleb's party that my dad's co-workers were at? The bitch who's in her twenties, who I saw flirting with my dad in the kitchen, well, guess who my dad fucked?"

Melanie answered for me. "Her!"

I remembered her from the party and from the lot next to my home, when I ran into Melanie's dad. I could tell she was a little on the trampy side. She had nothing on Melanie's mom, even if she was about twenty years younger.

"Melanie, he's still your dad. I wish I had my dad here. No matter what, this is their problem. Don't make it yours. You need to focus. You weren't with it today."

"Thanks, Elnando! I gave it my best. I'm sorry I didn't rise to your or Olivia's standards, but I gave it my all today."

"You're a beautiful dancer! You need to keep your head in the game. That's all. The rest of the shit going on around you will work itself out. I promise," I said, giving her a hug.

"I hope you're right," she answered. "I can't believe it's just three weeks away. I really want them both to be there."

"You know they'll both be there, and they are going to be very proud of you. You'll knock 'em dead."

271

"If they don't kill each other by then," she said, her mood lightening

Chapter 50

MaryAnn

I held on to Caleb's hand tightly. My palms were sweating and my heart was racing. The corridors of the Westchester County Medical Center Children's Ophthalmology Department were inviting, with murals hung of brightly colored flowers and open fields. The beauty of them did nothing to soothe my nerves. I hated coming here. I feared what the doctor would say about Caleb's limited eyesight, and how it keeps diminishing. I did not want to hear the words, "There is nothing more we can do."

Caleb had three corneal transplant surgeries thus far, his body rejecting each one. I knew that we had only one chance left. With Caleb's life given to chance, I made sure he was well prepared. With pre-school at the Center of the Blind, activities with other blind children at the community center, and his being able to read Braille, I knew, if worse came to worse, he would have somewhat of a productive life. Inside though, I wanted so much more for him—dates, proms, marriage and someday children; not that I thought blind people never experienced these things, and I knew in my heart that not all "normal children" attained these things. I thought if he had been blessed with sight there would be a greater chance of them coming true. Caleb was a brilliant, sweet soul, who enjoyed making his pottery and going to horseback riding lessons. I just prayed he could fully see the beauty in it all.

The Ophthalmology Department ran like a well-oiled machine. As soon as we arrived in the waiting area, a young nurse greeted us warmly and walked us to Dr. Zaidman's office. He was one of the leading surgeons in the country, and although I dreaded seeing him, I knew his knowledge and expertise was bar none, and if anything could be done to help Caleb, Dr. Zaidman was the one to do it.

Caleb had been complaining lately that the light was getting darker. I knew what this meant; what little sight he did have was going away. I prayed every night for a miracle, but with everything going on with Steven and me, God seemed a million miles away.

Caleb was not apprehensive at all about being here. I believe the promise of McDonald's afterwards, along with the fact that he thought it was another routine appointment, made it another day in his life.

I turned Caleb in the direction of the examination chair, and he lifted himself into it. Dr. Zaidman was in his late fifties and had a gentle manner. He asked Caleb about how he liked school, what his favorite games were that he played there, and how he enjoyed reading, now that he knew Braille. After the warm introduction, the good doctor examined Caleb with equipment that looked like something out of *Star Wars*. Caleb was patient, and when Dr. Zaidman announced that he was almost done, Caleb, said, "Good, I'm really hungry and my belly's rumbling. We're going to McDonald's."

Dr. Zaidman laughed, lowering the equipment, "In that case, I think we need to finish up now!" He patted Caleb's shoulder and said, "You did great! We recently added a new play area with a lot of neat things. How about you check it out, and in the meantime, I'm going to chat with your mom for a bit. Is that all right with you?"

Caleb said, "Okay," and the doctor led him out.

I felt panic, and slowly breathed in and out, in order to calm myself. Dr. Zaidman returned and took a seat in the rolling chair across from me. He rolled it forward, and in his warm manner, he confirmed my worst fears. "Mrs. Belezzi, it's not looking good. Caleb's eyes have gotten progressively worse. If he doesn't find a donor soon, whom his body doesn't reject, I'm sorry to say this, but he will be completely without sight."

The panic I felt now turned into fear. Barely able to speak, I thanked him, and told him I needed to sit with this for a minute before I got Caleb. He touched my hand, and said, "Take your time." I got out my cell phone. My voice quivering, I said, "Steven, I need you."

Chapter 51

Steven

I could feel the hurt and pain in MaryAnn's voice. It was the first time since I left the house that she spoke to me as a person, without instruction. I was shocked and relieved to receive her call. I missed her presence every day. I missed having her near my side on the couch, as well as in the bedroom. The thrill of Lauren was long gone. I missed the times that MaryAnn and I did have sex, how real it was, unlike the thrill ride that it was with Lauren. I missed *simple*. I missed Saturday morning breakfast with the family, even if Melanie was away at school. MaryAnn, Caleb and I were our own special group. I felt anguish in the fact that my actions destroyed it all; I never really knew what I had until it was all gone.

Whenever I thought of Lauren and our secret relationship, I felt sick to my stomach. I wished I could take back those days. I had resolved myself to the fact that MaryAnn was not going to take me back, much less forgive me. I would do anything to make things right with her. Most importantly, I wanted her to know how truly sorry I was for everything that I did.

Barkley's familiar bark welcomed me home. When I walked in, I could see MaryAnn curled up in a ball on the living-room sofa. I ran over to her. "What's wrong?" I asked, standing next to the couch. I could tell she had been crying; her eyes were blood-shot, and she had a scrunched-up tissue in her hand.

She looked up at me, sobbing. "Everything's wrong."

I bent down and grabbed her in my arms. "I'm so sorry for everything I did to you. I promise I will never hurt you again. I will try my hardest to make everything right. I will do my best to fix everything."

MaryAnn released me from my tight grip. "Steven, some things you can't fix."

"Don't you think we deserve a fighting chance?" I asked.

MaryAnn continued to sob even harder. "It's not about us, Steven. I can't even figure us out right now. It's Caleb! His eyes! They're getting worse!"

I didn't know how to answer her. We already tried to fix that in the past, but his body kept rejecting the implants. The doctor would only give it one more try, and both MaryAnn and I were petrified that the end result would still be the same.

I took her hands in mine. "MaryAnn, we'll do whatever we need to do. If it means getting a donor, we'll do it."

"I'm so scared, Steven. What if we can't find a donor? And, if we do what if it doesn't work? Caleb will be fully blind for the rest of his life."

"I know you're scared. I'm scared too! The only thing we can do is put it in God's hands."

The look of surprise to what I had just said showed on MaryAnn's face. MaryAnn was the faithful one in the house; she prayed and made it to church with Caleb and Melanie every Sunday, when most of the time I opted to sleep in. I thought my generosity and hard work was fulfilling my role to God. I now realized how wrong I was. Lately, God had been my go-to-guy. I prayed constantly to Him to restore my marriage and forgive me for everything I had done to MaryAnn, the rest of my family, and even to Lauren. I now know what it means to hit rock bottom. At this moment, I knew the only thing I could do was look up.

To my surprise, MaryAnn wrapped her arms around me, neither one of us wanting to let go.

Chapter 52

Melanie

The orchestra did their quick warm up. When the last note was played, the whole amphitheatre became silent. I put may hand on Elnando's shoulder and said, "Go get 'em."

Suddenly, a chaotic mixture of sounds began as Elnando tiptoed center stage. His technique was perfect as he danced across the stage. It was my turn to enter the stage and tantalize him as the firebird with my magic and beauty. From the moment I entered the stage I was in sync, and it lasted throughout the whole performance. Elnando captivated the audience with his facial expressions that played along perfectly with the story. What added to the performance was the exceptional job the fashion department did on the costumes, making the production top notch. The maidens wore contemporary ballet costumes—satin teal camisole leotards attached with a tulle skirt. Their whole costumes glittered with sparkling sequins. The other dancers, the extras, wore colorful deep yellow and blue leotards. Darnel looked like the perfect villain in a black suit and ruffled white shirt. The fairy princess, who wins my baby's heart, wore a beautiful sparkling white satin leotard and a tulle skirt, with a crystal beaded tiara. I glittered in all red, from my leotard to my tulle skirt, while wearing a massive high headpiece made with real white feathers. Elnando looked like the prince charming every girl dreamed of while growing up. He wore a gold and red English-style suit jacket with tight red dance pants and a small crown.

When the performance ended, the crowd rose to their feet and gave a standing ovation. And, when Elnando and I came forward and took our bow, the crowd roared. I felt a high like no other. It was truly one of the best moments of my life, and I'm sure Elnando's as well. When the curtain fell, Elnando grabbed me into his arms and spun me around, kissing my cheek. Then, without words, we looked into each other's eyes and kissed passionately.

~~~

Flashes from cameras, cheers, and big hugs awaited all the dancers as they exited the dressing room. An elaborate after-party sponsored by the school took place in the foyer. Elnando and I squeezed through the crowds looking for either of our loved ones. Suddenly, Elnando said, "Holy shit, you actually came!" It was Jewel, and I was as shocked as he was. Dressed in khakis and a blue striped shirt, he looked handsome and sincerely happy to be here. Elnando gave him a huge manly hug.

Jewel answered him, "You got me a ticket. By the way, you look good in those red tights," he said, kidding.

Elnando laughed and said, "My dance pants. You're damn right I look good!"

Elnando's mom, Birdie and Jewel's mom joined us with small plates overflowing with cheese and crackers. Hugging Elnando with one arm, while balancing her plate, Elnando's mom was ecstatic and said, "You were amazing!"

"Thank you, Mama," Elnando said humbly.

She then gave me a hug and told me how beautiful I looked and how well I did, as Birdie and Jewel's mom hugged and congratulated Elnando.

Out of the corner of my eye, I noticed my mom and Caleb across the room. I felt an ache in my heart, realizing my dad wasn't with them.

I excused myself from Elnando and his family, as they barraged him with questions.

As I made my way over to my mom and Caleb, I was surprised to see my dad joining them.

As I was about to approach them, I was suddenly stopped by an older gentlemen in his late fifties. "Hi, you're Melanie Belezzi, the Firebird?"

I nodded.

"I'm Jacob Waters," he said, extending his hand to mine.

"Hi," I answered, not sure if he was someone I met once and had forgotten.

"You did an incredible job tonight. I'm with the Gerwin Dance Company. Are you familiar with us?"

"Yes. You're in Dallas."

"That's correct. I'm here scouting today, and I really think you would make a good fit for our dance company."

"Thank you, but I'm only a freshman. I have three years left here and..."

He interrupted me and said, "From what I saw of you up on that stage, I think you may be ready for us now. I can tell your forté was in classical ballet."

I nodded.

"How about this? Finish up your semester. I'll be returning in the spring, because the company has some engagements here in the city. If you are interested, give me a call sometime around April. I'll set up some studio time. I would like to see how you perform in other dance styles. I understand this is Fillmore, but I know you understand how prestigious the Gerwin Dance Company is. Think about it," he said, handing me his card.

"I...I...will," I stuttered.

"Good, then I look forward to hearing from you," he said, patting my arm and walking away.

I stood in shock as my dad, mom and Caleb noticed me. Taking me away from my thoughts, all of them spoke at once. My mom and dad each hugged me and congratulated me.

Caleb handed me a huge bouquet of pink roses. "These are so beautiful. Thank you." I bent down and hugged him.

"Melanie, you were sensational up there!"

"She's something else," my dad added.

"Thank you," I said. "I'm really glad to see all of you."

With that being said, there was an awkward silence.

Breaking the ice, I said, "Mom and Dad, I want you to meet Elnando's family and some of my friends."

I led the way as my mom followed, while Dad picked up Caleb and followed behind. On our way, we saw Darnel, who was surrounded by a whole posse. I introduced Darnel to my family, and he introduced me to his mother, who happened to be a lot older than I expected. She was matronly, and gushed with joy as she spoke with Darnel and me about how proud she was of us kids. As we were standing there, Ming-Na came over with her parents, who were both Chinese and spoke with heavy accents. They had smiles that could light up a room, and had Ming-Na and I pose for pictures.

As we stood posing, Elnando and his family came over to join us.

I announced, "Mom, Dad and Caleb, this is Elnando's mom, Rosalie, and this is Birdie, a close friend who taught Elnando his moves, and this is Jewel, who is like a brother to him, and his mom, Anita."

Everyone greeted each other warmly. I looked over at Caleb who was resting peacefully on my father's shoulder, as my mother made small talk with Elnando's mom and Birdie. I was glad that my dad made it, not knowing if he arrived with my mom or not. I was relieved to see that he and my mom were in each other's presence. I glanced at my dad as he was stroking Caleb's hair; I realized I wasn't thinking of him as a horrible monster like I had the past few weeks. Maybe it was the high from my performance, but I found myself looking at him with kind eyes, feeling for him as a man who had fallen.

I rubbed the business card in my hand.

"What am I to do? Opportunity had found me. I didn't want to leave Fillmore, Elnando or my family, but the Gerwin Dance Company, that was every dancer's dream after Fillmore, and they are interested in me! Why now?"

I started to feel my high wear off, as I crinkled the card in my hand.

Part 3

The Final Act

"Take a Bow. The Ending is Really Only the Beginning."
                                    ~Jill Starling

Lauren

My hands were shaking out of control as I hung up the phone. It was Steven's wife, that wasn't the last voice I wanted to hear before my death. A group of men and women were huddled together like a mismatched football team going over their plays. Their plan was to take down the terrorists. I couldn't look at them. I crouched further down in a fetal position into my seat.

I lived through 9/11. I knew in my heart the reality of how all of this was going to play out. These were going to be my final moments. Without a soul even next to me, I was going to die alone. Too nervous to even speak, I sent Stefani a text. "I love you, my sister. Any time now, I am going to die. My plane has been hijacked. I want to thank you for always being so good to me. You mean the world to me! Tell Katt and Tiffany thank you for always being by my side and PLEASE in some way let Steven Belezzi know that I love him and will always be with him."

As I pressed send, I sat up. I watched the football team make their way toward the cockpit. I looked out my window. As the plane shuddered, I noticed beautiful green pastures. I closed my eyes, and prayed.

Please God, let me into heaven. Suddenly, the plane took a nosedive.

Melanie

What I remember...I was half conscious when I was wheeled into the ambulance. The drowned-out voices repeating "Stay with us" seemed so far away. I felt out of my body.

In what seemed like an eternity, I awoke in a semi-conscious state. I was frightened. The white sterile room, a beating sound of a monitor, machines, and being hooked up like a marionette, left me wanting to shout, *what is happening to me?* But the effort to even get the words out was futile. Feeling groggy and disorientated, I was relieved to see someone. An older woman, who appeared to be a nurse, walked into my room. I sat catatonic as she adjusted the monitors. Then a younger woman, whom I thought was a nurse, too, followed. She stood looking at me, scribbling on her clipboard as if I was some lab experiment.

"She's starting to wake up, her family should be here soon," the older nurse whispered and left the room.

My family and Elnando, where are you? I need you now, I am so confused!

As I became more coherent, I started to panic. The young nurse grabbed my hand and held it gently. Speaking softly, she asked me if I knew where I was here. I shook my head back and forth.

"Melanie, you are at the New York-Presbyterian Hospital. You have been in a terrible accident and have been in a medically-induced coma for the past five days."

I could feel myself starting to tear up.

"Your mom and dad are on their way. Dr. Eckelstein will be coming in to speak to you and your parents."

She squeezed my hand tighter. "You're going to be all right, Melanie."

286

I looked down at my body. As fear overwhelmed me, I asked, "But, my legs, will I ever be able to dance again?"

I could read the answer in her eyes, and as she was about to speak, my mom arrived. The nurse stepped aside.

My mom looked exhausted and worn out, she ran over to me and bent down next to the bed, as tears streamed down her face. "Melanie, Melanie."

"Mom, it's okay," I said, understanding how hard it was for her to see me.

She wiped her tears. "Your father will be here soon," she said, grabbing my hand.

The doctor came in. He appeared to be in his late fifties, early sixties. He had gray hair and glasses. He introduced himself to me and spoke in a no-nonsense manner. "Melanie, I understand you are probably feeling very disorientated and scared right now. As I'm sure the nurse explained to you, that you have been in a terrible accident. You probably don't remember it. You suffered a compound fracture to your left leg from your knee to your ankle. You also fractured your collarbone and had severe brain swelling. In order to relieve the pressure on your brain, we had to drill a hole in your skull. You are lucky to be alive."

I started to cry. My mom's grip on my hand tightened as the doctor continued. "Our staff has given you the best care possible, and will continue to do so. It will probably take a month or so of rehabilitation before you can leave here, and many more months of physical therapy. You have a long road ahead of you, but like I said, with the injuries you sustained, you are extremely lucky to be alive."

"Will I ever be able to walk again?"

"I believe you will."

"I'm a dancer..."

287

"I know, your parents told me all about you. Physical therapy is going to be like going through hell and back. From what I gathered from your parents, you are a determined young woman. If you don't lose hope, I believe you will lead a productive life again."

"I need to know. Will I be able to dance?"

"I can't answer that; no one can at this point. I have seen some pretty miraculous things in my twenty-five years here, and I believe there is a miracle inside of you."

My heart ached. His words did little to comfort me. My mom's presence did little to ease my pain. I needed Elnando.

Where was Elnando?

Elnando

I had finally regained consciousness. I was barely able to move as I lay in a fetal position on the floor. I looked over at the group of them. Some of them I recognized, and the others, barely teenagers, that I had never seen before. They were laughing, drinking while sitting around a card table, going through pictures on a phone. None of them even looked in my direction. Maybe they thought I was dead. I wasn't too far from the door, if I only had the strength to escape. Even if I could try, they were all armed, and they wouldn't think twice about shooting me.

One of them said, "That is one sweet piece of ass." Another added, "This bitch looks fine. What is she, some kind of fairy princess in this picture?" I realized it was Melanie they were talking about, and it was my phone they were staring at!

When I ran into Billion, why didn't I just make an excuse and immediately go to Birdie's place when he asked me to stop in? He was one of the leaders. Seeing me, he probably remembered how I hadn't been around in a long time. Did I think he was going to offer me a beer and have a friendly chat? I knew Jewel still ran with him.

A disturbing thought ran through my mind: *Maybe Jewel mentioned to him that at one time I was thinking of going to the police. Jewel was smarter than that, I hope. He was my brother, even though not by blood. He would never betray me, so I hoped.*

Suddenly, one of them looked over at me. "That *pendejo* is starting to wake up."

In a casual manner, Billion announced, "We'll finish him up. Let me finish my *40* first, and where the fuck is Jewel? I texted him, I even texted that bitch's *ho*."

One of the others remarked, "No shit."

"The *ho* never got back to me."

I felt absolute fear pulsate through my body.

Why the fuck would they text Melanie? What do they want with her? Where is Jewel? Only God and Jewel could possibly save me at this point.

Billion looked over at me with disgust, as he finished his beer. "I'm sick of this bitch bein' in my crib. Let's go," he announced, getting up and walking toward me.

Billion came over to me and gave a swift kick to my ribs. "Get up!"

Barely able to sit up, I said, "I'll do whatever you need me to do."

He kicked me again, as the others walked over. "You piece of shit! You think you're better than us?"

I cowered down, like an abused animal, hardly able to move.

Billion looked at the others, "Get his ass *outta* here!"

One of the others kicked me and said in a casual manner, "Get up."

I couldn't physically.

Billion yelled at them, "Grab his sorry ass!"

Two of them got me to my feet and dragged me down three flights of stairs, and out a back door that led to the vacant lot next to the project. It was pitch black out. I had no idea what time it was. In the distance, I noticed some passersby. Even if I could yell for help, no one would come; people around here minded their own business.

The two of them let go of me, as I fell to the ground. I knew this would be my final moment. I noticed the back of the Belezzi sign and thought of Melanie. I loved her; with her I had it all. Billion grabbed a baseball bat from one of the young members. He began bashing me, as each one of them took turns punching and kicking me.

I tried to get up but fell down instantly. Suddenly, I saw an outline of a figure walking toward us. Barely conscious, I knew it was Jewel. He stared at me intensely.

Billion held back the bat, to position himself for my slaughter. I looked at him for mercy. Bloody, and in gut-wrenching pain, I knew this was the end. Jewel's and my eyes met. His eyes looked dead with fear for me.

With Billion's final blow, he swung right below my waist. Nausea and dizziness overcame me. I couldn't take anymore.

I was in and out of consciousness, when I heard Billion say, "Jewel, you're going to finish him off. Do it right!" Barely able to open my eyes, I watched as they walked away.

Jewel looked at me, and then turned to make sure the coast was clear.

We stared at each other. I couldn't talk, but my eyes pleaded with him to save me.

Jewel dragged my barely conscious body toward the back of the fields. I whimpered in pain. Jewel didn't say a word.

Lying on its side was an old commercial refrigerator. Jewel opened it up and dragged my lifeless body into it. Jewel stood motionless, as he stared at my curled body. Moments later, he grabbed his cell phone. I was barely holding on to dear life, as I heard him say, "Come right, away. There is a dead body in the back of the lot next to the Carver Housing Project in Spanish Harlem."

Jewel bent down next to me. He took out his glock, and said. "I love you, my brother. I'm so sorry." He swung the refrigerator door closed. Suddenly, I heard the muffled sound of a gunshot.

Steven

"What's wrong?" I asked MaryAnn as she held my cell phone, with tears streaming down her face.

"I let you back into our home. I thought you were done with her."

"What's this about?

"*SHE* just called, confessing her love for you."

"There's nothing going on. I swear to you."

I rose from the bed to comfort and assure her that I was sincere and telling her the truth.

"Don't Steven. Don't come near me. Don't touch me. I've given you a second chance and..."

"MaryAnn, I swear I haven't seen or spoken to her." I wanted to tell her Lauren is supposedly living in California now, but I thought it might lead to even more questions.

"I can't handle this now, Steven. I can't," MaryAnn said, walking toward the bed.

"You don't have to. I promised you that I would never betray you again."

She sat on the edge of the bed. "I can't take anymore. Our poor Melanie, and Caleb may never fully see again and..."

"Everything is going to be all right. I promise."

"Is it, Steven? Not to mention us! It's going to be a long time until I fully trust you, if I ever do. I hope you understand that."

"I understand. I agreed to do whatever it takes—counseling, you can spy-cam my office, whatever makes you feel better. I just want us to be a family again."

Suddenly, a special report interrupted the program I had on. "We just learned an American Airlines jetliner traveling from Los Angeles to New York has been hijacked

292

by possible terrorists, and has crash landed in an open field in Westchester County just moments ago."

"Oh, my God," MaryAnn said, looking at the TV.

I turned up the volume, as the newscaster announced. "Passengers on board Flight #214 tried to overtake the possible terrorists, as the jetliner plunged into an open field. Ambulances, fire trucks, and police cars rushed to the scene. There were many first-responders to the scene, as many of the locals in the area witnessed first-hand, the plane crashing. Witnesses reported seeing dozens of people running off the plane in an attempt to escape the burning wreckage. It has been confirmed that 279 passengers were on board the Boeing 777 aircraft."

MaryAnn turned toward me and sighed. "I can't listen to this. I have to get out of here."

She handed me my cell phone.

"I'll go with you."

"No. I'm going to take Caleb. I have some errands to run, and then I'm going to drop him off at my parents. I'll meet you at the hospital later."

I grabbed MaryAnn's arm, as she was about to get up. "I promise you, MaryAnn. Everything is going to be all right."

"Steven, you shouldn't make promises you may not be able to keep."

I let go of her arm and watched as she walked out the door.

~~~

I lay in bed switching through the stations, but every station was reporting on the crash. I gave up and turned off the TV as my cell phone rang. It was Jack from the office. "Steven, I just got a call here from Lauren's sister. She was pretty frantic. I'm sorry to tell you this; Lauren was on that plane that crashed. Did you hear about it yet?"

"Yes, I just heard."

"I guess Lauren is still alive. She's at Westchester County Medical Center. Her sister wants you to go over there right away."

"I can't do that, Jack."

"She says it's pretty urgent that you get there as soon as you can. She may not make it."

"Thanks," I said, cutting him off and ending the call. I suspected that Jack now knew about the relationship Lauren and I had.

If I go over to the hospital and see Lauren, there would be no way MaryAnn would ever forgive me.

But, what if my visit could change our lives for the better? I thought, as I got up and walked out the door.

~~~

As I made my way to the hospital, I had mixed feelings about Lauren. She almost destroyed my life, but she still had a place in my heart. Not to mention the fact that I had been having sex with her for months on end, and now she was hanging on for dear life. It was hard for me to comprehend the reality of what was happening.

Why was she calling me? Was it from the plane? I'm glad I didn't answer her call. I didn't want to hear her voice or become tempted by her in anyway. Why couldn't she grasp the fact that I never wanted anything to do with her again, ever?

I was very familiar with Westchester County Medical Center. MaryAnn and I had brought Caleb there for his three failed corneal transplant surgeries.

As I made my way to the nurse's triage, I noticed a group of family and friends in one of the open waiting areas.

Could it be Lauren's family?

They were sitting in quiet disbelief. A man that appeared to be in his early sixties sat in the center of the

294

group. I had a feeling he was Lauren's father. He had his head down, looking like he was in deep prayer, while the woman next to him, whom I guessed was Lauren's mother, was tightly holding hands with a young woman who sat by her side.

I was about to ask the nurses about Lauren's condition, when I heard a voice from behind me say, "Steven."

I turned around. It was Lauren's friend whom I recognized. Her face was red and tear stained.

"I'm Katt. We met once. I'm Lauren's best friend."

"I am so sorry. How is she?" I asked.

"They are working on her right now. I have to get out of here," she said as her eyes began to tear up. "I really need to smoke." Reaching into her purse, she grabbed a pack of cigarettes. "I'm going to step out for a bit. Do you want to join me?"

I nodded and followed her, passing Lauren's family again. As Katt and I passed through the automated doors, *No Smoking Signs* surrounded the entrance.

Katt looked at me as she pulled a cigarette out. "Great!"

I noticed a picnic table a short distance away under a tall tree. It was a little island in the midst of the parking lot.

I looked over to the area and pointed, "There's a bench over there."

"Good," she said and hurried over to it.

I followed her. She lit her cigarette and sat on top of the picnic table, as I sat below.

"I just want you to know Lauren really loved you. She really did," she said, puffing away. "She wanted to be with you for the rest of her life."

I nodded and said, "A relationship like Lauren and I had was not meant to last."

"I know, because you're married."

"Yes, exactly, not to mention I was Lauren's employer. I should have known better."

Katt stared straight ahead, avoiding any eye contact with me. "I guess those things happen."

"It shouldn't have. You're young, if I can offer you any advice," I said, as Katt turned toward me. "Think before you act. By the grace of God, my wife has forgiven me."

"Your wife found out about Lauren?"

"She did."

"Damn!"

"I was going to get caught, eventually. My wife needed to know what I had done. I realize what I have with my wife is sacred. We made vows together. I broke them, along with my family's trust."

Katt stepped off the table, threw her cigarette on the ground and stepped on it.

In a fatherly manner, I said, "Bottom line, if a relationship has to be kept in secret, it shouldn't be one."

Katt nodded. "You're probably right. Unfortunately, you were the last love that Lauren had, regardless, if it was right or wrong. In Lauren's mind, she wanted to be with you for the rest of her life."

"There is a way Lauren can be with me for the rest of my life."

I caught her completely off guard. She looked at me puzzled. "I don't understand."

"My son Caleb is going to become fully blind soon, if he doesn't receive donated corneas and have surgery. If it's possible, I would like to have permission to have Lauren's corneas donated, should she not make it. I doubt Lauren was a donor, so I will need Lauren's or her parents' permission. I know this is a very difficult time for all of you. It is imperative, that if Lauren or her parents' give permission while Lauren is still alive, that the doctors know immediately that she will be a donor."

Her voice trembled as she said the words, "Would your son have her eyes?"

"No, he wouldn't have her eyes, but with her corneas, there's a chance he may be able to see."

"What do you want me to do?"

"Talk to her family right away." I got out one of my business cards. "My cell number is on here. If they agree, please let the staff know that Caleb's doctor is also at this hospital. He's the head of Ophthalmology. Please call or text me right away with their decision."

She looked down at my card with tears in her eyes.

"Katt, thank you."

She looked up at me, our eyes met, and I turned around and walked away.

I decided not to go back in and see Lauren.

I went to my car and prayed.

Dear God, if you don't grant Lauren a miracle, can you please give one to my son, Caleb?

MaryAnn

Seeing my baby girl in this state broke my heart. I kept reminding myself that she is alive, and that really is all that mattered. Whether she walked or even danced again was in God's hands. Melanie had fallen asleep and I wondered where Steven was. He didn't text me and I didn't feel like texting him.

Suddenly, I heard a light knock on the door, and a man dressed in a dapper suit peeked his head in and whispered, "Mrs. Belezzi, my name is Detective Vincent DeSantis, and I'm here with Prosecutor Carla LaRue. May we speak with you?"

I nodded and followed them out, assuming this was about Melanie's accident.

We took a seat in the visitor's lounge. They both had a no-nonsense look about them, and I wanted to ask them if this could wait, that Melanie had just come out of the coma, and I doubted she remembered any details about that fateful day.

The prosecutor was heavyset and wore a weave full of braids that she had pulled back in a ponytail. "Mrs. Belezzi, I am a prosecutor with the Attorney General's Office. We understand this is a very difficult time for you and your family."

"Yes, it is. You're here about my daughter's accident?" I questioned them.

The detective sat forward. He was tall, with dark hair and deep brown eyes. He had a look of urgency in him. "Not exactly. We understand your daughter was hit, walking in traffic. Again, we are very sorry. The reason we are here is because of your daughter's relationship with Elnando Boltares. Are you aware of her relationship with him?"

"Yes, I am. They have been seeing each other since Melanie started attending Fillmore."

Suddenly, we were interrupted as Steven walked over. "What's going on?" he asked.

They introduced themselves again. Steven took a seat next to me.

Detective DeSantis continued, "I was just about to explain to your wife. We are here regarding your daughter's relationship with Elnando Boltares."

I interrupted him. "I have been trying to contact him regarding Melanie. Melanie's friends at school haven't heard from him. They tried his cell phone. Melanie needs him here."

The detective asked, "Are you aware, that he is a member of the gang, the Latin Knights?"

I nodded, as Steven sat silent.

The detective continued, "Elnando was almost beaten to death in an abandoned lot next to where his family lives."

"Oh my God!" I gasped

"He is actually at this hospital. He is conscious. Miraculously, he only has a few broken bones. He will be okay."

"Thank God," I said.

"He has around-the-clock police protection outside his room."

I looked over at Steven and he looked as shocked as I was, and I'm sure he wondered what this was leading to.

The detective continued. "Elnando is lucky to be alive. We spoke with him. His life was spared by his best friend, who took his own life instead of Elnando's."

I covered my mouth in shock.

The prosecutor spoke up, "We want to prosecute the people who did this. They are also responsible for much greater criminal activity. We spoke with Elnando. He is aware that once he leaves the hospital, he is just as well dead. We offered him and his family to be placed in a witness protection program, if he agrees to testify. He accepted our offer. Elnando told us a great deal, even some crimes in which he was a participant in. He asked if Melanie could go with him."

Steven stood up. "No way! Are you kidding me?"

Very calmly the prosecutor responded, "We completely understand how you must be feeling."

"She is only seventeen!" I blurted out.

"I understand. I have a daughter around the same age," the detective answered. "If she did agree, she would no longer have contact with her family and friends again, as long as she chooses to stay in the program. She would receive a new identity, a new life..."

Steven interrupted him. Clearly agitated, he said, "No way!"

The detective said, "Like I said I have a daughter too. I understand. Ms. LaRue and I will not speak to your daughter regarding this. From this point on, your daughter will never hear from, see, or even know where Elnando Boltares is, as long as he stays in the program."

Steven said with a sense of urgency in his voice that actually scared me, "Please keep him far away. If it's possible send him to another country. I'll pay for it myself!"

There was an awkward silence. Then the detective looked over at the prosecutor and then looked at us. "I must warn you, your daughter's life could be in danger as well. These people have no mercy. They may take retaliation. They have Elnando's cell phone. Elnando remembers them sending your daughter a text and looking at photos of her on his phone."

I sat stone-faced.

The detective advised us, "If she were my daughter, once she recovered, I would get her the hell out of New York."

Steven let out a heavy sigh, as I put my head in my hands.

My poor Melanie! Please God, save us. We can't handle this without you.

~~~

The detective and prosecutor gave Steven and I their business cards should we have any questions for them.

I sat in shock.

Steven looked like he was going to explode. "We have a long road ahead of us, MaryAnn. No one is getting near Melanie. No one!"

I turned toward him and said, "What should we tell Melanie?"

"We tell her the truth."

"What if she is willing to leave all of us for him?"

"We don't tell her about that! MaryAnn, we don't say anything about him wanting her to go with him. You understand?"

"Then, we aren't really telling her the truth."

"No, we are telling her what she needs to know in order to move on, and hopefully be happy again."

Steven

MaryAnn decided to stay for the night by Melanie's bedside. I needed to get out of there. My mind was racing. I didn't feel like going home. I was frustrated.

Why did Melanie ever get involved with that boy? But, who was I to judge? Why did I ever get involved with Lauren?

Thoughts of Lauren raced through my mind all night. *Did she survive?* I was anxious to hear from her friend, Katt.

Truthfully, I didn't want her to make it. I wanted her to die. I wanted her out of my life forever.

Ironically, I needed a part of Lauren now; it was the only part I was willing to take. It would take time to find a donor for Caleb, and time wasn't on our side. Lauren may be Caleb's last hope.

I was driving what seemed to be on autopilot. I found myself in Spanish Harlem, at the site of where Elnando grew up and where his life almost ended. I knew it wasn't the safest area to be at this time of night, but there was a quiet stillness in the streets.

I pulled my car over and stared at the run-down tenement and abandoned lot next to it.

This was once someone's paradise. Now dilapidation and darkness is all that remains. In two weeks the big wrecking ball will be striking it. Maybe then, some light will enter this hell.

I started to pull away, when my cell phone vibrated. It was a text from Katt, "Lauren didn't make it. I did speak with her right before she died. These are her final words. "Steven I love you! I'm sorry our relationship has hurt you. I realize what you really want, and the answer is YES! That way, I know you will have a part of me with you for the rest of your life.""

Epilogue

Caleb

I saddled up Misty Mae, and she is as beautiful as I've always imaged. It has been five years since my corneal transplant. Being granted this gift of sight, I could never ask for anything more. Looking out into the grandstand confirms it even more. My dad and sister just arrived. He brought my mom a Dunkin Donuts' coffee, along with a peck on the cheek. When I was young and blind, I never felt that the love or faith that they shared together is as strong as it is now.

We all prayed and stood by my sister through years of therapy, as she not only regained her ability to walk, but also the ability to dance. She returned to school three years after the accident. She wasn't able to return to Fillmore, the school she loved so much. She now attends Carlilly Institute of the Performing Arts in Pennsylvania. She lives on campus. Life has been a test of strength for her the past few years, both emotionally and physically. She struggles with pain and is, unfortunately, not quite the dancer she once was. I regret never being able to see her dance.

Now, she is a theatre-arts major. I believe she is finally feeling the joy that only the stage and Elnando could bring her. I never got a chance to see Elnando. Melanie and my parents rarely speak of him, but I remember that he was Melanie's first real love. Melanie's newfound happiness seems to be due to a new love. The last time she was home from college, she was staring at a picture of him on her computer. I said to her, "That looks like how I imagined Elnando." I guess just hearing his name was hard for her. She slammed her computer shut and said, "Shut up, Caleb! Just keep your mouth closed," and ran to her room.

Her eyes told me—he was Elnando.

My family has been through many trials, but we have persevered. We'll never know whose corneas were donated to me. My mother always says, "We have a special angel watching over all of us." She looks forward to the day they meet in heaven, so she can personally thank them for the greatest gift that they have not only gave me, but our whole family.

Misty Mae is now ready for me. As we jump over these obstacles, hearing my family cheer me on is everything I need—*At This Moment.*

~ *The End* ~

Available on Amazon.com and jillstarlingnovels.com

Follow Jill Starling on:

 @jill_starling

 Facebook.com/JillStarling